A DEATH in CHELSEA

Lynn Brittney

A Death in Chelsea

Lynn Brittney

MIRROR BOOKS

First published by Mirror Books in 2019

Mirror Books is part of Reach plc
10 Lower Thames Street
London EC3R 6EN
England

www.mirrorbooks.co.uk

© Lynn Brittney

The rights of Lynn Brittney to be identified as the author
of this book have been asserted, in accordance with the
Copyright, Designs and Patents Act 1988.

ISBN 978-1-912624-20-1

1 3 5 7 9 10 8 6 4 2

CONTENTS

This book is dedicated to my paternal grandmother
Rosie Jones (nee Thompson), who used to lay out dead
bodies for her community, and to my maternal great-uncle
Charlie, whose inability to speak properly because of a
cleft palate saved him from conscription into WW1

MAYFAIR 100 SERIES

INTRODUCTION

Mayfair 100, the telephone number of Chief Inspector Beech's special secret team of amateur women detectives and professional policemen, had been silent for almost a month. After their first successful case, there had been no call to further action and the team were beginning to get frustrated.

Dr Caroline Allardyce, of course, had busied herself with her work at the Women's Hospital, as had her colleague, the pharmacist, Mabel Summersby. Victoria Ellingham had tried to occupy herself with making use of her legal training and drafting amendments to the Factories Act, in the hope that her mother, Lady Maud, might be able to introduce them to some influential member of parliament. PC Billy Rigsby seemed to spend a lot of hours down at the Metropolitan Police Boxing Association. He couldn't box any more but had decided he could train others. Or he spent time with his formidable mother and aunt, Elsie and Sissy, permanently ensconced as caretakers in an empty house in Belgravia. DS Tollman had been content to go to the Mayfair 'head quarters' of the team, just to play cribbage with Lady Maud and get away from his constantly squabbling daughters, but even he, Beech noted, had begun to get restless at the lack of another case.

As for Beech himself, he had been reluctant to pester the Commissioner for another case for the team. Sir Edward Henry had sanctioned the setting up of the team but on the strict terms that no one in Scotland Yard was ever to hear about women being used in detective work and that the team was only to be used when special circumstances warranted their attention. So, Beech waited and inwardly fretted – made excuses to the team and hoped for a new case to present itself. At last, his patience was to be rewarded…

CHAPTER ONE

A Family's Honour

Scotland Yard, 2ⁿᵈ July 1915

Chief Inspector Beech stared at the morning newspaper, almost unable to comprehend the figures on the page in front of him. The war was not going well. It appeared that the Russian allies had been defeated by the Germans on the Eastern Front at the cost of hundreds of thousands dead and captured. The carnage was appalling, and the sense of defeat sat on his chest to the point of suffocation.

He looked out of the window and tried to imagine the disappearance of most of the population of London, which almost equated to the Russian loss, and his mind struggled with the concept. Beech knew that he was not the most imaginative man, at the best of times. He preferred to try to forget about his own terrible experiences in Belgium, but his thigh wound, legacy of the First Battle of Ypres, eight months ago, was a constant presence in his life now. The dull ache that reminded him he would never be the same again. Every day he struggled with the fear that his leg would not heal, and his eventual fate would be amputation. It hung over him like a sword of Damocles and the daily reminders in the newspaper of the continuing carnage of the war did nothing to lift him out of his trough of depression.

His reverie was broken by a sharp knock on his door.

"Come in," he instructed, and the section sergeant put his head into the room, announcing briskly, "Commissioner requests to see you immediately, sir."

Beech nodded and swiftly followed the sergeant down the corridor, where they parted company, as Beech ascended the staircase to Sir Edward Henry's office.

Another sergeant nodded him through – "Sir Edward's expecting you, sir" – and Beech entered to find the Commissioner offering a glass of water to a distressed lady.

"Ah, Beech… good man," Sir Edward murmured. "I think we may have a case for your… er… *special*… team. Let me make the introductions. Ma'am, this is Chief Inspector Peter Beech… Beech, this is the Duchess of Penhere."

Beech inclined his head in a small obeisance. "Your Grace," he said firmly.

The duchess, struggling with her composure, similarly inclined her head and said, in a voice thick with grief, "Chief Inspector, I am grateful for your presence this morning. Sir Edward has intimated that you might be able to help me deal… no… extricate my family from a terrible situation."

Beech's interest was piqued. He had observed that the duchess was, to all outward appearances, firmly of the Victorian era. For a woman of her breeding to show such visible distress suggested a family 'situation' of dire proportions. "I will do my best, Ma'am," he responded, with as much reassurance as he could manage.

The duchess sipped some water and tried to regain some equilibrium. Seeing that she was finding it difficult, Sir Edward stepped in.

"Shall I explain, Ma'am, about the unfortunate events that have brought you here?"

The duchess nodded, gratefully, and Sir Edward turned to Beech and began the explanation.

"The Duchess of Penhere's daughter, Lady Adeline Treborne, was found hanged in her bedroom…" A small sob escaped from the duchess's handkerchief-covered mouth. Sir Edward continued. "The Duchess is convinced that her daughter did not commit suicide but that she was murdered. The Duchess came straight to me this morning, after the discovery of the body. The late Duke and I were close friends," Sir Edward offered by way of explanation.

Beech nodded and turned to the duchess, mustering as much gentleness as he could. "Ma'am, can you tell me why you believe your daughter was murdered?"

The duchess looked at Beech with a mixture of puzzlement and embarrassment. "Surely you have heard of my daughter… Adeline… Treborne?" Seeing the lack of recognition on Beech's face, she persisted, "'A Lady's View?'"

Sir Edward interjected, "The Duchess's daughter was a well-known… er… society commentator… in the *London Herald*."

Beech looked nonplussed and the duchess said patiently and with a certain amount of bitterness, "Chief Inspector Beech, my daughter peddled the worst kind of gossip in the 'society' pages of that dreadful newspaper. She had

3

created, I understand, a great many enemies by writing scurrilous things about perfectly respectable people. Her activities greatly distressed our family and we were barely on speaking terms. Nevertheless, Adeline would not have killed herself. She had too much self-regard and, whatever else she may have been, she tried to be a good daughter of the Catholic Church and would not have disgraced her family even further by committing the crime of taking her own life. She would never have put us in the position of being unable to bury her in our family crypt. Her position in society meant everything to her."

Beech tried to reconcile the picture of an individual who spread malicious gossip in print about others with 'a good daughter of the Catholic Church'. He could see that the duchess was struggling with her own inner conflict but, nevertheless, she seemed so firm in her belief that her daughter's death was murder that he realised it must be investigated.

"Ma'am, where is your daughter's body now?"

"She is still in her rooms in Chelsea. I thought it best not to disturb things too much. She was found…" – there was a small break in the duchess's composure before she uttered the next word – "… hanging from her bedroom ceiling by the live-out maid. The poor woman was hysterical when she contacted me by telephone. I haven't seen my daughter's body… I'm afraid I lacked the courage. My chauffeur cut her down and laid her on her bed and he is now standing guard outside her door, in case anyone should seek entry. I came here immediately, in a taxi, to see Edward. He tells me that you have a special group of people who can investigate this terrible business as discreetly as possible?" The duchess looked at Beech hopefully.

"Yes, I do." Beech looked at Sir Edward, unsure about the amount of detail he should reveal to the duchess. Sir Edward answered with a barely perceptible shake of the head, indicating that information should be kept to a minimum.

The duchess had one last request. "I would prefer it," she murmured, looking at the floor, rather than at either of the two men, "if my daughter's body were not cut up… mutilated… by a police surgeon. I would prefer it if that could be avoided."

Sir Edward raised his eyebrows at Beech, obviously looking to him to provide a response.

"Your Grace," said Beech earnestly, "I can assure you that no police surgeon will touch your daughter's body," and he was rewarded by a small nod of satisfaction from Sir Edward and a watery smile from the duchess.

The duchess rose to leave and both men rose also. "I wonder if you could take me back to my daughter's rooms?" the duchess asked Beech. "My chauffeur can give you the keys to the apartment and then take me home, while you start your investigations."

"Of course, Your Grace. If you will excuse me for a moment, I will order an automobile." Beech stepped outside of the office to get the Commissioner's sergeant to order up a police vehicle. Through the half-open door, he saw Sir Edward kiss the duchess's proffered hand, murmur some words of comfort to her and then, offering his arm for her to lean upon, he escorted her to the door. Beech noted the intimacy of old friends and wondered about this odd pairing of two unlikely people – the Commissioner who had risen from the lowly middle classes and the impeccably aristocratic duchess.

"Keep me informed at all times, Beech," Sir Edward said quietly as he transferred the duchess's hand to Beech's arm, and Beech nodded firmly.

Once settled in the police car, the duchess instructed the driver, "Trinity Mansions on Sloane Square," and they settled in to an awkward silence in the gloom of the vehicle.

"Chelsea is such a raffish area," the duchess murmured distastefully, "full of artists and writers and such. I should have preferred my daughter to live in Kensington or Knightsbridge. Much more suitable."

There was a silence, as Beech was unsure how to respond.

The duchess spoke softly again. "I apologise if I am speaking ill of an area in which, perhaps, you might live. People of my age are apt to speak without thinking."

Beech gave a small smile. "Please don't concern yourself, Ma'am. I do not live in Chelsea."

"Where do you live, if I may ask?"

"Albany, Ma'am."

"Oh?" The duchess seemed enlivened by this piece of information. "Those rather nice Regency bachelor apartments near Piccadilly? My husband resided there before we were married! Not, of course, that I was ever permitted to visit," she added hastily. "No, that would have been quite improper."

There was a small silence and the duchess folded and refolded her handkerchief in her gloved hands. Even Beech, with his self-confessed lack of understanding of women, knew that this was a sign of her inner turmoil and he felt that he should distract her in some way.

"Your husband was a friend of Sir Edward's, I understand?"

"Yes." The duchess visibly brightened. "From India. My husband's family had tea plantations. Edward was Inspector General of the Police in Bengal. He's a terribly clever man, you know. The Duke admired him greatly..." She tailed off and pressed her handkerchief under her nose. Beech realised that the car was drawing up by Trinity Mansions.

"Your Grace," he said quietly, "if you would be so good as to remain in this car, I shall go upstairs and find your man and send him down to you."

The duchess nodded and took a deep breath. "The rooms are on the second floor. Number twelve." Beech nodded. "Thank you, Mr Beech," she added.

"I shall have to speak with you again, Ma'am."

The duchess inclined her head in acceptance. "I shall await your visit in due course."

Trinity Mansions was a well-appointed cavern of sizeable apartments on the north-east corner of Sloane Square. It was now a minute past ten o'clock; Beech noted the time from the large clock above the opening to the department store across the square. There was a degree of bustle around the streets, a jam of three omnibuses outside Sloane Square Underground station and a long queue of men had formed leading into the Duke of York's Headquarters opposite the department store. Beech realised the men were waiting to enlist and this caused a momentary resurgence of the despair he had felt when reading this morning's newspaper headlines. He scanned the line of hopeful recruits and noted how many of them were woefully under age. And he knew, with certainty, that the Army would not turn them away, even if they confessed their tender ages. *Get on with your work, man,* he thought, swallowing hard and mentally closing off his emotions as he turned away and took the steps into the building.

It was apparent, from the foyer, the wooden panelling and the luxurious carpeting, that the occupants of the building were reasonably wealthy. There was a porter's cubicle with a sliding window but, at the moment, no occupant. There was a small lift, but Beech decided to take the stairs to the second floor. Scanning the door numbers, he followed them to the right and, as he turned a corner, he saw the chauffeur, seemingly deep in conversation with a uniformed man who was probably, Beech thought, the building's porter. Producing his warrant card, he said,

"Chief Inspector Beech of Scotland Yard. The Duchess is waiting for you in a police car downstairs. She instructs you to turn over the keys to the apartment to me before you leave."

"At once, sir," the chauffeur replied, producing a set of keys from his pocket.

Beech took the keys and asked the chauffeur to wait a moment.

"I assume you are the porter?" Beech enquired, turning to the other man.

"Bailey, sir. I am the day porter in Trinity Mansions."

"I see. And what time did you start today?"

"Seven o'clock, sir. I usually start at eight but Jenkins... he's the night porter... sent the boot boy down to fetch me when the maid found the body."

"You live down in the basement, Mr Bailey?"

"Yes, sir. My wife and I have two rooms – she's the housekeeper here. Mr Jenkins has a room, the boot boy, David, has another and we have a shared kitchen."

"No other staff?" Beech asked.

"Not living in, sir... for the whole building, I mean. Various tenants have their own arrangements. Some of the gentlemen have live-in valets, one lady in number seventeen has a live-in maid. Miss Treborne had a maid who worked from six thirty in the morning until five in the afternoon."

"Where is this live-out maid now?"

"Down in my rooms, sir. My wife gave her a sleeping draught, as she was so distraught, and tucked her up in our bed for a while."

"Right." Beech addressed both men. "I shall start my investigations and both of you will be about your business. You will not discuss the matter with anyone at all, is that understood?" Both men nodded. "Mr Bailey, some of my men will be along later today to interview you and the other staff. I would be grateful if you could keep Miss Treborne's maid in your rooms until we return."

"Yes, sir."

Beech turned to the chauffeur. "We will visit the Duchess this afternoon, as part of our investigation, and we may wish to speak to you further… I'm sorry, I didn't catch your name…"

"Hobson, sir."

"Well, Mr Hobson, just one last question. I understand that you cut Miss Treborne's body down and laid her on the bed. Is that correct?"

"Yes, sir."

"Did you touch anything else?"

"I opened a couple of large cupboards to find a sheet with which to cover Miss Adeline, sir," he volunteered, "and then I picked up her keys and locked the door behind me."

Beech noted that the man was wearing driving gloves. "Were you wearing your gloves all the time?"

"Yes, sir. I didn't think to take them off… especially when handling a dead body. It's not that I'm squeamish, sir, but… well… you know…"

"Yes, quite. Well, thank you, both of you. That will be all for the moment."

Beech waited for the men to disappear down the stairs, put on his own leather gloves and then let himself in. Sir Edward, with his introduction to Scotland Yard of the fingerprinting system a few years ago, had impressed upon all the police force that gloves should be worn at all times when investigating the scene of a crime.

The living room was gloomy, as most of the windows were swathed in thick, red, heavily tasselled curtains. The décor seemed to him rather bohemian, but he would rely on others' opinions on that matter. And certainly, untidiness could be added to the list of Adeline Treborne's character faults, he thought, as he surveyed the piles of magazines and newspapers on the floor. There were two used dinner plates on the table – one meal was only half eaten – and two wine glasses, one containing the dregs of what looked like red wine. There were table lamps everywhere. There was an envelope addressed to Adeline Treborne and a single sheet of blank paper in a wastepaper basket by the coffee table, but nothing else.

Beech went slowly around the flat, making a mental note of the contents of each room. The small kitchen was pristine, as though it was never used; the bathroom was cluttered with cosmetics and bore the tidemark of a recent bath, although the bath was dry. He noted the presence of a few crystals of bath salts on the side of the bath.

The small bedroom appeared to be part study and part storage. Two large cabin trunks were on their ends along one wall and a desk was on the wall opposite. Beech swung open one of the cabin trunks and noted that it seemed to be meticulously packed for a lengthy holiday. But where would one go, during a war? He found it odd. Ever since the *Lusitania* had been torpedoed by a German U-boat, two months ago, no one with any common sense was signing up for ocean-going cruises any more.

Lastly, Beech entered the main bedroom. The shape of Adeline Treborne's body underneath the sheet seemed very small. He lifted the sheet and was surprised to see that the body looked rather peaceful and composed, apart from the purple discolouration around her neck. The cut piece of a red curtain tie-back was draped loosely round her neck, like some macabre rope of beads. The bedside table was littered with all kinds of pills and potions. They would have to be collected and investigated. He looked up at the ceiling, where the rest of the curtain tie-back was dangling from a central light pendant. He noted with alarm that it was a gas fitment, which had started to come away from the ceiling owing to the weight of the body. There was no smell of gas but he nonetheless opened the nearest window and left the bedroom, locking the door behind him. Then he left the apartment as quickly as possible to find the porter.

"Is there still a gas supply to this building?" he asked urgently as he approached Mr Bailey's cubicle.

"Yes, sir," replied Bailey, "although we are in the middle of changing to electricity."

"Can you switch off the supply, at once," Beech ordered, his tone of alarm causing Bailey to move swiftly out of his cubicle and head for the stairs. Beech followed the porter down to a cupboard, where an elaborate set of handles had to be moved to the shut-off position for each apartment in the building.

"The tenants are not going to like this, sir."

"Well, it's better than them being blown up," was Beech's terse response. "Just let all the tenants know that there is a leak and you will endeavour to have it fixed as soon as possible."

"Shall I call the Gas Company, sir?"

"Not yet, Bailey. My people need some uninterrupted time in that apartment. I'll let you know when you can call them in. Do you have a telephone I can use?"

"Yes, sir. Follow me back to my cubby hole."

Beech lifted the receiver and asked the operator to connect him with Mayfair 100. After a short time, the telephone was answered by Detective Sergeant Tollman.

"Ah, Tollman, good man! Is the team all there, at the moment?"

"Yes sir," Tollman answered, "with the addition of Miss Mabel Summersby, who is currently taking photographs of the ladies."

"Is she, by George!" Beech said, thoughtfully. "That could be rather useful. Could you tell everyone that I shall be with them in about half an hour and to be ready."

"Yes, sir." Tollman sounded hopeful. "Do you wish Miss Mabel to stay then?"

"Yes, Tollman, I certainly do. I shan't be long."

The police driver was waiting patiently outside. Beech gave him the address in Mayfair, sat back in the passenger seat and smiled at the thought of being able to get 'the team' working together again. Their first case had been such a resounding success but the enforced idleness that had followed had weighed heavily with all of them.

Beech smiled, as he looked forward to being able to galvanise them into action. He realised that, although he had visited the house frequently in the last few weeks, he had missed the vibrant energy that they had all displayed while working on their first case.

Thankfully, that is all about to change, he thought content-edly as the car stuttered to a halt in front of the house.

CHAPTER TWO

The Team Prepare

Beech looked at his assembled team and relished their excited anticipation as he uttered the words, "We have another case."

Their relief was palpable, and an air of expectation filled the room as they waited for Beech to explain further.

"Last night, Lady Adeline Treborne was found hanged in her bedroom..."

"The society gossipmonger!" Caroline interrupted in astonishment.

"Yes," Beech continued. "She was..."

"That woman was disgusting!" This time it was Victoria interrupting, with some feeling.

Beech stared at the floor in resignation, as the two women vied with each other to remember the worst anecdotes they could about the unfortunate Adeline Treborne.

Victoria was first. "I've never forgotten the time when Millicent Cheshire – she was eighteen at the time – fainted at her own coming-out party – and the Treborne woman intimated in the newspaper that Caroline was pregnant..."

Caroline was outraged. "What about the time she wrote a piece about that orchestral conductor, Sir Emory Peters? She practically named every single one of his male lovers!"

"*If* I might continue…" Beech said, raising his voice, which made Arthur Tollman hide a smile behind his hand and Billy Rigsby flush slightly. Caroline raised her eyebrows and Victoria pursed her lips. Mabel Summersby, who only ever read scientific journals, had absolutely no idea who they were talking about and merely looked confused.

Beech continued, "Lady Adeline's mother, the Duchess of Penhere, is of the opinion that her daughter was murdered…"

"God knows there must be enough people who wanted to perform the deed…" muttered Caroline, refusing to keep her opinion to herself.

"Peter," asked Victoria, in a concerned tone of voice, "Are we only to be given crimes involving the aristocracy?"

Beech looked irritable and sounded even more irritable. This was not how he had imagined his announcement being received.

"Do you want to work on this case or not?" he asked bluntly.

"Yes!" came the unanimous response from the team.

"Then kindly allow me to explain the details of the case – *without interruption.*" He glared at Victoria and Caroline and a silence fell across the room.

"Right." He looked around, to make sure he had everyone's full attention, then he resumed. "As I said, Adeline Treborne seems to have hanged herself last night.

The live-out maid discovered her hanging from a light fitment in the bedroom and, understandably, became hysterical. She called the boot boy, who was outside in the corridor, I presume – we will confirm that today – who, in turn, called the night porter, who then roused the day porter. Lady Adeline's mother, the Duchess of Penhere, was called by telephone. She rushed around there by car but did not enter the apartment. Her chauffeur cut down the body, placed it on the bed, covered it with a sheet and then stood guard outside in the hallway. Meanwhile, the Duchess took a taxicab to the Commissioner's office – apparently, Sir Edward was a good friend of the late Duke – and the Commissioner called me in. All clear so far?"

Everyone nodded. Tollman, as usual, was taking notes. Beech continued, "I then escorted the Duchess back to Trinity Mansions in Chelsea. I spoke to the chauffeur and the day porter, a Mr Hobson and a Mr Bailey, respectively. They explained to me the chain of events, nothing more. Mr Bailey's wife had sedated the live-out maid and is going to keep her in their rooms until we question them today. I entered the apartment and found a certain degree of untidiness but nothing to suggest a struggle. She had had company for a meal. There were two dinner plates, one half empty, on the table and two used wine glasses. The bath had been used but not cleaned – but, presumably, that would have been the live-out maid's job, as soon as she arrived. There was a small bedroom, which contained two packed cabin trunks. In the main bedroom, the body of the deceased was on the bed, covered with a sheet. The gas fitment in the ceiling appeared to have become dislodged, presumably with the weight of the body, and I immediately opened a window and went downstairs to get the porter to turn off all the gas supply to the building. That's it. Any questions so far?"

Tollman spoke first. "Yes, sir. What makes the Duchess so sure that her daughter did not commit suicide – other than a parent's unwillingness to accept the act?"

Beech shook his head. "Not much, I'm afraid. She spoke of her daughter having a strong sense of self-regard, also of being very conscious of her position in society... and there was also the question of them being a staunchly Catholic family and her daughter would not be able to be buried in the family crypt if she was a suicide."

Tollman was not convinced. "Sounds like a case of wishful thinking to me, sir. It's hard for some relatives to cope with the fact that suicide is against the law and the Church frowns on it as well. I take it that the Duchess was aware of her daughter's reputation?"

"Apparently they had barely spoken for months and the Duchess said that Lady Adeline's activities had 'greatly distressed' the family. So, I think the Duchess harboured no illusions about her daughter."

Caroline interjected. "Can we have a copy of the autopsy report?"

Beech smiled broadly. "We can do better than that, Caro. How would *you* like to perform the medical examination of the body?"

Caroline was ecstatic. "Really?! How splendid! Why do I get the honour?"

"The Duchess pleaded that she did not want her daughter's body cut up by some police surgeon," Beech replied, "and I promised her it wouldn't be. Any surgery must be minimal and delicate, if you get my drift. Nothing visible once the body is dressed for burial, unless there is an absolute necessity to access the brain, for example. Unfortunately, you will have to conduct the autopsy at the scene. Not ideal conditions, I'm afraid."

"Can I help?" Mabel Summersby asked tentatively. "Only I've just finished reading Dr Hans Gross's book, *Criminal Investigation*, and I would rather like to put some of his knowledge into practice."

"I suppose you read it in German, as well?" said Caroline, half-joking.

"Of course." Mabel seemed surprised that anyone would ask. "There is no English translation at the moment." Caroline smiled and shook her head in amusement.

"Actually, Peter," Caroline said to Beech, "it would be very helpful if Mabel could assist me. And, also, I think it would be a good idea if she could bring her camera equipment."

Everyone looked over to the corner of the room where Mabel's bulky Graflex camera stood on a tripod.

"I agree. I think it would be jolly useful for us to have a visual record of the crime scene," murmured an impressed Beech.

"Ideally, I could do with another pair of hands as well... to help me move the body and so on. Perhaps Constable Rigsby or Mr Tollman...?" She trailed off as the two policemen shook their heads firmly. Caroline looked disappointed but then Billy had an idea.

"My Aunt Sissy could help you. She used to work as an undertaker's assistant – laying the dead out in their homes, like. Washing and dressing them and so on."

"She sounds perfect!" Caroline was thrilled. "Can you telephone her?"

"Straight away," said Billy, on his feet and out of the room in a flash.

"What is *my* task?" asked Victoria anxiously, beginning to feel left out.

"We shall *all* be going to Trinity Mansions." Beech was firm. "Tollman and Rigsby will interview the porters, while you and I will talk to the live-out maid. Then we must leave Caroline's team to their work, while you and I, Victoria, go and speak to the Duchess."

"Without wishing to incur your displeasure again, Peter," Victoria said pointedly, "can I just ask once more if we are only to be allowed to work on cases that involve the aristocracy?"

Beech drew a deep breath. "It is a fair point, Victoria," he conceded, "and the answer is, I don't know. Sir Edward has the final say on what cases we are to be given. This one happens to involve the family of a personal friend. I think, after our first case, he is aware that we can handle assignments that require extra discretion. I'm hopeful that, eventually, we will cover a broad range of crimes at all levels of society… but we must bow to Sir Edward's wishes. The last thing we want is to unnerve him by making demands at this early stage."

"Let's not rock the boat, eh, Mrs E?" Tollman gave her a friendly word of advice and Victoria nodded her understanding.

Billy came back into the room and said, with a grin, "Sissy's in a bit of a flap at being asked to assist – in her words – 'such refined and educated ladies', so I'm going to go and pick her up and reassure her, if that's all right with you, sir?"

"Of course!" Beech agreed. "I am surprised, Rigsby, that your aunt is capable of being 'in a flap' about anything!"

"Ah, yes, well, my aunt may be able to knock the block off some East End rough who looks sideways at her, but she can't always cope with those who may be termed 'her betters'," Billy said wisely. "She'll come around, once she gets to know the two ladies." With that, Billy put on his helmet and left.

"Fancy someone being nervous about meeting me!" Caroline exclaimed.

"Absolutely understandable," murmured Beech. "Frankly, Caro, you are the most terrifying woman I know!" – which earned him a punch in the chest from Caroline and amused everyone else.

Mabel suddenly found her voice and said, out of the blue, "We shall need equipment for the post mortem! I need containers for the stomach contents and bodily fluids."

Caroline agreed. "I need some equipment too. Mabel, make a list, and you and I will go to the medical suppliers in Wigmore Street first. Is it all right if Mr Tollman takes your camera equipment? He'll be very careful, I'm sure." She looked at Tollman for confirmation and he replied firmly, "Extremely careful, Doctor."

Mabel unscrewed the camera from the tripod and folded everything up into a small suitcase. Tollman carefully lifted it up, as though it contained fragile porcelain, and followed Beech and Victoria out of the door.

"We'll be there as soon as we can!" Caroline called after them and then she turned back to make a list quickly with Mabel.

***

Billy shot a glance at his aunt, sitting ramrod straight in the taxicab, and gave a small smile. He could tell that she was nervous because she had been completely silent throughout the journey so far. This was entirely unknown for the usually garrulous Sissy.

"I dunno what you're worried about, Aunty," said Billy, squeezing her hand. "You've met my governor…"

"Oh, yes, proper gentleman, Mr Beech," Sissy said hastily. She looked at Billy and furrowed her brow. "It's not *him* I'm worried about," she said confidentially. "It's these young women… they're posh and professional… whatever are they going to think of someone like me? I left school at ten. I've only ever been in service or done laying out. What am I going to say to them?"

"Listen." Billy tried to be firm but kind. "The lady doctor is all right. She's got no airs and she don't pull her punches. In fact," he added with a grin, "she reminds me of you."

"What do you mean, Billy?"

"She can give Mr Beech a right earache sometimes, but she makes me laugh."

"Gertcha, you monkey!" Sissy was beginning to thaw. "What about the other one… this pharmacist?"

"Well, I don't really know her that well," said Billy thoughtfully. "You might find her a bit odd. She's very clever and very scientific but she lives in a world of her own. She arrived at the house this morning with the buttons on her jacket done up wrong and she strikes me as being away with the fairies sometimes. But Doctor Caroline rates her, so that's good enough for me."

"Will I be meeting the widow lady, as well?"

"What, Mrs Ellingham? You might do."

Sissy was worried again. "She's *really* posh, isn't she? She's Lady Maud's daughter."

"Look, Aunty…" Billy tried not to sound exasperated. "This isn't like you at all! Since when have you ever worried about what people think of you? Mrs Ellingham and her mother, Lady Maud, are all right. They have a laugh and a joke like the rest of us. They might live in a house in Mayfair, with servants, but *you* live in a house in Belgravia now…"

"Yes, but we're the servants, your mum and I. We don't get ideas above our station."

"Oi, stop that!" Billy was annoyed now. "You don't realise how much this war has changed people. These ladies are working people now… *working*… just like the rest of us. Their fathers, husbands, brothers are dying out in France and elsewhere, just like the menfolk from the lower orders. God knows how many men will be left once this war is over and these women… educated women… might have to keep *on* working, cos they won't be able to find a husband to support them. Everything has changed, Aunty. We're all working class now."

There was a silence and Billy wondered if he had gone too far; but then he reasoned that Sissy had not clipped him around the ear, so he couldn't have upset her that much.

Finally, she spoke. "You're right, Billy. I'm just being foolish. I may not have the education of these other women, but I've got useful skills, haven't I?"

"Course you have. No one knows as much about boxing and dead bodies as you," he said, in a deadpan voice, and then they both burst out laughing.

It was a marginally more confident Sissy who stepped out of the cab in front of Trinity Mansions. She was regaling Billy with a tale of her friend Edith, who worked in the department store over the road, when Beech, Tollman and Victoria came around the corner, prompting Sissy to become quiet and a little flustered again.

Billy put a protective arm around her shoulders and Victoria, remembering that Billy had said that his aunt was 'in a bit of a flap', strode forward and held out her hand.

"Hello, I'm Victoria Ellingham. I'm so pleased to meet you," she said with a broad smile.

Sissy was unsure whether to curtsey or not, but as Billy had anticipated her urge and was holding her in a vice-like grip, preventing her from bending her knee, she tentatively held out her hand.

"How do you do, Miss," she murmured, as they shook hands.

Beech then held out his hand and said, "Thank you so much for agreeing to help us out today. We do appreciate it," and the bewildered Sissy found herself shaking his hand too.

Finally, it was Tollman's turn. He carefully put down the suitcase containing the camera and doffed his hat. "Detective Sergeant Tollman, ma'am. Pleased to make your acquaintance." He gave a rare smile and Billy found himself astonished that his aunt's cheeks appeared to glow.

Victoria eagerly continued, "Please call me Victoria."

Sissy looked shocked. "Oh, I couldn't do that, Miss!" she exclaimed.

Tollman said conspiratorially, "That's what I said, when she said that to me." Sissy looked bemused and Tollman continued, "So we agreed that I would call her 'Mrs E'."

Sissy looked expectantly at Victoria. "Is that all right, then? Mrs E?"

Victoria laughed. "Of course. Whatever suits. What shall I call you?"

"Oh, Sissy's what I've always been called, Mrs E, and I'm very happy with that."

"Well then, come along, Sissy. Dr Allardyce is relying on your expertise today," said Tollman, then he dropped his voice to a conspiratorial tone. "She's never done a post mortem before."

Tollman winked at Sissy, which was beginning to unnerve Billy, and he waited for Tollman to go into the building before he murmured to his aunt, "I think old Tollman's taken a shine to you... either that or he's sickening for something. A smile and a wink out of him in less than ten minutes! He'll have a heart attack if he carries on like this."

Sissy laughed and elbowed Billy in the ribs. "Leave it out, you silly sod! I think they're all lovely. I don't know what I was worried about."

"Well, don't get any funny ideas about walking out with Tollman, now, cos he's a widower with three grown-up daughters at home, who lead him a merry dance. You don't want to be doing with any of that."

"Oh, shut up, Billy... as if I'd be interested in Mr Tollman!"

As they ascended the steps into Trinity Mansions, Sissy asked, "How long's he been a widower then?"

When Caroline and Mabel arrived, carrying baskets of bottles, jars and Caroline's medical bag, Sissy and Billy were waiting for them in the foyer, the others having gone downstairs to conduct various interviews. All concerns about introductions and formalities were abandoned as Sissy scrambled to relieve Caroline of a basket she was about to drop, and Billy did likewise for Mabel.

"Oh, thank you so much... er..." Caroline looked harassed.

"Sissy."

"Sissy. I'm Caroline and this is Mabel. I think we have far too much equipment here but neither of us have ever done a proper post mortem before."

"I'm sure you'll have no problems, Doctor," said Sissy encouragingly, refusing once again to be drawn into using Christian names.

"Have you got my camera equipment?" asked Mabel anxiously, and Billy pointed to the corner of the foyer.

"All safe and sound, Miss Summersby. Shall we take the lift up to the second floor?"

Billy picked up the camera suitcase and opened the two metal grilles of the lift. Everyone stepped inside, and he pressed the button.

"Bit of a squash in here, eh, ladies?" He was trying to be jovial, but he could see that they were not in the mood. Everyone, including Sissy, was thinking about what had to be done when they entered the apartment.

Before he opened the door with the keys Beech had given him, he instructed the ladies to put on gloves. "There is going to be someone coming down here from the Yard later on today to try and find some fingerprints – if Mr Beech feels that further investigation is needed."

"Oh yes, of course," Mabel commented. "Important standard procedure. Excellent."

All the ladies, suitably gloved, were then ushered into the gloom of Adeline Treborne's apartment. Billy set down the camera case and left to resume his duties as support for DS Tollman.

They set all the equipment down in a corner of the living room and Mabel began to assemble the camera and tripod.

"Mabel, you carry on here, while Sissy and I go and have a first look at the corpse." Caroline was anxious to get under way. "I've never seen a corpse from a hanging before," Caroline confided to Sissy, "have you?"

"Yes, Doctor," was the surprising answer, as Sissy took her coat off and revealed that she was wearing an oilskin apron. "The undertaker I used to work for did two burials of clients who had hanged themselves. One was in 1912 and the other was just last year. It was a shock the first time I saw a corpse like that, but I knew what to expect the second time."

They reached the bed and Caroline drew back the sheet, exposing the body of Adeline Treborne.

"And I can confidently say, Doctor," said Sissy firmly, "that this lady did *not* die from hanging."

CHAPTER THREE

"The Lady Had Very Few Visitors."

Mrs Bailey was making a huge pot of tea when Billy arrived down in the staff quarters and everyone else was seated around a large, well-scrubbed kitchen table. It was quite a crowd. Aside from Beech, Tollman and Victoria, there was a pale-faced girl (Billy assumed she was the live-out maid who had discovered the body), a thin lad, about fifteen years of age – probably the boot boy – and a man who kept yawning, presumably the night porter who needed his bed.

"Oh, and here's another one!" Mrs Bailey said brightly, as Billy took his helmet off and sat down in a vacant chair. She began dispensing tea into a battery of china cups and then placing them on the table for everyone to help themselves. "Milk and sugar are over there, Davey. Go and fetch them, there's a good lad." The boy obediently trotted over to a large dresser and returned with a milk jug and sugar bowl. Mrs Bailey settled herself down in front of a cup of tea and Tollman got out his notebook.

"Right." Beech took the lead. "Mr Jenkins..." – he looked at the yawning man – "I can see that you are struggling to stay awake, so perhaps we should start with your version of events."

"Sorry, sir." Jenkins tried to stifle a yawn. "I'm not normally this tired but it's been a very difficult night, hasn't it, Mrs Bailey?" He looked at her for support.

Mrs Bailey sighed. "Not one of our best, Mr Jenkins. Not one of our best." She turned to Beech and elaborated. "You see, sir, although the staff down here are not *servants*… we are paid employees of the landlords… some of the tenants treat us like servants and we are expected to respond kindly."

"Please elaborate, Mrs Bailey."

"Well, last night, for example, David went round the building at ten, to collect all the boots and shoes. Well, he had to make two trips last night, didn't you Davey?" David nodded his head furiously.

There was a small silence and, realising that David was not going to elaborate, Mrs Bailey took up the baton again. "It was on account of Mr Ledbetter, in apartment nine, putting out six pairs of shoes. Six! The poor lad didn't have enough room in his basket. And then Miss Cavendish in number eleven had left a note out for him and he had to bring it down to me. Davey don't read, you see," she added by way of explanation.

"What did the note say?" asked Tollman, always a stickler for the details.

"Huh. Complaint, of course! It always is with number eleven. She was complaining that Davey got polish on her shoelaces and she marked her gloves putting them on. Poor Davey! He tries very hard and she's always got some complaint."

Beech was trying to progress the investigation. Jenkins seemed determined to deflect all questions to Mrs Bailey and Beech sensed that she could get easily sidetracked. "Well, that was at about ten thirty. Then I got a summons from her in number seventeen." She pointed over to the wall of numbered bells by which the tenants summoned the staff. "That was at about eleven. So, I goes up there and she's got bad indigestion, so I came downstairs to get the bicarbonate of soda, to take it back up to her…"

"Is this normal?" Tollman interjected, with a tone of disbelief in his voice. "Only it seems to me that you're running a hotel here, not an apartment block!"

Mrs Bailey looked triumphant. "That's exactly what I said to the management company, the last time they visited. If you want this place to be run like a hotel, then you'll have to employ more staff! The tenants are not supposed to bother housekeeping services, which is me, after ten o'clock at night. They're supposed to ring the duty porter if they have a problem. But no, her in number seventeen says, 'Ooh, I couldn't discuss my digestive system with Mr Jenkins! That wouldn't be ladylike!' Silly mare! So, it was nearly midnight before I climbed into bed."

Billy grinned, and Mrs Bailey winked at him. "More tea, love?"

"Don't mind if I do, Mrs Bailey."

"What about you, Lily, love?" she said, in a voice of concern, addressing the pale-faced girl at the corner of the table. Lily nodded. "Plenty of hot sweet tea, eh? When

31

you've had a shock, like you have." Lily nodded again, and tears began to well in her eyes. Victoria put a protective arm around her.

"Perhaps Lily should go back to bed with her cup of tea, and she and I can have a little chat. What do you think?" She looked at Beech for approval.

"I think that would be a good idea," he replied.

"Yes, you take Lily back to my bedroom, Miss, and I'll bring the tea through." Mrs Bailey directed them along the hall and came back to making a fresh pot of tea. "Is she a lady policeman, then?" she asked Beech, in reference to Victoria.

"No. A trained nurse," he answered quickly. "We sometimes bring them with us on our investigations when we feel someone may be in need of assistance."

"Oh, that's a good idea!" Mrs Bailey was impressed, and she turned her attention to stirring the large pot. "Tell them about *your* night, Mr Jenkins, afore you fall asleep on us!" she chuckled, as she swept out of the kitchen bearing a cup of tea for Lily.

"Yes, well, normally it's very quiet – except during the London season," he said, with reference to the social season enjoyed by the upper classes during the summer. "Then you get tenants coming in at all hours, with no regard for the amount of noise they make. But, anyway, last night, I had two tenants ring me. One at one o'clock in the morning to say that he was awoken by the sound of a door banging constantly and another tenant rang me at six this morning to say that her gas supply had stopped working…"

"Did you say six o'clock?" Beech interrupted. Jenkins nodded. "And where is this tenant's apartment in relation to Miss Treborne's?"

"The one directly above, sir. Mrs Amory in apartment thirteen. She is right above Miss Treborne."

"And what about the banging door?" Tollman asked.

"Oh, yes. That was because someone had left the staff entrance slightly ajar and it was moving in the breeze. Hardly what I would call *banging*, but then Major Sutcliffe reckons he's got incredibly sensitive hearing and, of course, his apartment on the first floor is right above the staff entrance."

"Where is this staff entrance and who has keys to it?" Billy could see that Tollman was getting interested.

"I can take you down there, if you like," Jenkins volunteered, rising to his feet.

"Billy." Tollman rose also and nodded to Billy to follow.

Jenkins led them down the corridor, past the bedroom – where Billy noted that Lily was sitting up in bed, weeping, and recounting her story to Victoria – and then through a door and up a flight of stairs, which brought them out beside the porter's cubicle. Mr Bailey was sorting the day's post into the tenants' pigeonholes and nodded an acknowledgement as they swept past and down an uncarpeted flight of stairs in the corner of the foyer. At the bottom of the stairs, there was a door to the outside world and two further uncarpeted staircases led up either side of the door.

"This is the staff entrance," explained Jenkins, "so that all servants, whether live-in or live-out, can enter or leave without coming through the front foyer. In fact, it is not allowed, unless they are accompanying a tenant. For example, there are three ladies in this apartment block that have live-in maids and companions, who go everywhere with them. *They* can pass through the front foyer, if they are accompanying their mistress, but not if they are on their own. Unless, of course, they have to come down to see the porter. These staircases…" he continued, pointing up one and then the other, "lead to either end of each floor in the building."

Billy walked up a few steps and his studded boot falls echoed loudly around the stairwell.

"Noisy, isn't it?" he commented.

Jenkins agreed. "That's what the Major says, because he's right by all of this, on the next floor. Mind you, his flat is the cheapest in the block." He lowered his voice confidentially. "He can't afford no more rent than he pays now, I heard him say once to another tenant, so he has to put up with it."

They turned their attention to the door. "Mm. Basic pin tumbler lock," said Tollman knowledgeably, "easily picked, if you know what you're doing. How many people have keys to this door?"

Jenkins looked uncomfortable. "I couldn't rightly say, to be honest. Over the years, the tenants have asked for keys for their personal staff – live-in and live-out. It's easy to lose track…" He tailed off when Tollman gave him a disapproving look.

"No second lock or bolt, I note," Tollman added, still fixing Jenkins with a look that implied negligence on behalf of the management.

Jenkins became somewhat defensive. "It's not possible, Detective Sergeant, for us to bolt the door from the inside. Too many people coming and going. We'd soon have complaints from the tenants if their staff couldn't come and go at all hours!"

"So, in other words, it's a complete free-for-all down here, then?" Tollman commented, and Billy could see that he was becoming exasperated. "Show me one of the keys for this door."

Jenkins lifted up a bundle of keys attached to his belt and separated out one flat silver key from the rest.

"As I thought." Tollman's tone was contemptuous. "The sort of key you can get any locksmith to copy easily. You and your mate, Bailey, are going to have to go around all the tenants in this building and find out exactly how many keys to this door are in circulation… and I want a list… by tomorrow!"

"Oh, what?!" Jenkins was not best pleased.

"I could always do it, Mr Tollman," said Billy grimly, not making a serious offer, merely pointing out the alternative. Jenkins quickly grasped its significance.

"All right, all right." He put his hands up in submission. "Last thing we want is a hulking great copper banging on everyone's doors. Bailey and I will do it."

Billy gave a subtle wink of satisfaction to Tollman.

"We'd better speak to this Major, then," said Tollman.

"Sorry, Mr Tollman," was the reply, "he went out just after seven this morning and he won't be back until late – if at all."

"Know where he's gone?"

"Hurlingham Club, probably, Mr Tollman. The Major's a top-class polo player. That's why he's always broke. Very expensive sport to maintain, I hear. Them ponies cost an arm and a leg to keep."

"I thought the cavalry had taken all the horses for the war," commented Billy.

"Apparently not," said Jenkins, as he led them up the back stairs again. "According to the Major, he and some of the other players had to fight tooth and nail to keep their ponies safe and sound in Britain. Obsessed with horses is our Major."

***

"It must have been a terrible shock for you, Lily," said Victoria softly, as she urged Lily to drink some more tea. "I don't know what I would have done in those circumstances."

Victoria assessed that Lily was probably about fifteen years of age. She appeared fragile – a slim, blonde wisp of a girl – but there were already lines on the face that betrayed a few years of hard work.

Lily's bottom lip trembled.

"I wouldn't have known, Miss, if I hadn't heard a creaking noise coming from the bedroom. I usually go straight into the bathroom and clean the bath and then quietly go about my other cleaning. Miss Adeline used to sleep until very late in the morning and she didn't like to be disturbed."

"So, you heard a creaking noise and went to investigate?" Victoria was gently insistent.

"Yes." Lily's voice dropped to a whisper. "She was swinging from the light fitment…" Lily put her hands up to her mouth at the memory.

"Lily, I'm sorry to ask you this horrible question… but was Miss Treborne in her death throes?"

"What do you mean, Miss?"

"Was she struggling, or twitching in any way?"

Lily's eyes grew wide at the thought of possible further horrors, but she said firmly, "No, Miss. Her body was perfectly still, and she just looked as though she was asleep… swinging up there, like a rag doll."

"And you saw no signs of a struggle in the apartment? No chairs turned over or tables upset?"

"No, Miss."

"What about signs of a burglary? Any drawers opened? Anything missing?"

Lily thought for a moment. "I can't say as I noticed, Miss. But everything seemed fine to me, when I walked in through the front door. I took my coat off and I was going to hang it on the coat stand by the door when I heard the creaking. Everything seemed normal."

Victoria nodded. Then Lily added, "But I think… I'm not sure… because I was so shocked by what was in the bedroom…I think that a couple of cupboards were open." Her eyes grew wide again as another thought occurred to her. "Do you think a burglar did this to her?"

"I doubt it." Victoria was quick to reassure her. "Miss Treborne probably left the cupboards open herself. She was probably looking for something." Victoria then thought to ask, "Lily… why did you ring the Duchess? How did you have her number?"

"The Duke gave it to me. Some time ago."

"The Duke?" Victoria was confused. She thought that Peter had reported that the Duke was dead.

"Miss Adeline's brother," Lily explained. "He used to visit now and then. I don't think he really gets on with his sister. I think he disapproves of her. One day, about a year ago, he said to me, 'Lily, if anything happens to my sister – anything untoward – you must ring her mother immediately.' I think he knew that the war was about to start, and he was going to be away."

"What did he mean 'untoward'?" Victoria was astonished.

Lily became confidential. "I shouldn't really say anything, Miss, but as Miss Adeline is gone… well… she lived a right rackety life, you know."

"Go on."

"Well, she spent a lot of money on clothes, booze and… well… drugs. She was always a bit addled – no matter what time of day. I think she used to get a special supply of drugs. There were rumours that someone used to come, late at night, with packages."

"Did anyone ever see these deliveries?"

"Mr Jenkins said he saw a man slip out of the back stairs door to the second floor one night, when he was late doing his rounds, but the man pulled his hat down over his face, so Mr Jenkins couldn't see him." Lily thought for a moment and then said, "I think Miss Adeline was quite lonely. She hardly ever went anywhere, except to shop for clothes, and she had very few visitors. I don't think the Duke would have come at all but for the fact he was stationed over the road before the war, at the Duke of York's Headquarters, and it was easy for him. He's on leave at the moment, and he came twice this week. On Monday, and the night she died. He arrived about six o'clock. Miss Adeline had asked me to stay a bit later and prepare a supper for them. Just cold cuts and potatoes, which I left covered over in the kitchen. So, I left about ten minutes after the Duke arrived. Apart from that, I never saw anyone visiting."

"But Miss Treborne must have gone out to a great many society functions," Victoria observed. "After all, it was her job to write about them."

Lily shook her head. "I never heard her say that she was going out to a function. I suppose she could have gone out to parties in the evening, when I wasn't here, but she would have told me. She used to tell me everything... her opinions about everything... used to drive me mad. I didn't listen half the time. I was just trying to get on with my work and she would follow me around telling me things. Like I said, I think she was lonely."

Victoria was puzzled. "So, all she ever went out for was shopping? You are positive about that?"

"Yes, Miss. She would say to me, 'Lily, I'm going out,' and off she would go. Then she'd come back a couple of hours later with some expensive item of clothing, a handbag, or some shoes."

"Well, thank you, Lily, you've been most helpful. Now you must get some more rest before you go home. Can you write down your address for me, in case the police want to interview you later?"

She furnished Lily with a pencil and a notebook and watched the girl write her details down.

Most curious, Victoria thought to herself. Whoever heard of a society columnist who never actually went to any of the events she wrote about?

***

When Tollman and Billy arrived back in the downstairs kitchen, without Jenkins, who had gone off, grumbling, to start the inventory of back door keys, Mrs Bailey and Beech were deep in discussion about sport.

"My husband's aggrieved cos there ain't going to be no more cricket – *anywhere*. I mean, Lord's Cricket Ground is a military depot now, Trent Bridge is a hospital, Headingley too…"

"There'll still be some club cricket though," Beech interjected.

Mrs Bailey was dismissive. "*If* they can get the men… anyway, that won't satisfy Mr Bailey. He lives for his top-notch cricket, does Mr Bailey. Whereas I am partial to a bit of horse racing – and that's disappearing as well! I knew it would be the death knell when the King announced he wasn't going to go to Ascot and then they said they were moving the Derby and the Oaks to Newmarket! I mean, what's the use of that! I could put me best hat on and go down to Epsom for the day and enjoy the races. I ain't going to go all the way up to Newmarket! Most of the racecourses have been taken over by the Ministry of Munitions now and made into training camps and all sorts."

"Well, Mrs Bailey, if you like the gee-gees, you must have had some good conversations with Major Sutcliffe then," said Tollman casually, pitching into the conversation.

"Who says I did?" Mrs Bailey seemed amused at the thought.

"Well, no one, but Mr Jenkins said that the Major is obsessed with horses and I would have thought he might have struck up a chat or two."

"Gaarn! Major Sutcliffe don't know nothing about horses!"

"Oh?" Tollman raised an eyebrow.

"Nah!" Mrs Bailey's scorn was mounting. "I was brought up around horses. My dad was a saddler in the big stables up at Camden Lock. Thousands of horses passed through there every week, when London was mainly horse-drawn transport. I spent my childhood helping my dad out and there ain't nothing I don't know about horses. Nothing. I said to the Major once, being friendly like, 'So what kind of polo pony have you got then, Major? Is it a Manipuri or maybe an Arabian, only I hear they're the best?' So, he looked at me like I've slapped him in the face and says, 'It's none of your business, my good woman!' and huffs off. Well, I said to myself, he don't know *nothing* about polo ponies. He's avoided me ever since."

Tollman began to scribble furiously in his notebook, his face set in what Billy called 'Mr Tollman's dog with a bone look'.

Mrs Bailey uncharacteristically lowered her voice and leaned forward. All three men, without thinking, leaned forward as well. "And I'll tell you something else…" she said in a loud whisper, "I would lay odds that the Major has never served in the military in his life, either."

CHAPTER FOUR

"What You Can Learn From a Dead Body, Eh?"

The three women stood and stared at the body of Adeline
Treborne. After Sissy's firm announcement that she did
not die from hanging, Caroline was unsure as to where to
begin. Mabel ventured a suggestion.

"I think I should photograph the body before we move
it."

"Good idea," said Caroline. Then she seemed to
awaken from her agony of indecision and said, "I must
close that window!" As she moved over to do so, she asked,
"Sissy, tell me why you made that statement, please?"

"Well," Sissy began, gaining confidence through being
the most experienced in matters of death. "The two bodies
I dealt with had terrible facial distortions – swollen, like.
The faces were red, the eyes bloodshot and bulging and, in
one of the cases, the tongue was swollen and blue, sticking
out of the mouth. Also, the second case I saw, the lady had
been hanging up for the best part of a day and her neck
was stretched and her head was pushed to one side. You
couldn't straighten it. Also, she had blood coming out of
her ears and nose and the corner of her mouth. There's also
the matter of the bladder and bowels…"

"Yes!" said Caroline and Mabel in unison and all three women looked at the floor directly beneath where the body had been hanging. There was nothing. No staining. But there was a smell of evacuated bowels in the air and Caroline suddenly said, "Sissy, help me roll the body on to one side."

"Oh, she's started rigor mortis, Doctor," noted Sissy, as she rolled the body of Adeline Treborne towards her and realised that the neck and shoulders were completely stiff.

"So, I notice, Sissy. But not yet in the leg muscles," Caroline observed, prodding the thighs. "I would say that this woman has been dead about four or five hours. Ah…" she trailed off as it became apparent that the smell was coming from beneath the body. "Evacuation of the bladder and bowels means that she died in her bed, not at the end of a rope. Mabel, I think we need photographs of this. Sissy, you'd better put her back down again, while Mabel sets up her camera. Photography does not appear to be a speedy job."

Sissy and Caroline stood to one side and Caroline began to make notes, while Mabel brought in her equipment and set everything up. "Ready," she said eventually, and Sissy once more rolled the body to one side. Then Mabel took photographs of the floor beneath the light fitment and of the light fitment itself, with the piece of cord still attached. Then, finally, a picture of Adeline Treborne flat on her back, the corpse's face now beginning to set into a grimace as creeping rigor mortis tightened the facial muscles.

"Right. Now, Sissy, I think we need to strip the body and start the proper examination. If you could do that for me, please, while I put my surgical gloves on."

"Yes, Doctor. Should we keep the clothing? Only I may have to cut the straps of the nightdress." Sissy began struggling to get the silk nightdress straps around the already rigid shoulders.

"Yes, keep the clothing for the police. There's some waxed paper in one of the baskets to wrap the nightdress in. Mabel, could you give Sissy some scissors, please?" Caroline was now sorting out her surgical instruments.

The nightdress was duly cut and pulled off the body and Mabel said, "What's that on her foot?" They all looked at a bulging vein on the victim's right foot. Caroline spread the big toe and the one next to it apart and peered at it through a magnifying glass. "There is a puncture in between the toes. My guess would be that either Adeline Treborne has been injecting herself with drugs or someone has administered drugs to her in this way. I think I should take some blood." She began preparing some syringes. "I'm going to have to cut into her femoral artery to get it, as her arms are beginning to stiffen. But, before I do that, could you just roll her over again, Sissy?"

Sissy obliged and now that the body was naked, they could see that the skin on the woman's back and buttocks was purple. "Well, she definitely died on her back, Doctor," pronounced Sissy.

"Yes, pronounced lividity," Caroline agreed. "But there are also the beginnings of lividity in the lower part of her legs and in her feet." Her lower limbs did indeed have a touch of purple about them.

"Wouldn't that suggest that the body was moved some time after death but within the six-hour mark?" ventured Mabel.

"Can I ask what that means, ladies?" asked Sissy. "Only I like to learn new things."

Caroline smiled at Sissy, her admiration for the older woman gaining momentum every minute. "Well, you know that lividity, the purple staining, happens when the blood pools in the part of the body that is lowest, after death?"

Sissy nodded and Caroline continued, "Well, if you change the position of a body within six hours of death, then it will change the pattern of lividity. Which means that this lady was dead for almost six hours before she was strung up. It was not enough to completely change the pattern of lividity, but it was enough to show that the body had been moved."

"Well I never," Sissy marvelled. "The next time I'm called out to a body I shall note anything suspicious like this, so I can tell the undertaker. They're supposed to report anything dodgy to the police. You can't rely on the doctors to spot it. No offence, Doctor," she added hastily.

Caroline laughed. "None taken, Sissy. If you hadn't been here, I should not have known what I was looking at, probably! Mabel, we need another photograph or two. Relax, Sissy, until Mabel's ready." Once again, they stood to one side while Caroline made more notes and Mabel's camera was set up. Then the body was rolled to one side to show where the blood had pooled in the lowest point of her body after death.

"Can you take a photograph of the foot and then one of the lower limbs too, please, Mabel?"

Mabel frowned. "We need a standard by which to judge the lividity in the lower limbs because it may not be apparent in the photograph without a comparison."

"Got you!" Caroline quickly took off one boot, hitched up her skirt and rolled one stocking down and off. Then she laughed and laid on the bed next to the body, with her own white limb next to the corpse's legs, providing a perfect contrast. Sissy was filled with admiration at such bravado.

Caroline continued the examination of the corpse, making notes as she went. "No marks of any kind on the head, scalp or face. No contusions or abrasions. So, no signs of an attack."

Mabel had spotted something, and she was approaching the corpse's feet with a scalpel and glass jar. "There's some white powder residue on most of the toenails. Is it all right if I collect it?"

"By all means. I'll write it down. Have you noticed that the toenails, fingernails and lips all look blue? Sissy, would you say that was normal with a corpse?"

Sissy peered at the hands and feet and then looked at the face. "I'd say it was more unusual that the mouth is blue, Doctor. If she had hanged, those lips would be very red or dark purple due to the blood congesting in the face. But those blue lips remind me of someone who's died of a chest complaint – you know, like pneumonia or TB."

"Sissy, you're a genius," said Caroline matter-of-factly. "Exactly what I was thinking. If this lady died from a drug overdose – a drug that depressed her breathing – then her lips would show lack of oxygen like this. What do you think, Mabel?"

"I would say that, judging from the colour of that vein in her foot and the other factors, she was injecting heroin and she gave herself way too much, which caused her to slowly asphyxiate and her heart stopped."

"Well I never," Sissy said. "What you can learn from a dead body, eh? But who strung her up… and why?"

"Mm. I'm afraid Miss Treborne's body is not going to tell us that… and yet…" Caroline had another idea. "Sissy, can you try to completely lift her body off the bed? Lift her as though you were trying to make her stand up?"

"I'll give it a try, Doctor." Sissy went around to the side of the bed and rolled the body towards her. Then she sat up the naked corpse. "We're lucky that she ain't stiffened up too much yet," she commented, then she put one arm under the body's far armpit, which Caroline could tell was not easy as the shoulders had stiffened to a degree that the arms were clamped firmly to the torso. Then, with a great deal of shuffling of the body on the bed and a few huffs and puffs from Sissy, she managed to get the corpse upright and on its feet. Eerily, the neck muscles had stiffened and the head remained upright. Sissy appeared to be holding a shop window mannequin and the late Adeline Treborne did not look lifelike at all. Sissy, on the other hand, was beaming in triumph at completing her task.

"Are you strong, Sissy?" Caroline asked.

"I think I am, Doctor."

"Then can you try to lift the body up, as high as you can? Can you try that?

Sissy took a deep breath, grasped the body firmly round the waist and lifted with all her might. She managed to get the body about three feet off the ground before she had to concede defeat and let it drop.

"Yes, as I thought," said Caroline, furiously scribbling some more notes. Mabel and Sissy looked nonplussed. "You can put the body back on the bed now, thank you, Sissy. You've been a tremendous help." Caroline turned to Mabel and explained. "This proves that even a strong woman would not have been able to lift the dead weight of Adeline Treborne and put her in a noose. It must have been a very strong man."

"Or two people," commented Sissy, which caused Caroline's eyes to widen at this fresh thought and she added yet more to her notes.

"Now, we had better get started on the surgical stuff, otherwise rigor will take over and we will find it impossible. Sissy, do you want to stay for this or would you rather not?"

"I've never done it before, but I'm game for anything!" said Sissy brightly.

"You really are a gem." Caroline was so impressed. "Perhaps you could help Mabel by passing her jars and bottles while she collects stuff. She may need an extra pair of hands."

"Righto." Sissy stationed herself behind the basket holding all the storage vessels that Mabel would need. She noted the sheaf of labels in the corner. "Do you want me to write on the labels and stick them on as well, Doctor?"

"Oh, could you? That would be a tremendous help."

Sissy chuckled. "As long as you spell out any difficult words for me."

"Right! Time for the first incision!" Caroline picked up a scalpel. "Where do you want me to start, Mabel?"

"Could we do the bladder first and see if there is any urine left in it? If there is, I may be able to distil it down and get a drug residue."

"The bladder it is." Caroline slowly made her first incision on the body of Adeline Treborne, while the other two women were poised to play their part.

CHAPTER FIVE

The Comings and Goings of the Night Before

"Rigsby, take the boot boy to one side and have a word with him, will you?" asked Beech confidentially. "Only he hasn't spoken a word since we've been here, and I think he is overwhelmed by too many people. He seems a bit shy."

Billy nodded. "Will do, sir." Then he moved back to the table and said, "David? How about you and me have a little chat about last night and this morning. Maybe, go to your room for a quiet word?" Billy smiled at the boy by way of encouragement.

A look of sheer terror came over the boy's face, which alarmed Billy. "Hold up, lad! Nothing to be frightened of!"

David looked at Mrs Bailey and she said, "It's all right, Davey, I'll be there. Let's you and me go with the nice policeman." She got up and took his hand and led him out of the kitchen. Billy raised his eyebrows in puzzlement at Tollman and Beech and then followed.

They went into a spartan bedroom, with pictures of trains on the wall.

"Oh, you like trains, do you, David? Me too." Billy tried to put the boy at his ease.

Mrs Bailey sat down on the bed and pulled David down beside her, patting his hand.

"Davey has a speech impediment, Constable," she explained. "He don't talk much, cos people can't understand him. Except I do, cos I had a sister with the same problem, so he talks to me."

Billy was sympathetic. "So, what causes this speech impediment then?"

"Tongue tie," was the reply. "The bit under his tongue is very short, so he can't move his tongue about to make sounds like you and me do."

Billy found himself unconsciously moving his own tongue around in his mouth, trying to imagine what it would be like not to be able to do so.

"Isn't there anything that can be done about it?" he asked.

Mrs Bailey smiled. "No, lad. Least I've not heard of any cure." She patted David's hand. "Sometimes we just have to put up with what God hands out, don't we, Davey? Anyway, the boy's all right. He's got a job, a roof over his head and food in his belly, and I make sure no one treats him badly. Can't ask for more, can you, Constable?"

"S'pose not." Billy agreed. "Right, so let's get started, shall we?" Billy got out his notebook and checked over his notes. "So, Mrs Bailey, you told us about David going to bed late because he had to make two trips to collect all the boots and shoes from outside the tenants' doors."

"That's right."

Billy turned to the boy. "David, when you were around and about yesterday, did you see anyone going in or coming out of Miss Treborne's apartment?"

David nodded and began to speak. His speech was not as bad as Billy had expected. When explaining later to Tollman, he would say, "It was like someone with a really bad lisp because they've got cotton wool wrapped round their tongue and made worse because he doesn't really want to open his mouth and he mutters."

Between David's explanation and Mrs Bailey's translation, Billy was able to gather that, on his first trip to collect boots and shoes, at about ten, he had seen a man, in military uniform, leave Adeline Treborne's apartment in a temper, judging by the way he banged the door behind him. He said he thought he heard her laughing through the briefly open door. Then, when David did his second sweep of the floor, at about ten thirty, to pick up the extra shoes that the man in apartment nine had left out, as he came to the top of the back stairs, he saw Major Sutcliffe going down the tenants' staircase.

Billy remembered that Mrs Bailey had been called out to a tenant at about eleven and asked her if she had seen anything or anyone.

"No, nothing at all, I'm afraid."

"Right, so then we come to this morning, David," said Billy. "Tell me what happened this morning."

David explained, again with the help of Mrs Bailey, that he had done his first trip with the cleaned and polished shoes and boots at about six fifteen. Then he had to come on a second trip to the second floor with the six pairs of cleaned footwear for Mr Ledbetter in apartment nine. As he was laying out the pairs of shoes outside the door, Lily arrived, and they smiled at each other.

"Davey's sweet on Lily," said Mrs Bailey mischievously, which made the boy go red and Billy grin.

Then the boy said that just as he was leaving, Lily gave this terrible scream and came rushing out of the apartment, sobbing. David went over to help her and realised something was wrong in the apartment. He went to go inside but Lily slammed the door and wouldn't let him go in.

Mr Ledbetter came out of his apartment in his dressing gown to see what all the fuss was about, and Lily asked him to call the porter. "She was yelling and screaming, 'Miss Adeline's dead! Miss Adeline's dead!'," explained Mrs Bailey, translating for David. "So, he called Mr Jenkins, who rushed upstairs," she continued. "He apparently went into the apartment, not to view the body, which he said he didn't want to do, but to call my husband up... and you know the rest."

That was as much as the boy knew, so Billy closed his notebook and patted David on the shoulder. "Thank you, lad," he said simply, and the boy nodded.

***

Caroline and Mabel's work was done. Samples had been collected of bodily fluids – fortunately there had been some urine left in the bladder – and Caroline had removed the liver, one kidney and part of the pancreas. Sissy had watched it all with fascination and diligently written labels for the jars and vessels containing the samples.

Caroline had been very careful to make minimal incisions and she was now sewing up the corpse with her very best and neatest stitches.

"Don't worry, Doctor," said Sissy, after Caroline had explained that the duchess did not want any visible marks of an autopsy on her daughter's body. "Once I've washed and dressed her, done her hair and put a bit of rouge on her cheeks and lips, she'll look like Sleeping Beauty who's just dropped off this minute." Even Mabel managed to laugh at that remark.

"Will it be all right if I rustle up a bowl of hot water and a cloth to wash her?" she asked. "Only I don't want to disturb any evidence."

"The kitchen looked virtually untouched," observed Mabel. "I'll come with you, Sissy, and make a note of anything that we disturb."

Caroline was finished, and she surveyed her handiwork before removing her blood-caked gloves and apron. When Sissy and Mabel reappeared, she carefully washed her hands in the bowl and dried them, before putting her outdoor gloves back on.

"You carry on, Sissy. Mabel and I will look through the drawers and cupboards for suitable clothes to dress her in." Caroline and Mabel began to carefully sift through the contents of the bedroom furniture but to no avail. "All this stuff is much too glamorous for a burial," Caroline observed, holding sequinned dresses in either hand.

"Have you noticed that a lot of her clothes appear to have never been worn?" observed Mabel. "Such extravagance," she added disapprovingly.

"Let's look in the other bedroom," suggested Caroline. "Peter said that there were cabin trunks of clothes in there."

The two women sifted through all the neatly folded and stored clothes and eventually found a plain, high-necked blouse, a long black hobble skirt and some black stockings.

"Shoes?" asked Mabel, opening a nearby cupboard and displaying an extraordinary number of pairs of shoes.

"Again, none of these appear to have been worn," commented Caroline, displaying the smooth soles of the shoes to Mabel. She selected a pair of plain black pumps.

"Perhaps she was just obsessed with shopping? You do hear of such women," said Mabel, making it very clear by her tone of voice that she found such behaviour objectionable.

"Mm. But all of these items of clothing are from exclusive fashion houses and the shoes are handmade. It takes an awful lot of money to be able to do that." Caroline was intrigued.

"Huh. Money from the family coffers probably," replied Mabel dismissively.

When they returned to the main bedroom, Sissy was towelling off the body and had removed the soiled sheet from the bed. "Do you want to keep that sheet, Doctor?" she asked.

Mabel said she would take it, just in case there was a need to try to extract something from it, and she duly folded it and wrapped it in waxed paper, while Sissy and Caroline struggled to dress the body.

"It's no good, Doctor," panted Sissy, after her third attempt to get the blouse on the corpse. "Rigor's too far advanced now. We'll just have to wrap her in a clean sheet and put the clothes and shoes next to her. The undertakers will make her look presentable."

It was agreed that that was the best they could do, and Sissy would telephone an undertaker to come over straight away. "I'll ring Netherfield's. They know me there and they are used to dealing with upper-class clients. They'll be discreet, when I tell them what's happened. I'll wait here until they turn up and explain everything. Get Mr Beech to telephone the Duchess and tell her what's happening. Tell her that Netherfield's will be in touch when the body is ready to be seen in the Chapel of Rest."

"Sissy, I don't know what we would have done without you," said Caroline with feeling and, to Sissy's great surprise, she gave her a big hug. Mabel echoed the sentiment but shook Sissy's hand instead.

"Any time, ladies," replied Sissy, a bit flustered and pink. "I'm always ready to help out. You just get Billy to fetch me. In fact, could you get Billy to come up and wait with me? Then he can take me home afterwards."

"We will, we will." And gathering up all their equipment – camera, samples, packages and baskets, Caroline and Mabel left.

When Billy came up to the apartment, he found his aunt sitting in an armchair in the living room, smiling contentedly.

"Went all right then, I hear?" he said, giving her a peck on the cheek. "Doctor Caroline couldn't stop singing your praises downstairs."

"Billy," said Sissy, stroking Billy's cheek, "I haven't felt so useful since July 1890."

"1890? What happened then?"

Her eyes grew a little moist and she said, "You daft 'aporth! That was when I delivered you, on the kitchen floor, when your mum unexpectedly went into labour."

CHAPTER SIX

What Do We Know About Adeline?

Over dinner that evening, Beech, without going into any of the details of the case, asked Lady Maud if she knew the Duchess of Penhere.

Maud frowned. "Not really. I know *of* her, of course. An old Catholic family, which meant that our paths never crossed in Church society because we moved in different circles. But I did serve on a committee, briefly, with her. The Royal Homes for Officers' Widows and Daughters. I joined the committee in September 1912 but the Duchess resigned six months later. I presume it was because of the activities of her daughter. The poor woman could barely hold her head up in public once those scurrilous columns started being printed."

Caroline interjected, "Maud... are they moneyed... the Trebornes?"

"Not at all! In fact, absolutely the opposite. I heard that the late Duke lost quite a lot of money in India – bad investments or something. He had to sell his two tea plantations and the Treborne country estate in Berkshire. The dreadful Adeline had to be brought back from spending her way around Europe, so I heard, and the son... the present

Duke… had to give up most of his horses and stabling, could no longer ride to hounds or play polo."

"Polo again!" muttered Tollman.

"I beg your pardon, Mr Tollman?" Lady Maud asked.

"Sorry, Your Ladyship. Just talking to myself. Only polo has cropped up quite a bit today. Sorry for the interruption."

"That's quite all right." Lady Maud looked bemused. "I think, anyway, I had finished. I really don't know any more about the Trebornes than that. The Duchess keeps a very low profile – well, you would, wouldn't you, if your daughter was the most hated person in London society?"

Everyone around the table murmured their agreement.

Lady Maud continued. "Anyway, I shall retire to my bedroom now, as I have a great many letters to write, and leave you good people to your deliberations. May I say that I am *so* pleased you have another case! Although I shall miss the regular games of cribbage with Mr Tollman, it is far more important that you are all usefully employed and enjoying your teamwork!"

Lady Maud rose, and the three men rose, and she swept out.

Beech smiled and said, "Well, now we have had Lady Maud's blessing, shall we retire to the study and deliberate our findings?"

Earlier in the day, Caroline had presented her initial evidence from the autopsy and everyone had agreed that Adeline Treborne had not committed suicide. Beech had duly informed Sir Edward Henry, who had given them permission to pursue the case further.

"I think I should keep my distance, for the moment," Sir Edward had said. "So, I'm afraid that will mean that you, Beech, will have to tell the Duchess the news about any developments. I just feel that it would be... politic... for me to keep in the background while the investigation is under way."

Beech had said that he understood. "Of course, Miss Summersby is, at the moment, conducting her tests and printing her photographs, so we will have a more detailed picture in a couple of days," he had added.

Sir Edward's eyes had lit up. "Yes! I'm very interested in this sort of work. This lady pharmacist seems to have embraced the entire concept of scientific police work. I should like to have a discussion with her, after this case is concluded. Well done for adding her to your team, Beech."

Finally, Beech had said, "A fingerprint officer will go to the apartment this afternoon, sir, and once the fingerprints have been processed, they will check them against any known criminals. But in this case, I'm not hopeful that we are dealing with any suspects with fingerprints on file. After all, we only have the prints of known criminals here at the Yard."

Sir Edward had nodded. "In the fullness of time, that will all be remedied," he had said, and the interview had concluded.

That evening, as the team reviewed the evidence they had gathered in the morning, they all agreed that Adeline Treborne was a complete mystery.

"If, as Lady Maud suggests," Beech ventured, "the family was short of money, I suppose that might account for her taking the job at the *Herald*. It's a terribly drastic thing to do, though. To cut yourself off from polite society like that."

"She had a huge amount of exclusive and expensive clothing and accessories," commented Caroline. "I would guess that any fee from the newspaper would not be enough to pay for more than a handful of the dresses I saw hanging in her wardrobes."

Victoria agreed. "Lily, the live-out maid, said that Adeline was always going shopping. She said Adeline would say to her 'I'm going out' and then she would return with bags of shopping."

"Perhaps because she was well-known," Tollman suggested, "fashion houses gave her clothes?"

Victoria and Caroline looked doubtful.

"They only do that when a famous personality – like an actress – is actually liked and admired," said Caroline. "No one would want a hated and despised gossip columnist wearing their clothes." She seemed amused at the thought.

Victoria spoke again. "The one thing Lily said that really bothered me was that Adeline Treborne never went anywhere – except shopping. In other words, I would have expected her to be out constantly, mingling with high society, in order to gossip about them. But according to Lily, who was there every day, Adeline never went anywhere and received almost no visitors that she knew of, apart from her brother. I mean, how does anyone tell tales about people when they don't actually mix with them?"

Billy suddenly spoke. "But why, Mrs E, would you invite someone to a party when you knew they were going to gossip about it in the newspaper afterwards? It seems to me that no one would want her at their functions, would they?"

"Very true," observed Beech. "So where did she get her information from?"

"Servants?" suggested Tollman. "They're always the best source of gossip, in my experience."

"Yes, but how and when would she get information out of servants?" asked Victoria. "She couldn't just waltz into the servants' quarters of all the aristocratic households in London! Any self-respecting butler would show her the door!"

"I suppose she could have met them somewhere and paid them for their information?" ventured Billy.

"No. I don't think so, lad," said Tollman, his face set in a frown of puzzlement. "It can take years to set up a network of informants… believe me, I know. Adeline Treborne was not old enough or in the right position in society to do that. Someone must have been helping her."

"Well…" Beech was tired, and his leg was aching; he wanted to make plans for tomorrow so that he could get home to his bed. "We have several things that must be done tomorrow. Victoria, you and I must see the Duchess and her son… Tollman and Billy, you need to interview the other tenants to see if they saw or heard anything."

"Yes sir," Tollman agreed. "I'm particularly interested in interviewing this Major chap."

"Oh yes!" Beech smiled. "The one that is supposed to be a fanatical polo player, except the housekeeper reckons he doesn't know one end of a horse from the other and he isn't really a major! I shall look forward to developments on that front. Caroline? What about you?"

"I'm afraid I'm on duty tomorrow, Peter," was the reply. "But I shall consult with Mabel during the day and see if she needs any assistance to process her material."

"Yes, you both did a splendid job there." Everyone in the room murmured their agreement with Beech.

"Entirely down to Billy's aunt, Sissy… and I'm not just saying that," Caroline admitted. "Sissy's experience with dead bodies, and her observations, absolutely pointed me in the right direction, because, frankly, I didn't have a clue. So much so that I am thinking of enrolling on the next course in pathology that comes along, because we barely touched on it in medical school. You do know, Peter," she added, "that the evidence from the autopsy we performed will be inadmissible in court, because I am not a registered pathologist or police surgeon?"

"Yes, I know," Beech replied gravely. "Although we could probably use some of your basic evidence about the body before surgery. The registrars will want a death certificate from you as an attending physician, and in court, if it comes to that, you can explain why you came to the conclusion written on the certificate… which will be?"

Caroline looked into the distance. "At the time I examined her – before surgery – I can only say for sure that she probably died from a drug overdose, not hanging – this is what the physical evidence showed me. But I don't know if she accidentally administered an overdose herself and I don't know at what point she *actually* died. I mean, it could be that she was seconds away from death when she was strung up and that just finished her off – in which case someone would be technically guilty of murder. We know that she could not have hanged herself. She was, probably, already a corpse when she was strung up, so I would have no concrete evidence to put something like 'murder by person or persons unknown'. If I put 'accidental death due to drug overdose', might that not generate a coroner's inquiry? I don't think the Duchess would be very happy about that."

"No, she wouldn't," Beech agreed, "but then I think that Sir Edward would probably squash any attempt to hold an inquiry. I think go with the accidental death description and we will just have to hope that we can nail the perpetrator with a confession, which will explain the murder process."

"Just one more thing, sir," added Tollman. "I think Billy and I should, if we can fit it in, go and see the editor of the newspaper Miss Treborne worked for. We need to find out what he knows and also caution him to keep his mouth shut. We don't want him finding out and splashing it all over the newspapers before we have had a chance to investigate. We should probably see him first before he starts preparing the early edition. The *Herald* does a print run twice a day."

"Good idea, Tollman. If he gives you any trouble, just intimate that Miss Treborne stumbled across some information that affects national security during wartime and he could find his whole newspaper slapped with a D Notice if he doesn't co-operate."

"Yes, sir," Tollman smiled grimly.

"Right!" Beech was firm this time. "Bed for us all, I think. We've done a good job today. Let's make further advances tomorrow." Then he made for the door.

"Peter, you're limping again," said Victoria in a voice of concern. "Why not stay here tonight and give your leg a rest."

"Nonsense!" said Beech, looking embarrassed. "I'll get a taxicab home and climb into bed. Nothing a good night's sleep won't cure."

Victoria followed him to the front door and put her hand on his shoulder. "You must take care of yourself, Peter," she said softly. "None of us can do without you."

Beech looked at her intently. "Could you do without me, Victoria?" he asked boldly. He knew he was risking a rebuff. His last attempt to resurrect their past relationship had led Victoria to ask him gently to be patient.

But this time, she returned his gaze without embarrassment and said simply, "Never."

Beech felt a surge of relief mixed with hope. He kissed her lightly on the cheek and limped out of the door. The ache in his leg seemed to have greatly diminished and he smiled as he made his way towards Park Lane to hail a taxicab.

***

Billy was replete with tea, toast, eggs and bacon and standing outside the Mayfair house when Mr Tollman arrived – just as he had been instructed.

"Good." Tollman was approving. "Let's not waste any time, lad. We've got a hell of a lot of fish to fry today."

"Raring to go, Mr Tollman," said Billy cheerfully, and they strode out towards the bus stop.

"First stop, Fleet Street," said Tollman firmly. "I'm just in the mood for a barney with a gobby editor."

Arthur Cranham did not disappoint. He was a typical Fleet Street newspaper editor. Loud, opinionated, clever and tough. When told that the Detective Sergeant and the Constable wanted to see him privately, he began to protest.

"You can discuss anything with me, anything private, in front of my staff," he said loudly and waved his arms expansively to encompass his not inconsiderable stable of employees. "I have no secrets." The 'staff', made up mostly of grizzled middle-aged men, with a smattering of female typewriter operators, paused in their endeavours, with interest, to see how their boss would win out over the coppers.

Tollman gave the sort of small, mirthless smile that made the hairs on the back of Billy's neck stand up and he waited for the sucker punch that would take Arthur Cranham down.

"How about Maisie Skinner?" said Tollman quietly, and Billy was fascinated to see all the air knocked out of Cranham as though he were a balloon in the hot sun.

"This way," was the editor's surly response, and the two policemen followed.

"Bloody hell, Mr Tollman," murmured Billy, barely moving his lips. "What have you got on this man that felled him so quickly?"

"I'll tell you later, son," Tollman murmured back as they entered Cranham's office and then closed the door.

The editor of the *London Herald* looked uncomfortable as he said, "I paid my dues on that score. Why has it all reared its head again?"

Billy had no idea what the man was talking about, but he was intrigued to see Tollman manipulate him by mentioning a name.

"Actually," Tollman said briskly, "I haven't come about Maisie Skinner…" Cranham looked visibly relieved. "That was just to stop you playing silly buggers and give us a bit of privacy to discuss another matter."

"Sit down," – Cranham motioned to the chairs by his desk – "and tell me what you really want… Detective Sergeant Tollworth, is it?"

"Tollman. We're here about Adeline Treborne."

Cranham's face broke into an exasperated expression. "I don't believe it!" he almost shouted. "What?! The bloody aristocracy paying the police to fight their libel suits now, are they? Forget it! I've had QCs in here threatening me with High Court actions if I print something about their clients, and they never follow through because they know that the dirty little secrets will have to be spelled out in detail if it goes to court. So, you can tell your Commissioner that threatening police action isn't going to work either. Got it?"

Tollman sat calmly through the tirade, while Billy tried to repress the urge to thump the aggressive Cranham.

"Finished, have you, Mr Cranham?" Tollman asked sarcastically. "For your information, we are not here on behalf of some of Miss Treborne's aggrieved victims. We are here because, last night, Adeline Treborne was found dead in her flat and we believe she was murdered."

Cranham's face turned ashen and he said, "Good God! That's impossible! Her copy was delivered this morning!"

It was Tollman's turn to be surprised. "Show me."

Cranham opened the door and bawled into the newsroom, "Miss Taylor! Bring me the original copy for *A Lady's View*!" A young typewriter operator scuttled across the room with a sheaf of pink notepaper and thrust it into the editor's hand. He turned back into the room waving the pink paper. "Eight thirty this morning, it was on the mat, as usual. On pink paper, as usual. In a pink envelope. And in her handwriting, as usual. See for yourself." He handed the papers over to Tollman.

"Could they have been delivered last night?"

"Nope," was the firm answer. "I was here until gone midnight and there was nothing pushed through the letter-box last night. And I was here at eight this morning and there was nothing on the mat. Perhaps her ghost delivered it?" Cranham guffawed at his tasteless joke. Then his news journalist's instincts kicked in. "So, how did she die? Strangled by a lover? Knifed by an irate debutante? Was it gruesome?"

Tollman's lip curled in distaste. "You said that you were here until after midnight. Have you any witnesses?"

"Hold on a minute! Why would I kill the goose that lays the golden eggs, eh? Do you know how much our circulation's gone up since she started writing for us? The hoi polloi love a bit of dirt – especially when it's about their betters. Don't try and frame me for this murder, Tollman. You're looking in the wrong direction. Start looking among the people she wrote about. Some of them threatened to kill her, take my word for it." Cranham suddenly bounded over to the door again. "I can do better than that… Miss Taylor!" He bawled again. "Bring me the Complaints File!"

"What, *all* of it?" she bawled back, astonished.

"Yes! And be quick about it!"

There was a pause as Miss Taylor struggled up to the doorway with her burden and then Cranham turned around to Tollman with a heavy, bursting at the seams box file, which he dumped on Tollman's lap.

"There you are," he said triumphantly. "Fill your boots with that lot!"

"Is this all to do with Adeline Treborne?" Tollman was incredulous.

Cranham laughed. "Absolutely! Every bit of it. And that's only the file for 1915. She's been writing the column now for two years. That woman is… sorry… *was*… hated by all London society. Never known anything like it."

"Did you discuss this with her?" Tollman asked. "Did you offer her protection?" he persisted. "I mean, if she was worth so much to your circulation figures, wouldn't you want to protect your investment?"

"Never saw her. I didn't even know where she lived," was the surprising answer. "She waltzed in here, about two years ago, all dressed in her finery and makes me an offer. She produced a load of incredibly racy society stories from her handbag and asked me how much they were worth. I looked at them and realised that, if they were not complete fiction, they were gold dust. I made her an offer. She bargained a bit and we agreed on a sum..."

"What was that sum?"

"Three hundred pounds a year." Billy couldn't help himself and whistled. Cranham acknowledged Billy's disbelief. "It's a lot of money, I know. But, like I said, the stuff was gold dust and I took a punt. She made a few conditions. She said she didn't want to see me any more, or visit the office, nor did she want me visiting her home. Made me laugh. Here she was, dishing the dirt on all her school friends and their parents and she's trying to make *me* feel like I'm the lowest of the low. She said she would put her name on the articles... I said to her, 'Why would you want people to know it's you? Do it under a pen name, otherwise they won't invite you to functions and you won't be able to get the stories.'"

"What did she say to that?" Tollman was puzzled.

"She just shrugged and said she had ways of getting the information anyway, and not to worry about that side of things. She said she wanted everyone to know it was her. She didn't care. Then she said that the copy would be delivered by hand, every Thursday, for the weekend editions. And it has been, without fail. And like it was this morning."

Billy and Tollman looked at each other and Tollman handed over the heavy complaints file to Billy with an exasperated sigh.

"So, when can I run the story about Treborne's murder?" said Cranham hopefully.

"You can't," said Tollman flatly. "There's a possibility that she was involved with a spying ring," he lied creatively, "and there's going to be a D notice slapped on it."

Cranham made a noise of disgust. Adeline Treborne was nothing but a good story to him now. Billy realised that the man had absolutely no scruples.

"Right… well, when you get this case sorted out, I want the full SP on this one. Otherwise I'm going to come down like a ton of bricks on your Commissioner. This paper needs to run the story first, or I will want to know why!"

Tollman rose, and Billy did likewise, clutching the heavy file in front of him. "You do that, Mr Cranham, you do that," Tollman said in a patronising tone of voice. "I'll give the Commissioner the Maisie Skinner file and you two can have a nice chat about old times."

Cranham scowled. "All right. You've made your point. Now hop it, there's good little policemen." He eyed Billy up and down. "Or, in your case, son, good *big* policeman."

Out in the street, Billy waited for a beat and then said, "Well, are you going to tell me or not, Mr Tollman? About this Maisie Skinner?"

Tollman's face took on a grim set. "Prostitute, lad. Matey in there was friendly with her, very friendly, if you get my drift. She was found face down in the canal up by Regent's Park, barely a stone's throw from Mr Cranham's residence. He came up with an alibi. We couldn't prove otherwise, so we had to let him go. But, judging by the reaction when her name is mentioned, he's still in fear of being collared again."

"Do you think he did her in, Mr Tollman?"

"Nah." Tollman shook his head. "I think she thought she'd do some more business on her way home and she picked a wrong 'un. Either that or her pimp did her in. Too near King's Cross for my liking. Crawling with vermin round that station, it is. Come on, lad, let's take that file back to Mayfair, get a cup of tea off Mrs Beddowes, and then sally forth to nab this major. I'm feeling in the mood to make a collar today."

CHAPTER SEVEN

The Missing Major

The major was not there. "Didn't come back yesterday," said Mr Bailey, shrugging. "Not seen him, Mr Tollman. You can try his apartment, but I really don't think he's there."

Billy knocked loudly and then put his ear to the door to hear if there were any sounds from inside. After a while he shook his head and pronounced the place empty.

Tollman looked frustrated. "Best get on with interviewing the other residents," he said, "then if the Major hasn't returned by lunchtime, perhaps we might pay a little visit to the Hurlingham Club and see if we can find him."

"Where *is* this Hurlingham Club, Mr Tollman?" asked Billy, relishing the thought of a trip somewhere exotic.

"Fulham, lad, on the river, near Putney Bridge."

"Oh." Billy was disappointed. Fulham and Putney, to him, were definitely not exotic locations. Middle-class, in parts – maybe, but nothing special.

The first person they interviewed was Mr Ledbetter – 'Six Shoes' as Billy called him – and the neighbour opposite Adeline Treborne's apartment.

Ledbetter was a thin-faced, pernickety man, whose apartment bore testimony to his parsimonious and well-ordered life – no comfort, very few chairs, no pictures on the walls – nothing.

"So, sir," said Tollman, resigned to the fact that he wouldn't be offered a seat. Billy began to take notes. "The night before last. Did you see anyone coming or going from Miss Treborne's apartment?"

"No," said Mr Ledbetter.

Tollman sighed inwardly, realising that Mr Ledbetter was a very pedantic man and would need specific questions in order to respond.

He tried again. "Did you *hear* anything, sir?"

"Yes. Several things." Then there was a silence.

Resisting the urge to smack him, Tollman continued, "Could you please talk us through the sequence of events that evening and explain to us, in detail, what you heard."

Mr Ledbetter pursed his lips. "I put six pairs of shoes out at nine forty-seven. At about nine fifty-eight, I heard Miss Treborne's door slam and heard the lift being summoned. I did *not* hear the boy pick up my shoes, which made me very cross. I waited for fifteen minutes, I heard a knock on the door opposite, and then I opened my door and looked out. My shoes were still there," – he sounded aggrieved – "and I noticed that Major Sutcliffe was entering Miss Treborne's apartment…"

"Was he?" muttered Tollman grimly, catching Billy's eye, who nodded.

"Yes. Do you want me to continue?" Mr Ledbetter obviously didn't like being interrupted.

"Yes, please."

"I waited another fifteen minutes and was on the point of summoning the porter to complain that my shoes had not been picked up by the boot boy, when I heard Miss Treborne's door open and close again. Then I heard the boy gathering up my shoes. Then I was able to go to bed finally – half an hour later than my usual time – and I heard nothing further until I was awakened by that girl screaming."

"So, that would be at ten thirty, sir?" Billy was anxious to get his notes right.

"What? When I went to bed?"

"No, when you heard Miss Treborne's door open and close."

"I said so, didn't I?"

"Right." Billy realised that there was a lack of co-operation looming and gave up.

"Well, we won't trouble you any further, sir," said Tollman firmly and motioned Billy to follow. Once outside and out of earshot, he murmured, "Gawd, that was hard work!"

"Good witness, though," said Billy, looking at his notes. "He may be a pain in the arse, but he's very precise."

They ascertained from Mr Bailey that, of the six apartments on the second floor, one was unoccupied and two tenants were away for the summer. They had spoken to Mr Ledbetter in number nine, and that only left Miss Cavendish in number eleven.

She turned out to be a sour-faced middle-aged woman with a permanent air of disapproval. She had plenty to say about Adeline Treborne.

"The woman was a disgrace. In my opinion, she lowered the tone of this building. And she was a terrible neighbour. Sometimes I would hear her raucous laughter. Very unladylike. Sometimes I would hear her arguing with someone and sometimes, if I happened to be in my bathroom at the same time she was in hers, I would hear her sobbing loudly."

Billy looked up from his notes with a face of concern and frowned at Tollman.

"Did you ever go into her apartment when you heard this sobbing – to see what the matter was?" asked Tollman, knowing full well what the answer would be.

"No!" Miss Cavendish was outraged by the suggestion. "I prefer to limit my acquaintances to people of moderation. Miss Treborne was a complete stranger to politeness. Everything she did and said was outrageous. I caught her wandering the corridor in a robe with bare feet one evening. She looked dazed – probably intoxicated – and when I looked at her, she just said 'Boo!' and laughed."

Billy stifled the urge to smile and continued writing.

"So, Miss Cavendish, what did you hear, the evening before last?" Tollman asked.

"I saw her brother arrive at about six o'clock – I've seen him before – and then I heard the maid leave a little while later. I heard raised voices several times during the evening, between the Treborne woman and her brother, culminating in a very loud argument at about ten, when her brother left, I assumed, and slammed the door. I heard the boot boy pick up my shoes and then not long after that I heard a knock on her door and she let someone in. I think I heard a man's voice. He must have stayed about fifteen minutes because the door opened and shut again…"

"Any raised voices that time?"

"No. But I did hear her laugh loudly at some point."

"Did you hear anything else at all, Miss Cavendish?"

"Well… I woke up at about midnight… very briefly… and I thought I heard two women talking… but my bedroom window was open, and it could have been coming from the street. I'm not sure. I went back to sleep again fairly quickly. I can't be certain. But my bedroom shares a wall with the Treborne woman's living room and I can't help hearing things sometimes."

"Thank you, Miss Cavendish. We'll call on you again, if there are any further developments."

"If her death does turn out to be murder, I shan't sleep a wink until you catch whomever is responsible. Supposing it is just some itinerant villain who murders lone women at night and robs them? Was she robbed?" she asked as an afterthought, as she showed them the door.

"Not as far as we know, Miss," Tollman said reassuringly. "I'm sure you are quite safe."

"Well, that's an interesting addition," he said quietly to Billy as they descended the stairs, "hearing women's voices about midnight."

Billy nodded and looked back through the notes he had made at the team meeting. "Mrs E said that the live-out maid suspected that Adeline Treborne got deliveries of drugs late at night. She reported that Mr Jenkins saw a man on the stairs once, but that could have been completely unrelated. It could easily have been a woman who delivered the drugs."

"Mm. Meanwhile, the Major is looking more and more dodgy to me. Let's have a pie and a pint and then take the bus along to Fulham. See if we can't collar this character in mid-chukka."

"Eh?"

"Polo term, lad. Don't worry about it."

***

Beech and Victoria had walked to the duchess's house in Knightsbridge. Beech had decided that he would present Victoria as a discreet legal consultant, approved by the Commissioner to advise in cases that required delicate handling. Victoria was happy with that role, but she privately wondered whether the duchess would be open-minded enough to accept a female legal expert.

The duchess was seated, pale but composed, when the butler showed them into the drawing room. Standing beside her, in uniform, was her attractive son. Victoria estimated that he was probably in his late thirties and his amused manner, as Beech explained Victoria's presence at the meeting, demonstrated an effortless charm, self-assurance and sense of privilege. Victoria decided that she disliked him intensely.

The duchess accepted Victoria's presence without demurring in any way, and they sat. Victoria was aware of the Duke's eyes scanning her face and form and it made her slightly uncomfortable.

Once coffee had been served by a maid and the door was closed, Beech said simply, "Your Grace, our investigations thus far have been very thorough, and we have every reason to believe that your daughter did not commit suicide but was murdered."

The duchess's hand flew to her mouth and she murmured, "I knew it!" The Duke appeared to lose some of his self-assurance and muttered, "Good God!"

Victoria took some small pleasure in saying, "In fact, sir, *you* would appear to have been one of the last people to see your sister alive."

"Henry?" the duchess asked in alarm. It appeared that she was unaware of the Duke's visit.

"It's nothing… nothing… I'll explain later, Mother." He seemed rattled. Beech and Victoria exchanged glances. "Perhaps you should have a rest now," he continued. He turned to Beech. "The undertakers have said that we can visit the Chapel of Rest this afternoon. My mother needs to … emotionally… conserve her strength. If you will excuse me for a moment." He lifted the duchess to her feet and guided her to the door. He turned back. "I will just take my mother upstairs and then we can resume our conversation."

After the door had closed, Beech said gently, "That was rather brutal of you, Victoria."

"I'm sorry," she confessed, "he was just so full of himself. I don't like that kind of man at all. I just wanted to put him in his place."

Beech looked perplexed. "How can you make that sort of judgement in so short a time?"

Victoria smiled ruefully. "Believe me, it is quite possible. But," she added briskly, "I can assure you that I will be much less impulsive when he returns."

Beech shook his head in confusion. The instincts of women were quite beyond him.

The Duke returned – this time, Victoria noted, with a little less swagger than before.

"Now," he said, in a businesslike manner, "where were we?"

"Your visit to your sister, sir," Beech responded in an equally brisk tone. "We believe you arrived at about six o'clock, ate a prepared meal with her and left, after an argument, at around ten."

The Duke looked irritated. "Servants' gossip?" he said with a sneer.

"No. Witness testimony of neighbours and housekeeping staff."

"Damn busybodies! Yes. I visited my sister, as you say, at around six o'clock, ate a meal with her... although she barely ate anything... and, yes, we had an argument and I left. But I can assure you that she was very much alive when I left her." He laughed, which made Beech and Victoria both react in astonishment. "Do you know," the Duke continued bitterly, "when I heard Adeline was dead, part of me hoped that she had seen the error of her ways and killed herself. It would have been the honourable way out of the situation and, despite what my mother would wish, suicide would be preferable for the family name than this mess we find ourselves in now."

Victoria felt a surge of distaste. "Did your sister ever explain to you why she chose to write her newspaper column?"

"Oh, some damn silly nonsense about being treated badly by society when our father lost all his money!" The Duke made it quite clear that he found it a poor excuse. "Yes, it is true that when my father had to declare bankruptcy, Adeline was cut dead by young women who, frankly, should have behaved better. But it was equally hard for me. I had to resign my membership of several clubs, sell my hunters, take up a commission in the Army – that sort of thing. As I said to her time and time again – one just has to weather these storms. People will come around once we have remade the family fortune. Sorry, I know it's early, but I need a drink…"

He got up and strode over to the sideboard, pouring himself a large Scotch with just a whisper of soda. Downing it in one gulp, he poured another and returned to his chair.

"Frankly, and this is what I tried to get through to Adeline and what the argument was about on the night she died, I could have revived the family fortunes a lot quicker if she had not chosen to blacken our family name with her activities. I have put together several investment opportunities but as soon as men hear the name Treborne, they turn away. Don't blame 'em." He took a deep breath and another mouthful of Scotch. "Truth be told, I'm not sorry my sister is dead," he said brazenly, "but I am fearful of what terrible muck your investigation might turn up."

Victoria looked at him in disbelief, almost as though he were some unknown creature that came from another world. She could not comprehend the level of callousness that a brother could display towards a sister – even if that sister was Adeline Treborne.

The Duke caught her looking at him intently and, almost as if he had read her mind, he said suddenly, "You know, it's a terrifying thing to go to war." He held Victoria's stare and, for a moment, she glimpsed a flash of fear in the normally brash face. "Many men find it makes the horror more bearable if they persuade themselves that they are doing it to protect their women and children back home." He paused for a moment, as if to gather his emotions. "Women become idealised… I've seen it. Women become lovelier, more fragile, more precious in the minds of the soldier about to go over the top."

Victoria saw, out of the corner of her eye, Beech drop his head in discomfort at the recognition of the emotions being described.

The Duke continued, all the while his gaze never leaving Victoria's face, "Imagine then, if you come home from that place in Belgium or France, that place full of fear and anguish, and you find that your own sister is not a flower of womanhood but a malicious and vile slattern whose only joy in life is making other people unhappy? How would you feel?"

He then turned to Beech and said simply, "Chief Inspector, you may regard me as a suspect, but I tell you honestly that I did not kill my sister. But I also tell you, with equal honesty, that I *wanted* to kill her. I just lacked the courage."

***

Billy was impressed. Just a hop, skip and a jump away from the grime of the New King's Road was a hidden world of rolling acres, greenery, horses and money.

"I never knew this place existed," he marvelled as they walked briskly up the long drive to the gleaming white neoclassical mansion that served as the clubhouse.

"Some one hundred acres, so I believe," said Tollman authoritatively. "Shame about the view of the Imperial Gas Works over the top of the trees, though."

They passed a group of horses being ridden slowly back to the stables. They were steaming gently in the sunshine and Billy wrinkled his nose at the pungent smell.

"I don't get on with horses," he said confidentially to Tollman. "Temperamental buggers."

"Can't say as I'm desperately fond of them myself, lad, but the manure is good for my roses."

They reached the clubhouse and were directed by a young officer to the steward's office, where an elderly man was quietly doing some accounts.

Tollman produced his card and the steward rose to his feet, extending his hand in welcome.

"Major Sutcliffe," he said breezily.

Billy could tell that this was not what Tollman was expecting. There was a moment of awkwardness before Tollman recovered enough to ask, "Major Sutcliffe of 5 Trinity Mansions, Chelsea?"

"What?" The major seemed puzzled.

"Do you live in Chelsea?"

"God, no! I live here… I have a cottage here. What's all this about?"

"We are looking for a Major Sutcliffe, who resides at number 5, Trinity Mansions, Chelsea," Tollman persisted, "and we were led to believe that said Major Sutcliffe was an avid polo player."

The major looked even more confused. "I *am* an avid polo player – or I was, in my younger days, but I don't live in Chelsea and…" Then suddenly he broke off and remembered something. "Ah! Wait a minute… I wonder if this is anything to do with the chap in question?" The major produced a letter from his desk drawer and handed it to Tollman. "I was just about to write to the lady to say that she must be mistaken…" He tailed off as Tollman opened the envelope to reveal a letter and a cheque for £10 from a Mrs Emilia Warren.

Tollman read the letter out. "'Dear Major Sutcliffe, I have thought better of my decision not to subscribe to saving the dear polo ponies from the ravages of war and I enclose a cheque for £10, which I hope will help to avoid the poor animals suffering at the front line. Yours faithfully, Mrs Emilia Warren.' I take it, Major Sutcliffe, that you did not ask this Mrs Warren for a donation?"

"Absolutely not!" exclaimed the major. "Not altogether sure what the lady is on about. The horses here are privately owned by our members, for them to ride when they are on leave. Polo ponies are tremendously expensive animals and our members pay a lot of money to have them stabled, ridden and generally pampered in their absence. Cavalry horses are altogether a different breed, don't you know? Can't imagine where she could have got the idea that our members' horses were being sent to the front line!"

Billy could see the cogs and wheels going around in Tollman's brain as he processed this information. He was clearly piecing together something.

The major spoke again. "I suppose there could be a Major Sutcliffe at Windsor maybe. Household Cavalry there. Here and Ranelagh tend to be Hussars and Lancers, you know. I suppose there could be another Major Sutcliffe in a regiment I'm not familiar with… but I doubt it. I know most everyone involved in polo."

"No, sir, I don't believe there is another Major Sutcliffe anywhere," said Tollman, with a look of triumph. "I believe that you are being impersonated by a criminal."

"Good Lord!"

"May we keep this letter and cheque?"

"Absolutely. Whatever you need, Detective Sergeant. Just let me know when you've cleared it all up, there's a good man. It's a bit worrying to think there is someone out there impersonating me. My good name could be dragged through all sorts of mud!"

"Don't you worry, Major, we'll sort this one out very quickly. PC Rigsby, let's be on our way!"

As they marched up the driveway, at a faster pace than before, Billy was itching to know what Tollman was thinking.

"Do you know who it is? This so-called Major in Sloane Square?" he asked.

"Not yet, Billy, but I've got a few candidates in my head." He stopped dead and looked at his watch. "We're too late for the banks, they'll be closed now. But we need to go back to Sloane Square and find out which bank the so-called Major pays his rent from. Ten to one he will make regular payments into that account of monies he has conned from little old ladies, by making them believe they are saving the polo ponies from being massacred by the Germans." He gave a grim smile. "It's the old Spanish prisoner con."

"The what? How did Spain come into it?" Billy was confused.

As they reached the bus stop and waited for the next bus, Tollman explained. "It is the oldest confidence trick on record, Billy. It goes back to the Spanish Armada in 1588…"

"1588! You're having me on!"

"It's absolutely true. Even though the English beat the Spanish Armada, confidence tricksters would go around England telling people that English sailors had been taken prisoner by the Spanish and, in order to bring these brave boys home, they would need to be ransomed. So, gullible and kind-hearted people all over Elizabethan England would stump up their hard-earned pennies to bring the 'prisoners' home. Well, this is a variation on it. Only this time, it's polo ponies needing to be rescued, not Spanish prisoners."

"So, what do we do, Mr Tollman?"

"Plain-clothes job in the morning, Billy. We stake out the bank in question and see if we can nab him in the act of paying in his ill-gotten gains."

"What about the post? Shouldn't we go through his post?"

Tollman shook his head firmly. "No. A confidence trickster would never give out his home address. Normally, he would leave a meeting with the money, or a cheque, in his hand. This..." – he pulled the lady's letter out of his pocket and waved it under Billy's nose – "is a mistake he hadn't counted on. He obviously mentioned the Hurlingham Club when he met with the lady, but she wasn't convinced by his patter, and he left empty-handed. Then she changes her mind and decides to send the cheque by post. He made two mistakes. One, he should never have used the name of a real person and two, he should never have mentioned the name of a specific club, he should have left it vague."

"Do you still think he has something to do with Adeline Treborne?"

"I do, Billy, I do. He could have been the last person to see her alive. Perhaps he was trying to persuade her to save the polo ponies, who knows? Or perhaps he was so desperate for money, he killed her for it. We won't know until we nab him."

CHAPTER EIGHT

"An extraordinary level of distress."

There was to be a team meeting that morning, after breakfast. Tollman arrived early and, for once, partook of the meal, exchanging views with Lady Maud about the war and Germans in general.

"There is an article in *The Times* this morning, Mr Tollman," she said, turning over the pages of the newspaper as she sipped her tea.

"Mother! Reading at the breakfast table! Tut! Tut!" Victoria teased.

Maud smiled. "I know, I know. My standards are slipping daily, it's true. Anyway," she continued to Tollman, "the editor quotes an article by a Baron von Hügel, which obviously appeared in some magazine. It says, and I quote, *Theory and system is, for the average Englishman, something that instantly puts him ill at ease…*" She paused while Tollman made a noise of disapproval, then continued, "*or at least something that he disbelieves and avoids. For the German, it is in his very blood. It is this innate need of a system that renders the German steady but also obstinate; virile and brutal; profound and pedantic; comprehensive and rich in outlook, and rationalist and doctrinaire.*" Maud stopped to savour the looks of astonishment from everyone around the table.

Caroline spoke first. "I should think that Mr Tollman disproves that theory, wouldn't you?"

"Well, quite," agreed Beech. "There is no one who loves a system as much as Detective Sergeant Tollman."

"I agree with the bit about 'brutal' but I'm not sure that Germans are any more 'virile' than any other nationality, are they?" Victoria added.

Lady Maud smiled again. "I am sure you will agree with this next piece. I quote again: *Germans seem to have but little faculty of self-criticism; or perhaps it is the absence of any sense of humour that enables them to say or sing things that trend perilously near balderdash.*"

There was a general ripple of agreement around the table and Maud looked pleased with herself.

"Well, despite this baron's obviously German name, he seems to be batting for the British team," observed Tollman.

"He does indeed. It's a very interesting article," Maud observed. "Well, I shall leave you now to your meeting," and she rose from the table. "Although," she added ruefully, "I do wish I could help in some way. I'm feeling rather surplus to requirements at the moment. All my committees have adjourned for the summer and I feel the need of some occupation."

"Actually, Maud, there is a way you can help us," Beech said hopefully.

Lady Maud beamed and sat down again. "I'm all yours. What is it? Some more undercover work? Following a suspect?"

"Nothing so dashing, I'm afraid. Tollman and Rigsby came back from the *London Herald* yesterday with masses of letters of complaint about Adeline Treborne. I wondered if you and Victoria could read through them all, this morning, and isolate any letters that you feel represent a genuine threat to the deceased. I'm sorry but it may not be very pleasant." Beech sounded apologetic.

Lady Maud was enthusiastic nonetheless. "Wonderful!" she pronounced. "A whole morning reading about gossip. I shall relish it. Let me know when you are ready for me. I shall be down in the kitchen discussing the week's meals with Mrs Beddowes."

The team then discussed the day's tasks. Tollman and Billy had discovered that 'the Major' banked with the London County and Westminster Bank in the King's Road. They were going to stake it out all day, in the hope that he would turn up to either deposit or withdraw money. Beech, meanwhile, was going to Scotland Yard to obtain a warrant to search 'the Major's' apartment. Caroline had pronounced that Mabel, who had 'got the bit between her teeth about the scientific side of criminal investigation', wanted to do some further examination of Adeline Treborne's apartment and Caroline had agreed to accompany her before they both started their shifts at the hospital in the afternoon.

"I don't know what we will find, but Mabel seems to think we should scour every inch of the place looking for anything untoward."

Beech felt it couldn't hurt and had given permission. Victoria and Lady Maud were, of course, going to sift through the letters of complaint sent to the *London Herald*.

Caroline, Tollman and Billy decided to share a taxicab to Sloane Square. On the way, Billy said casually, "Dr Allardyce, is there anything that can be done about someone who is tongue-tied?"

"Do you mean emotionally or physically?"

"Physically."

"It depends. If the condition is suitable, then a small snip of the frenulum – the bit under the tongue – can solve the problem. But I would have to have a look at the tongue in question. Who is it?"

"David, the boot boy at Trinity Mansions. He's had a rough old time in life, I reckon, because of his speech impediment. He can't read or write but that's probably cos they didn't bother with him at school. Marked him down as a dummy, because he couldn't speak properly."

Caroline patted Billy's hand. "I'll have a look at him, when Mabel and I have finished. Would I find him down in the kitchen?"

"Yes. Just ask Mrs Bailey. But, mind, she's fiercely protective of him. Reckon he's the son she never had, or something."

Caroline smiled. "If I mention that *you* sent me, do you think she would let me have a look at him?"

Billy grinned and nodded.

Trinity Mansions hove into sight and the redoubtable Mabel was standing on the pavement with another basket full of glass vessels.

"Bless her, she's so keen," murmured Caroline.

"Ah, well, she's like Lady Maud," said Tollman. "Some people just like to be needed."

They piled out of the taxicab, exchanged pleasantries and then the women went into the building and the men sauntered down the King's Road to start their stake-out.

"I'll have a word with the branch manager," instructed Tollman, "and then we must make ourselves inconspicuous and wait it out."

"What if he doesn't turn up today, Mr Tollman?"

"Well, then we'll have to come back tomorrow. But if he hasn't turned up by the time the banks close, we'll go and see if Mr Beech is at the apartment and see what we can turn up there."

They turned into the palatial banking hall of the London County and Westminster Bank and Tollman made a beeline for the nearest banking clerk. Discreetly showing his warrant card, he said, "We need to see your manager immediately," and the clerk scurried off to find him.

Billy noted that there were four banking windows and three of them were staffed by women. The fourth was staffed by a middle-aged man. He felt a little pang of sorrow as he wondered how young bank clerks, with their soft hands and their sedentary lives, were faring in the brutality of the trenches. When Billy was fighting at Ypres, he had been among, mostly, hardened professional soldiers, like himself, and it had been grim. *Nope, the front line is no place for soft civilians,* he thought. *Not at all.*

***

"I have never read such an extraordinary level of distress, in my life!" exclaimed Lady Maud, now on her twenty-seventh letter. "These are not letters of complaint, they are cries from the heart! And what makes it worse is that I *know* some of these people!"

"Mm. I can't say that I *know* them but I know *of* them," Victoria agreed. "Have you come across a letter from Lady Hetherington? Only I've got one here where she refers to her previous letter, so there must be another one in the pile." Victoria shook her head in dismay. "She talks about Adeline Treborne's scurrilous piece about her daughter actually causing the girl's engagement to be broken off by the man she was supposed to marry."

"Disgraceful. I have one here that is heartbreaking," replied Maud. "All the more so because I know the woman in question. The letter is from Mrs Barrington, the daughter of Ida Toller-Bridge. Well, the daughter talks about the fact that her father left her mother for some American heiress, and divorced her. It was absolutely no fault of Ida's. I mean, she had no say in the matter. She was abandoned and then divorced and played no part in the scandal. They tried to keep it quiet, of course, but Adeline Treborne wrote about it before it was common knowledge and before Ida had had a chance to tell the Queen. Ida was serving on the Committee of Queen Mary's Work for Women Fund and regularly went to the Palace to have tea. She had been hoping to explain matters to Queen Mary and gracefully retire from the committee, but Adeline Treborne scuppered all that. Before Ida knew it, she received a letter from the

"An extraordinary level of distress."

Palace saying that in keeping with protocol over matters of divorce, she could no longer serve on the committee or be received at Buckingham Palace. Ida was heartbroken. That committee was everything to her. She really is quite a broken woman. Do you think I should set this letter aside for Peter to look at?"

Victoria shook her head. "No, Ma. I'm sure that Ida Toller-Bridge's daughter felt like killing Adeline Treborne but Caroline has proved that it would have had to have been a strong man who lifted up her body and put it in a noose. Besides, I have a dozen equally heart-rending tales here," – she waved a sheaf of letters – "all from victims or relatives of victims of Adeline Treborne's vile gossip column. I think Peter may be looking for something a little more sinister than that. A sort of Jack the Ripper type letter, if you will. One that threatens Adeline with harm."

Maud sighed. "Righto. I shall carry on. But I shall have to have a large brandy when we have finished. This is positively harrowing!"

***

Mabel peered at the carpet underneath the place where Adeline Treborne's body was found hanging. She got out a magnifying glass and Caroline stifled an urge to make a Sherlock Holmes joke. Suddenly, Mabel said, "I thought I felt something underfoot, when we were moving around here yesterday. I only hope we haven't degraded it too much."

"What is it?" asked Caroline, peering at the place on the carpet that interested Mabel the most, but not really being able to see anything.

"I think it's some sort of plaster or cement. That's what it looks like to me," said Mabel, getting out a scraper and a paper envelope.

"Might it be from the damaged light fitment?" Caroline suggested, pointing upwards.

"Mm. Could be. I'll take a sample from the carpet and then, if you can steady me while I climb on the bedstead, I'll see if I can reach the ceiling fitment and take a sample from there."

Mabel assiduously scraped away at the carpet and deposited the cement particles, or whatever they were, into the envelope, sealed it and labelled it. Then she climbed on the bed and was about to place her boots on the thick wooden bed-end when she stopped and got out her magnifying glass again. "Look!" she said excitedly, "more residue of something." Caroline peered again and, this time, she could see two marks on the varnished wood, about twelve inches apart.

"I think they are boot marks," Caroline suggested. "If someone were to climb up there to rig up a noose, they would plant their feet right where those marks are – don't you think, Mabel?"

Mabel agreed, and another envelope was labelled, and a fresh scraper was used to take the residue off the bed frame. Then Mabel recommenced her climb on to the frame, while Caroline held her around the legs, to stop her from wobbling.

"I can just about reach," said Mabel, the effort of stretching up to the ceiling evident in her voice. "Someone taller than me would have no problem." She scraped at the cracked ceiling plaster and added it to another envelope. Then she carefully unwrapped the cord from the ceiling light. "I can't do much with this, other than to soak it in a salt solution and see if any blood comes out. But we already know that she was almost certainly dead when she was hanged, so there probably won't be any blood. One can only prove by elimination, says Dr Hans Gross."

"What do you mean?" asked Caroline.

"Well, if Adeline Treborne had been alive and died as a result of hanging, it would not be unreasonable to assume that the cord would have bitten deep into her flesh as she struggled, and extracted some blood from the tissue around her neck. So, the fact that the cord may not hold any blood proves by elimination that she could not have been alive or been hanging up here for very long."

"I see." Caroline was impressed. "You really do seem to have a vocation for this sort of work, Mabel."

"If it were a proper science, I'd sign up for training straight away," announced Mabel firmly. "Hang on to me, Caroline, while I get down…" Caroline took Mabel's hands and helped her navigate from bed to floor.

"I can already tell," observed Mabel, slightly breathless from the exertion, "that the ceiling plaster is not the same as the other material. It's white and the substance on the carpet and on the bedstead is grey. I can't wait to analyse it," she said cheerfully. "Now, we'd better make a note of the food left on the plates in the living room, so that I can match them with the stomach contents. If I do that, could you put all the medicines on the bedside table in the basket? I'd better check that they are what is actually described on the labels. Then we'd better scout around for any other drugs, hidden away in cupboards or drawers."

"Yes, ma'am," said Caroline, saluting and laughing.

"Oh dear, am I being bossy?" Mabel asked, looking worried.

"Mabel, you can be as bossy as you like. I am filled with admiration at your cleverness and organisation." And she laughed again as Mabel blushed.

***

Billy was getting bored. They had spent the last two hours on guard at the bank and, so far, nothing. It had all started so well. The manager had confirmed that a Major Sutcliffe had an account with the branch and, upon looking at the daily ledgers, noted that he had made regular deposits of cheques and cash, every few days in the last month. It was estimated that he visited the bank roughly every three days and now he was overdue.

The four bank clerks that manned the windows were summoned, one by one, and told that Major Sutcliffe was a confidence trickster and that if he presented himself at their window, they were immediately to offer an apology and absent themselves from their post. Tollman and Rigsby would then know that the man standing by that window was the Major.

Tollman could see that Billy was restless and he strolled over to him. "Patience, lad," he murmured. "If we don't get him today, then we'll get him tomorrow." Suddenly Tollman stiffened and rapidly turned his back. "Billy! The man walking in the door now! I recognise him, and I don't want him to recognise me. Keep your eye on him and shout for me when you've collared him."

Tollman walked towards the desk in the corner and sat, facing away from the counter, while pretending to write. Billy fixed his eye, casually, on the man who had just entered the bank and then slowly followed him towards the counter. He was aged about fifty, a little bit portly, with an extravagant moustache. He was clutching a briefcase. The man spoke to one of the women clerks and passed some banknotes across the counter. The clerk greatly impressed Billy by not getting in a flap but simply leaning forward to the man, murmuring her apologies and then walking away from her post.

Billy was almost behind him when the man, irritated, leaned forward towards the window and called "Excuse me, Miss!" in a loud voice.

Billy tapped him on the shoulder and said in a friendly tone, "Expecting to be served, are you?"

"What?"

"I think she left because she was too embarrassed…" Billy continued.

"What are you talking about?" The man was getting really irritable now.

"Too embarrassed to watch you being nicked," Billy said with a grin as he deftly put the man in a half-Nelson. "Mr Tollman!" he shouted, and Tollman was immediately at his side.

"Well, well," said Tollman sarcastically, "if it isn't the Reverend Todd!"

"Eh?" said Billy, with a puzzled smile on his face.

"Oh yes, Constable Rigsby," Tollman continued, as the fascinated bank staff and customers became transfixed by the drama. "Meet Reginald Ingham, also known as the Reverend Todd, who collects money on behalf of a mission in Swaziland, also known as Mr George Bywaters, a solicitor who has some very good news about dead relatives, also known as Sergeant Percy Matthews, wounded veteran of the Boer War who needs some money so that he can have an operation and now, it appears, also known as Major Sutcliffe, the saviour of polo ponies." Tollman drew a deep breath. "Reginald Horace Ingham, I am arresting you for larceny by obtaining money under false pretences and also on suspicion of murder…"

"No!" Reginald finally found his voice and it held a note of terror. "I never laid a finger on her! You're not stitching me up for that bitch's murder!"

There was a gasp of shock from the onlookers and Billy clipped the side of Ingham's head with his free hand. "Oi! Language! There's ladies present!"

"We're going to take you into the bank manager's office and detain you there until we can get a police vehicle to come and pick us up," said Tollman matter-of-factly. "We shall take all the details of your transactions as evidence and we shall count the money you were attempting to pay in today… including this cheque from a Mrs Emilia Warren, which she sent to the Hurlingham Club." Tollman produced the letter from his pocket.

"So that's how you found me," muttered Ingham. "Stupid woman! She should have given me the money on the spot."

"Strikes me that *you're* the one who's been stupid. And you can tell us all about it when we get you down to the Yard."

***

Mrs Bailey eyed Caroline with suspicion. "With all due respect, you don't look like a doctor, miss."

"I assure you that I am, Mrs Bailey. I work at the Hospital for Women in Euston Road and I'm a very good friend of Constable Rigsby's."

Mrs Bailey softened. "Well, I suppose that's all right then. Sit down, Doctor, and have a cup of tea." Tea was Mrs Bailey's solution to everything.

Caroline sat and waited patiently for the tea-making process to be completed. She wondered if she had made the right decision to come down and see the boot boy, after waving Mabel and all her samples off in a taxicab. Mrs Bailey seemed a bit of a dragon. Susceptible to Billy's charms but probably not to the dubious charms of lady doctors.

"So, what was this again, about my Davey?" asked Mrs Bailey, once she had fortified herself with a gulp of hot, sweet tea.

Caroline noted the use of the word 'my'. Billy was right. Mrs Bailey had claimed possession of Davey.

"Constable Rigsby felt that I might be able to help Davey overcome his speech impediment."

Mrs Bailey looked suspicious once more. "How?" she asked bluntly. "Because I have to say, I have a sister who is tongue-tied, and no doctor has ever offered to help her."

Caroline decided to be cautious. "Well, not every case is suitable for surgery. I would have to examine your sister, to see what might be done… as, indeed, I don't know whether I can help Davey, until I examine him. But if he is a suitable candidate, the surgery is very simple and quick. There shouldn't be any risk."

"And if you performed this surgery, what would be the outcome for Davey?"

"Very good. He should be able to speak normally after a period of healing. That, I'm sure, would make his life so much better." Caroline tried to sound encouraging.

"No."

Caroline was shocked and then outraged. "Mrs Bailey, I don't think you have the right to deny the boy the possibility of a decent life!"

Mrs Bailey's mouth was set firm. "I don't have the right to condemn him to certain death either."

Caroline was confused. "I don't understand…"

"Then let me explain, Doctor." Mrs Bailey's eyes were gleaming with determination. "My other sister has just lost her boy. Sixteen years of age. He was an apprentice stoker on a merchant ship called the *Bayano*. It was sunk off the Scottish coast by a German U-boat in March. Two hundred crew died. My sister is beside herself with grief. She doesn't even have the body of her son, to bury him."

"I still don't understand." Caroline couldn't see where Mrs Bailey was leading.

"I don't want to stop Davey from having a normal life, Doctor," – the tears had begun to form in her eyes – "but the way he is at the moment – a dummy who can't speak properly, nor read or write – the Army won't have him, neither will the Navy. As long as he is the way that he is… he's safe."

Caroline finally understood. There was a silence while she thought.

"I'll make a bargain with you, Mrs Bailey," she finally said, softly. "When this war is over, you bring Davey to me, and we'll give him his voice back."

Mrs Bailey smiled through her tears and nodded. "Yes, Doctor. It's a deal. When this war is over, Davey and me will come and find you."

CHAPTER NINE

It's All in the Book

Beech eyed the surly individual in front of him. Reginald Ingham had just been brought into the Yard by Tollman and Billy Rigsby. It had taken Beech all morning, wading through Scotland Yard's finest tiers of bureaucracy, to obtain a warrant to search Ingham's premises and he was not in a mood to be trifled with.

"So…" – Beech was leafing through a file filled with Ingham's previous convictions – "It looks as though, this time, you are facing the hangman rather than another spell in prison."

Ingham shook his head vehemently. "I'm not a murderer! You can't pin that woman's death on me!"

"Then who *is* responsible, Ingham? It appears that you were the last person to visit Adeline Treborne. You were seen and heard by the neighbours. You stayed about fifteen minutes – plenty of time to have killed her. How *did* you kill her, by the way?" Very few people outside of his team knew how Adeline Treborne had been found and he thought he would test Ingham, to see if he knew the method of death.

Ingham looked confused. "Look, Chief Inspector, I *didn't* kill the woman! I'm not capable of doing such a thing! Look at my record! I'm a confidence trickster... I con women out of money... I don't kill and have never killed anyone."

"There's always a first time for everything," commented Tollman, who was taking notes in the corner.

"Quite," agreed Beech. "So why, exactly, were you visiting Miss Treborne, Ingham? Was it to extract money from her?"

Ingham gave a small mirthless laugh. "You've got it all wrong, Chief Inspector. I wasn't trying to get money out of *her*. She was extracting money from *me*. She was blackmailing me... and a few others."

Tollman and Rigsby looked at each other in surprise. As startled as he was by this news, Beech calmly asked Ingham to explain more fully.

Ingham began his tale. "She had found out, somehow, what my business was, and she came to me, about six months ago, and said that if I didn't pay her ten pounds a month, she would tip off the police. So, I paid her. What else could I do? But ten pounds is a lot of money, Chief Inspector. I'm lucky if I make thirty pounds a month and my rent is five. It put a lot of pressure on me."

"I can understand that." Beech was sympathetic. "So, perhaps you felt that the sensible thing to do was get rid of your blackmailer, once and for all."

"No!" Ingham was exasperated. "Look, I didn't kill her! I went to see her to ask if she could let me off that month's payment. Business hadn't been so good. I needed a breather. She wasn't having it. She laughed at me and waved her bloody great book at me and said, 'Hard luck, Major. Everyone else has to pay up. I don't make exceptions.' I could see I wasn't getting anywhere, so I left."

"Wait. You said a book… she waved her bloody great book at you?"

"Yes. Big brown book. Like an accounts ledger."

"Where did she produce this book from? A cupboard, drawer, handbag?"

Ingham struggled to remember. "I think it was just on the table… I don't know. Maybe she'd been looking at it when she let me in."

"Right," said Beech, rising. "We are now going to search Miss Treborne's apartment and we have a warrant to search yours. If we find that book in your rooms, we will assume that you killed her and took it…"

"You won't find it in my place!" Ingham was insistent. "I didn't kill her, and I didn't take her book. I swear on my life."

"Tollman, take him back to his cell and then meet me outside. Rigsby, come with me." Beech gave Ingham a final warning look and then left the room, with Billy in tow.

"You've got to speak to your guv'nor, Sergeant Tollman." Ingham was desperate now. "You've known me a long time. You know that I have never been involved in any violence. You know that!"

"Like I said before, there's always a first time. Particularly if a man is desperate enough."

***

Victoria and Lady Maud were exhausted. Reading letter after letter, cataloguing the terrible spite of Adeline Treborne, had been draining.

"I cannot understand why the girl did such a thing," commented Maud. "I mean, to set oneself outside the bounds of decent society by betraying all their secrets... well, it is beyond my comprehension."

Victoria was puzzled and had been since they started work on this case. There was just something that didn't add up. "Mother," she said, "have you ever been to a function where Adeline Treborne was present?"

"Good Lord, no! Well, at least not to my knowledge. Surely no one *would* invite her to their private functions, would they?"

"Well, exactly! She may have gone to parties and balls in the early days, before people realised what a snake she was, but not once she started the newspaper column. Besides, her maid, Lily, said that Adeline never went *anywhere*. And that she was very lonely and had almost no visitors. So, *how* was she getting her information? I mean, some of this stuff..." – she waved a handful of letters – "... is very specific. Information about divorces that were being kept secret – not something that would have been chatted about at a party... I mean, this one, here..." – Victoria rummaged among the letters and found the one she was looking for – "... which is a letter from a young woman's sister complaining about a private conversation that had been reported by Adeline. This," Victoria tapped the letter with her finger to emphasise the point, "is not something that she would have overheard at a party. This is about two people talking in the privacy of a bedroom."

"It has to be servants, Victoria," Maud said simply. "There's no other explanation for it. People of our class know that we should *not* have conversations in front of servants but so many of us forget. We are so used to having servants floating around in the background that we forget they are there. It's the only possible explanation."

"I agree with you. But there is still something that does not add up. There is no evidence that Adeline Treborne *met* with any servants. How would she do that anyway? She could hardly loiter around the servants' entrance of every large house in London, could she?"

"I suppose not," Maud agreed. "I don't know. Is there some place that servants go? Like a social club or something?"

"Maybe we should ask Mrs Beddowes and Mary. Perhaps they can shed some light on the matter."

Down in the kitchen Mrs Beddowes was baking and prevailed upon Victoria and Lady Maud to sit and partake of warm scones, homemade jam and cream. "Cream is getting scarce now, milady. Apparently, they're mixing the cream in with the milk now and then turning it into evaporated milk for the troops."

"Perhaps we should get a couple of cows for the end field in the country house," said Maud, trying not to speak with her mouth full. "I'll look into it. Although I somehow can't see William coping with cows at his age," she added, referring to her elderly coachman back in Berkshire.

Mary poured some tea and Victoria asked, "Mrs Beddowes… Mary… is there any sort of social club that servants in London go to? You know, somewhere where they could gather and chat, on their days off?"

Mrs Beddowes and Mary shook their heads.

"No, Miss Victoria, I've not heard of anything like that," Mrs Beddowes said. Then she said thoughtfully, "Mind you, some of the footmen and valets used to go to the Workers' Educational Association for classes… the ones who wanted to better themselves, like. But I don't know if that's still running, what with the war and everything. Oh… Mary, what was that thing you heard about… from Annie at number thirty-two?"

"Oh yes! Some woman had persuaded some of the households in Mayfair and Knightsbridge to send their parlour maids and ladies' maids to a sewing circle once a week. Annie said she wanted to go but it's not for kitchen staff, only upstairs staff. It didn't cost anything, Annie said. One of their parlour maids went and she said it was lovely. You got tea and cakes and a chat and they only did a little bit of sewing."

"Interesting," said Victoria. "Mary, do you think you could find out a bit more about it for me? Like where they meet and who runs it?"

"Yes, Miss. I'll have a chat to Annie this afternoon, when Lady Donaldson is having her nap. It's usually quiet in the kitchen then for about an hour."

"Good girl! And come and tell me all about it, straight away."

"Yes, Miss."

***

Tollman had found a large cache of, seemingly, unused handbags in the top of Adeline Treborne's wardrobe. They were all lined up in an immaculate row. Some were large and capacious and some were small and bejewelled. All in pristine condition and, to Tollman's eye, representing a sizeable amount of money. He tutted and sighed, before dragging over a chair to stand on, to enable a more thorough examination.

He began to open them, one by one, and then, in one of the oversized bags, he came upon the large brown accounting book, as Ingham had described. As Tollman's fingers closed around it, his heart sank.

"I have found this book, sir," he said in a glum voice, "but it looks as though we are too late."

Beech, Tollman and Rigsby stared at the book in despair. They had been searching for nearly an hour, only to find that someone had got there before them.

Tollman laid the book down carefully on the living room table and switched on a lamp to illuminate the blank page.

"Billy," he said quietly, "go down and see the boot boy and borrow some of his blacking and a soft rag for me."

Rigsby nodded and left. Beech understood the possibility that was forming in Tollman's mind.

"Do you think there might be an impression, Tollman?" he asked hopefully.

Tollman ran his fingers lightly over the top blank page. "I think I can feel something, sir."

When Rigsby returned, he and Beech stood, almost holding their breath while Tollman deftly smeared a light coating of boot blacking over the page. Magically, words and numbers began to appear and Beech murmured "Good man!" in relief.

They peered at the book and Tollman tried to decipher the impression of Adeline Treborne's erratic handwriting.

"Make notes, Billy," he said, then he read out loud, "top line looks like – capital letter S, small letter r – looks like a space then capitals A, J, M full stop P … thirty pounds. Second line is capital A, small m… space, then the whole word… wife… then space, capital Q and capital C… thirty pounds. Third line is capital M small j small r… ah, I think this is the 'Major'… ten pounds."

On Tollman went, reciting what he could see on the page, with Billy carefully writing down every instruction until he ended up with a list that almost perfectly matched the scribble revealed by boot blacking.

It read:

Sr AJM.P	£30
Am wife QC	£30
Mjr	£10
Kit B, Peachtree	£10
SR M jew	£30
Ruth B baby	£10

"One hundred and twenty pounds!" Beech was staggered. "If this is just one month's extortion fees, then

Adeline Treborne was a very rich woman indeed. And most hated by this list of people."

"This might not be the full list," commented Tollman. "I could only get what was written on the last page. There could have been more people she blackmailed but we won't know until we find the missing pages."

"That's a hell of a lot of money," said Billy with feeling. "She was collecting, in one month, far more than I earn in a year."

Tollman tapped Billy's list. "It's these three that interest me the most. The ones who were paying thirty pounds a month. You have to be very wealthy to be able to afford three hundred and sixty pounds a year in blackmail fees."

Beech decided that the team needed to put their heads together to decipher the list and come up with some ideas. Meanwhile, he would visit Adeline Treborne's bank and ascertain just how much money the dead blackmailer was worth, while Tollman and Rigsby combed through everything in Ingham's apartment to make sure that he wasn't the one who had taken the missing pages from the book.

Billy opened a drawer in Ingham's bedroom and said in disgust, "I can't stand this!"

"Pornography?" asked Tollman, busying himself with searching in the bedroom.

"No. Pictures of half dead and dying horses." Billy curled his lip.

"Ah," said Tollman, giving them a cursory glance and pulling a face, "Ingham used these to wring money out of his little old ladies. Nothing like a distressed animal to get the womenfolk to part with their money. My wife used to singlehandedly support Battersea Dogs Home. I think they were more distressed than her family when she died."

"How did he get hold of these? They look as though they were taken at the Front." Billy was annoyed.

"Son," said Tollman, taking the pictures from Billy and putting them back in the drawer. "Concentrate on what's important. We haven't got time to worry about dead horse pictures. Have you searched all this room?"

"Yes, Mr Tollman."

"Looked behind all the drawers... under the mattress... under the rug?"

"Yes, Mr Tollman."

"Good lad. Well, there isn't anything here. Let's get back to Lady Maud's and have a nice cup of tea and sort out the evidence so far, shall we?"

***

"At the moment, we have two suspects – Ingham, aka The Major, and the Duke of Penhere," Beech said. "And yet," he continued, "neither of them really fits the bill."

"The problem we have, Peter," chipped in Caroline, "is that we seem to have two separate actions. The death from drug overdose and the fake suicide from hanging. It's difficult to attribute both to one person but then, if the drug overdose was an accident on the part of Adeline Treborne and someone arrived in the early morning, with the intent to kill her, why bother to string her up? She must have already been dead!"

"Yes, I know. But someone obviously hung her up at six o'clock in the morning, because that was when the dislodging of the gas pipe cut off the gas in the apartment above."

"And her body was still swinging when the maid arrived at six thirty," added Victoria. "Obviously, she had only just been hung up and someone had been in and out very quickly that morning."

"I have a problem with Ingham being our murderer, sir," offered Tollman.

Billy added, "Me too, sir. He's not fit enough to lift the dead weight of a body up to ceiling height. He looks a flabby beggar to me."

"And I'm sure the Duke of Penhere will have servants who can attest to serving him breakfast at the very time of the 'hanging'," offered Victoria.

Beech exhaled loudly in frustration. "Let's turn our attention to this blackmail list, shall we? By the way, according to Adeline Treborne's bank manager, the worth of her bank account was a staggering three thousand pounds."

Billy whistled, and the others murmured disbelief.

"And that was despite the expensive rent on the apartment and her endless shopping for clothes and accessories," Caroline reminded everyone.

There was silence as they each pored over a copy of the list, as provided by Tollman.

Sr AJM.P	£30
Am wife QC	£30
Mjr	£10
Kit B, Peachtree	£10
SR M jew	£30
Ruth B baby	£10

"I can't make head nor tail of it," confessed Beech.

"Well, we know that Mjr is the Major," observed Victoria, her analytical mind working smoothly as usual. "The others must be abbreviations as well."

There was another silence.

"Could Sr be short for Sir?" commented Tollman. "Sir AJM.P?"

Victoria sounded excited. "Wait a minute! When you read it out like that, I hear Sir AJ… M.P… member of parliament. Sir AJ…? AJ?"

"Anthony Jarvis," said Beech firmly. "Used to be Governor of Hong Kong, then became MP for Wapping, I think? He would fit the bill. What else do we know about him?"

Tollman delved into his encyclopaedic memory. "In his mid-fifties, runs a shipping company, confirmed bachelor. That last factor could be the reason for black-mail," he added.

"And I think I may have deciphered another name," said Victoria triumphantly. "I think the second one is American wife of a QC. Now there are two QCs I know of that have American wives – one is Sir Amory Barton, who is nearly eighty, I believe, and the other is Sir Michael

Patrick, who has close ties with the Royal Family – he is quite young for a QC – forty something and quite brilliant."

"Well done, Victoria!" Caroline was always impressed by Victoria's deductive brain. Then she added, "Oh, I almost forgot! A message from Mabel!" She dug out a piece of paper from her bag and read, "All the drugs on the bedside table were as described on the boxes and were mainly sedatives to help with sleep. The substance on the carpet, and on the bed frame, was definitely cement and, in particular, *waterproof* cement. This is cement that has sulphates and other substances added, to make it waterproof for use in construction in or near water. She also wanted me to remind you that, as we did not find a syringe anywhere in Adeline Treborne's apartment – not in her rubbish bin or hidden anywhere – then someone else must have injected her with a drug and taken the syringe away with them. She was injected with heroin, by the way. Mabel was left with a powdery residue of heroin when she distilled the bladder urine. The stomach contents matched the half-eaten food on one of the plates we found. Residue of bath crystals was found by Mabel under the toenails, which showed that Adeline Treborne had recently had a bath. Oh, and no blood came out of the hanging cord, so Mabel feels that proves she was dead when strung up."

Tollman started to applaud and the others joined in. "Well done to Miss Summersby," he said generously.

"There is something else that is bothering me," said Victoria, puncturing the sense of achievement everyone was feeling. She went over to the study table, where the notebook, with its boot blacking reveal, was displayed next to Adeline Treborne's pink notes for her gossip column. "I don't know if anyone has noticed, and I realise that the notebook discovered today only contains an approximation of what was written on the actual page, but the two examples of Adeline Treborne's handwriting are markedly different. The notebook is scrawly and undisciplined writing. The pink paper notes are uniform and very precisely formed letters. They don't match at all."

CHAPTER TEN

The Evasive Member of Parliament

The morning dawned a little chilly and drizzly, which was unusual for July, but Beech was happiest when it was cooler, as his injured leg gave him less of a problem. He had telephoned ahead to the Duke of Penhere to request an appointment and he walked at a moderate pace to the meeting, enjoying the fact that his leg was free of pain today and his limp was barely noticeable. Then he made the mistake of buying a newspaper, which detailed, on its front page, the news that the Germans appeared to have perfected a synchronised machine gun for their Fokker fighter aircraft, which shot bullets in between the propeller blades. They had already managed to down several French aircraft. *German science and engineering is outsmarting us at every turn*, thought Beech, and his positive mood evaporated.

The Duke was finishing his breakfast and offered Beech a cup of tea, which was gratefully accepted.

"What, may I ask, is the purpose of this visit?" asked the Duke, eyeing Beech warily.

"Just a couple of quick questions, if you wouldn't mind, sir." The Duke shrugged, and Beech continued, "Could I ask you where you were at approximately six in the morning on the day that your sister's body was discovered?"

The Duke looked amused. "In my bed, of course! I'm not in the habit of rising before nine when I'm on leave. Ask any of the servants. My valet drew my bath at nine and I had breakfast at nine thirty."

"I see. Can any of the servants attest to the fact that you were in your bed, asleep, at six o'clock?"

"They have strict orders not to disturb me before nine," said the Duke tersely. "I would have thought that my word as to my whereabouts was sufficient." He glared at Beech for daring to question his probity.

"There is one other matter, sir," said Beech, retrieving a sheaf of papers from his inside pocket. "Could you verify for us that this is your sister's handwriting?"

The Duke looked amused again. "On *pink* paper? I hardly think that my sister would be so middle-class, but let me have a look." He glanced at all four pages and his face darkened. "Such scurrilous rubbish!" he muttered. "No," he decided, handing back the papers to Beech, "this is nothing like my sister's handwriting. My sister wrote like a doctor, in a mostly unintelligible scrawl. How she managed to pass through one of the best finishing schools in Europe without having her handwriting corrected was always a great mystery to my mother and I. Where did you get these papers?"

"From the newspaper she worked for. This was how she provided her gossip column every week. According to the editor, it was always the same. Notes written on pink paper and dropped through the letterbox early every Thursday morning."

The Duke shook his head. "Well, then, she must have had an assistant. Someone who wrote this stuff out for her and delivered it. You should know that my sister was usually heavily intoxicated or sedated every night. She had great difficulty sleeping. She never rose before about eleven o'clock in the morning and would not have been capable of delivering a letter by hand early in the day."

Beech nodded. Frustratingly, the mystery just kept deepening and he had yet to see a glimmer of light that would shine on to the murderer.

"There is one other thing, sir…"

"I hope this will be the last thing, Beech. I have a meeting this morning." The Duke was beginning to get impatient. Beech ignored him and continued.

"Did you give your sister any money at all, to supplement her income?"

The Duke looked dumbfounded and then laughed out loud. "Good God, man! I don't *have* any money to give! All of this…" – he spread his arms wide to encompass the world in which he lived – "…is financed by loans. My father died a bankrupt. My mother was distraught. It became incumbent upon me to find a way of enabling my mother and I to live in a way befitting our status in life. We sold our country estate, bought this house on a mortgage and I borrowed money from every financial institution that would open its coffers to me. I never gave money to Adeline. In fact, I believe that, once, she offered *me* money."

"Did you accept it?" Beech asked bluntly.

"No, I did not!" The Duke sounded bitter. "My mother would have died if she had found out that I had accepted such tainted money from Adeline."

"Your Grace, I'm afraid that what I have to tell you now will not be pleasant..." Beech warned.

The Duke looked defiant. "Just get on with it, man!" he said with a great deal of irritation and, Beech detected, not inconsiderable anxiety.

"Your sister was able to maintain her lavish lifestyle because she was blackmailing prominent citizens. We have uncovered a list that includes a member of parliament, a QC and, possibly, other high-ranking members of London society. She was receiving from her victims in excess of one hundred pounds a month and her bank account, at this moment, contains over three thousand pounds."

The colour had drained from the Duke's face and he sunk his head into his hands in despair. Beech could think of nothing further to say. Finally, the Duke said hoarsely, "How will I ever be able to pay these people back?" and Beech was impressed that that was his first thought and not a comment about the damage to his family's reputation.

"That will be taken care of, sir. The courts will discreetly divide the funds of your sister's bank account among the victims, once we have established the full details of her murder."

The Duke nodded, still stunned by the news, and Beech thought it best to depart and leave the man to his confusion and anguish. Besides, he had an urgent appointment at the Houses of Parliament.

He thought back to his conversation with the Commissioner yesterday evening. He knew that the Commissioner would be working late and, after the team had mulled over the evidence, he had gone back to Scotland Yard to report to Sir Edward on progress.

"Well, this is proving to be a bad business, isn't it, Beech?" was Sir Edward's assessment after listening to the details of the case. "Society gossip, murder and now black-mail. Astonishing!" Sir Edward had then made his request for discretion, all the while looking a little uncomfortable. "It goes against my principles, really," he had confessed, "but I can see no value – especially now that you have uncovered the blackmail situation – of allowing any of this to reach the ears of the press and public – until you have solved the case. Especially if, in the case of Sir Anthony Jarvis and Sir Michael Patrick, you find that the reason for the blackmail may affect national security."

Beech had understood, of course.

Sir Edward had continued, "Therefore, I suggest that you, personally, Beech, conduct private interviews with the gentlemen in question and only bring in your police-men if there is a suspicion of a crime. Do *not*, however, attempt to arrest anyone in a place of continuous interest to the press, such as the House of Commons or the Royal Courts of Justice."

Beech had nodded, and they had parted, each with the understanding that the Adeline Treborne case was becoming more 'delicate' by the day and, therefore, required the utmost discretion.

As Beech strolled past Buckingham Palace, he could see that there was an orderly demonstration in progress. It seemed to be led by a lone suffragette, wearing the purple, green and white sash of the movement, but the crowd behind her comprised men and women – at least four of them seemed to be men of the cloth, wearing dog collars. They were carrying placards saying 'Stop the War' and 'Stop the Barbarity in France', and another read 'Bring our Young Men Home'.

It was very civilised. Two Palace policemen were keeping a baleful eye on the small crowd, who were now chanting, "Stop the War!" Beech idly wondered if the King and Queen were watching from a window or were even aware that the demonstration was taking place.

He had witnessed other anti-war demonstrations and speeches during the last few months, usually in and around the stations where soldiers left and arrived. Such demonstrations usually ended badly, with pro-war people taking exception to the sentiments expressed by the anti-war brigade, and fights often broke out. The pro-war brigade always won because, at the moment, despite the news of daily carnage, gassings and the fear of Zeppelin raids over London, most people regarded it as their patriotic duty to support the war. Beech wasn't sure any more. Men who had been invalided out of the war faced a terrible period of indecision. They wanted to condemn the war as a barbaric loss of life, but they couldn't quite bring themselves to acknowledge that their own effort had been in vain. It was a painful place to be.

As he passed through Admiralty Arch and into Whitehall, the place bristled with old men in uniforms. These were the men behind the desks at the Admiralty and the War Office. The men who made life and death decisions without ever having to leave the comfort of luncheon at their clubs in St James's. Beech pressed on. He faced a daily battle of 'not dwelling on things'. These had been the words used by his commanding officer, when he had visited him in his hospital bed in Belgium. "Best not to dwell on things, Beech," the colonel had said. "Be glad you're out of it and get on with your life." Easier said than done.

Finally, he arrived at the Houses of Parliament and was ushered through the side gates by the duty policeman and into the cavernous corridors of power. Sir Anthony's office was through the labyrinth around the House of Commons Chamber itself, past the Commons Library and nestled by the Speaker's Court. A female secretary in a room the size of a broom cupboard opened the door to a windowless inner office that was just large enough to hold a desk, a filing cabinet and two chairs. Sir Anthony Jarvis stood up behind his desk, offered his hand to Beech and apologised for the meagre accommodation.

"They squeeze us in where they can," he said jovially. "I would have met you in one of the general seating areas, but you did insist on privacy. So, sit down, Chief Inspector, and tell me how I can help you."

Beech tried to sound as sympathetic as he could. He explained to Sir Anthony that the matter was confidential and that he was about to discuss a crime that was not yet a matter of public knowledge. As soon as he uttered the name of Adeline Treborne, the member of parliament's smile wavered and then resumed. It was a very practised recovery, but Beech noted the few seconds in which self-assurance was replaced by panic.

"Sir Anthony," he continued, "we have found a document that lists individuals, in some kind of makeshift code, that we believe were being blackmailed…" This time it was the unconscious movement of the MP's Adam's apple, as he swallowed hard, that betrayed his tension. Beech marvelled at the man's ability to mask any conflicting emotions with a veneer of assumed calm.

"I'm sorry, Chief Inspector Beech, but how is this my concern?" Sir Anthony interrupted. There was no hostility or defensiveness in his voice. His tone was smooth and unruffled. "Is it perhaps to do with one of my constituents? Is that how I can help you?"

Beech decided to be a little firmer in his response. "We believe that it is *you* that was being blackmailed by Adeline Treborne."

Sir Anthony laughed. "*Me?* That's ridiculous! Why on earth would anyone blackmail me? I mean, I don't even know the woman. I've *heard* of her, of course. Who hasn't? But I think you are mistaken if you think that I could have possibly been of any interest to such a woman. How did you say she died?"

"I didn't," said Beech simply. "Suffice it to say that we have every reason to believe she was murdered."

"Murdered?" Beech noticed the little slip in the façade again. There was no doubt that Sir Anthony was rattled.

"Can I ask where you were, sir, between the hours of ten thirty p.m. on the first of July and six thirty a.m. on the second?"

"I… was… in my apartment in Tothill Street."

"Can anyone bear witness to that, sir?"

"I shouldn't think so. I live alone."

Beech could see that the interview was not going to progress any further, so he stood up. "Thank you very much for your co-operation, sir." Sir Anthony inclined his head in reply. "In case I should think of any further questions, can I ask what time you will be leaving the House today?"

"I have a Committee meeting until four this afternoon, so I shall probably be gone by five."

"Thank you, Sir Anthony, for your time. I will be in touch."

It was just a short walk from the Houses of Parliament to Scotland Yard. As soon as he was in his office, Beech rang Mayfair 100 and spoke to Tollman. "I need you and Rigsby to do a plain-clothes assignment. Meet me outside the Houses of Parliament at four thirty."

***

Mary had had her little chat with her kitchen maid friend up the road and discovered that the sewing circle met in the hall behind St Columba's Church near Hyde Park Corner on two afternoons a week.

"Is there any age barrier?" asked Victoria. Mary didn't quite understand the question, so Victoria rephrased it. "Is it only *young* maids who attend?"

"Oh no, Miss," Mary replied. "Annie says there are a couple of quite elderly ladies' maids who attend, an older head nurse and an older parlour maid. But she won't allow governesses or housekeepers or below stairs."

"Mm. That seems extraordinarily discriminating for a sewing circle," commented Lady Maud.

"Doesn't it?" observed Victoria. "Thank you, Mary."

After Mary left, Victoria thought for a while. "You know, mother, if I were someone who wanted to find out as much gossip about wealthy households as possible, I would seek the company of above stairs staff who wait on tables, serve canapés and drinks at parties, or body servants who remain invisible while hanging up clothes, brushing their mistress's hair or a thousand other personal services, while their employers have important conversations in front of them. I wouldn't seek the company of below stairs staff, housekeepers or governesses because they don't have enough contact with their employers. And I wouldn't seek the company of male servants because they never pay attention to gossip usually. Do you see what I'm getting at?"

"I do indeed, Victoria," agreed Maud. "We need to infiltrate this 'sewing circle' but who can we send?"

"We can't send Mary, I'm afraid…"

"Oh no! The girl is too dim!"

"Well, I was going to be a little more charitable, mother, but you are right. We need someone who will pass for a servant and has the quick wit to find out what is going on. I wonder if Billy's aunt is available?"

Victoria and Maud swept down upon Billy as he was fetching coal into the kitchen for Mrs Beddowes.

"Billy, we need a word," said Victoria conspiratorially.

"Come up to the study, when you're finished," said Lady Maud.

Billy washed his hands and duly presented himself upstairs. Victoria explained their suspicions about the female servants' sewing circle.

"We need someone to infiltrate the organisation," said Lady Maud, relishing her part in the planning of the operation.

"Do you think your excellent Aunt Sissy would help?" asked Victoria.

Billy shook his head ruefully. "Sorry, ladies, but my Aunt Sissy can't thread a needle to save her life. Sewing is just not her forte, as it were. She leaves all that to my mum."

"Well… what about your mother, then? Would she help us?" Victoria persisted hopefully.

Billy screwed up his face into an expression of doubt. "I could ask her…" he said tentatively, "but don't get your hopes up."

Billy was duly despatched – without delay – to telephone his mother and was astonished to find her eager and willing to play her part. He suspected that Sissy had been boasting about her day with Caroline and Mabel and this had made his mother a little jealous. He heard her say to Sissy, while she was still on the telephone, "Ooh, now *I'm* being asked to help!" with a note of excitement in her voice. Not only that, but she was being invited to come and have tea with Lady Maud and Victoria to discuss the matter.

"Oh, and Ma," Billy added before he put the receiver down, "come to the front door, please, and not the kitchen entrance. You're not being interviewed for a position."

At three o'clock, a breathless Elsie Rigsby, in her best hat and coat, rang the front doorbell of Lady Maud's Mayfair house and was astonished to find the front door being answered by Victoria herself.

"Mrs Rigsby!" she said, extending her hand, "I'm Victoria Ellingham. Do come in! Billy has told us so much about you!"

"Ooh, how do you do, Miss. I wasn't expecting you to answer the door."

"Ah, well, you will learn that we are very informal in this house. Mother did not bring her butler with her to London, so whomever happens to be nearest to the door when the bell rings, answers it! I think that's fair, don't you?"

Elsie was ushered into the drawing room and the presence of Lady Maud, who greeted her as though she were a long lost relative. "Mrs Rigsby! We are so delighted that you could come to see us! We have lots to talk about, don't we, Victoria? Sit down, sit down. Let us take your coat and make you comfortable. We have one of Mrs Beddowes's best cream teas on the table here and we shan't be disturbed." Maud was determined to charm Elsie Rigsby into submission at all costs.

"No Billy?" asked Elsie, looking around.

"No, I'm afraid he's been summoned out on a job, by Mr Beech," explained Victoria. "But he said to us that he was sure you were capable of making your own mind up about our suggestion and didn't need any help from him."

"Sounds like Billy," Elsie chuckled as she accepted a cup of tea. "Now, Your Ladyship... Miss Victoria... how can I help you?"

***

Tollman and Rigsby, dressed casually, like a father and son out on the town for the afternoon, met with Beech at a café at the top of Whitehall, near Parliament Square.

"When I interviewed Sir Anthony this morning," he explained quietly, "I was convinced that, even though he said he did not know Adeline Treborne and the thought of him being a blackmail victim was ridiculous, he was lying. I may not have your instincts, Tollman, but I definitely felt that he was hiding something."

"Mm." Tollman nodded and said cynically, "I'm surprised we've only got one MP on the list. In my experience, at least half the House of Commons and two-thirds of the House of Lords are taking bribes, keeping mistresses, visiting prostitutes or generally involved in mucky business."

Billy grinned and even Beech managed a small smile. "I think that's a rather sweeping generalisation, but I take your point. Anyway," Beech continued, "I have instructed the duty policeman to give us a signal when Sir Anthony leaves so that you can both follow him, and I will discreetly follow you. He knows what I look like, so it will be up to you two to handle the close observation work."

Tollman nodded. "Leave it to us, sir."

Rigsby and Tollman took up position opposite the side gates to the Houses of Parliament. Beech stood to one side, immersed in a newspaper and occasionally glancing at the duty policeman. Finally, he was rewarded with a one-finger salute to the helmet, which signalled that Sir Anthony was about to exit the gates. Beech nodded to Tollman and Rigsby and they casually crossed the road to be closer to their target.

Sir Anthony seemed distracted when he came out and he immediately turned on to Parliament Square and hailed a taxicab. Tollman and Rigsby sprinted across the square and hailed another one, which slowed to pick up Beech as it turned into Whitehall.

"The driver has been instructed to follow the vehicle in front," murmured Tollman.

"It will be interesting to see where this leads us," muttered Beech, his eyes fixed on the road ahead.

The traffic was slow as it went around the bottleneck of Trafalgar Square and Sir Anthony's cab led them up the Strand, into Fleet Street and towards St Paul's.

"Heading to the City of London?" ventured Tollman, but then they found themselves being led away from the City, past the Tower of London and into the grimy world of the riverside docks and wharves of Limehouse.

Sir Anthony's taxicab seemed to be slowing down and Tollman quickly instructed Billy to get out and follow him on foot, while Tollman and Beech carried on beyond the now stationary vehicle and turned a corner before alighting. Tollman pulled Beech into a dank alley, just as Sir Anthony rounded the corner, hurrying past, looking neither to left nor right. Billy sauntered past about one minute later, tipping his hat at Tollman to signal that he knew they were there.

"Stay with me, sir," muttered Tollman, "this is a very rough part of town," and they slipped out into the street to follow the tall figure of Rigsby in the distance.

Beech looked around. The street was filled on either side with dark, towering warehouses. The wind then hit them sideways on, as they crossed a bridge over the wharf and became exposed to the open river. In the wharf and all along the river, as far as the eye could see, were ships tied up, their cargoes disgorging on to the docks and into the warehouses. Customs men with clipboards were checking the consignments; other dockers were loading cargoes on to canal barges that were tied up two and three abreast, ready to transport the goods up the canal system that fed into the Limehouse Basin. So many of the men working on the ships were testament to Britain's vast empire – Lascars, Chinese, Indians, Africans.

There were men lounging in doorways, looking with suspicion at any stranger that passed. Women were hanging out washing on lines strung between the buildings and operated by pulleys fixed by the side of windows. The odour of strange food cooking, with foreign spices, lingered in the air. Grubby children played on the greasy cobbles with pieces of rope and other rubbish that came from some of the many ships moored along the Thames.

Up ahead, Billy had ducked into a doorway and they could see that Sir Anthony was entering one of the large merchants' houses that ranged along the river, next to offices that bore the name Chen Shipping Company. Once he was in the house, Beech and Tollman ran up to join Billy. He had chosen a vantage point in the shadows of a warehouse doorway, which was partly obscured by a horse and cart but gave a full view into the window of the house that Sir Anthony had entered. They were rewarded with the sight of the member of parliament clasping a young man, who looked Chinese, in an embrace.

"Aye, aye," murmured Tollman, "looks like a secret boyfriend…"

But then, to their confusion, a Chinese woman, exquisitely dressed, entered the room and Sir Anthony gave her a lingering kiss.

"A girlfriend as well?" Billy asked in a whisper.

"Gentlemen," said Beech, with a note of triumph in his voice, "I think it is time that we asked Sir Anthony Jarvis to reveal his secrets, don't you?"

CHAPTER ELEVEN

A Man Gone Native

Sir Anthony Jarvis's face was a picture of dismay when he was confronted by Beech, Tollman and Rigsby. The Chinese woman and young man looked confused.

"I think it is time for the truth, Sir Anthony," said Beech firmly. "We are, after all, conducting a murder enquiry."

The Chinese woman gasped and swayed, as the young man rushed to her side and helped her to a chair.

"Anthony, what is this?" she asked in perfect English.

"I'm sorry, my dear," he answered, "I have not been entirely honest with you." Then he turned back to the policemen and said, "I will answer all your questions, of course, but may I first introduce my wife, Mei Li, and our son, Harold."

There was a stunned silence from the policemen. This was not what they had been expecting.

"Sorry, Sir Anthony... this lady is your *legal* wife?" Beech, alone, understood the implications of a knighted member of parliament being married to a Chinese wife. Social death and resignation would be on the cards if the information became common knowledge.

"And has been my wife for a very long time, Chief Inspector," said Sir Anthony defiantly. "My son was born in wedlock and he is now twenty-seven years old."

Billy looked at the son, standing by his mother. He was tall and powerfully built and he looked angry.

"And this was why Adeline Treborne was blackmailing you?" Beech asked.

"What?!" Harold Jarvis looked as though he was about to explode, and his mother looked even more distressed. It was obvious that Sir Anthony had neglected to tell his family about the Treborne problem.

Sir Anthony looked miserable. "I'm so sorry..." he said plaintively, "I didn't want to worry you..."

"*Worry* us?!" The son advanced on his father angrily. "It's not enough that we have to hide away in this foul area, where my mother cannot walk the streets without an escort; or that I had to be sent away to school under an assumed name, but now you tell me that you were being *blackmailed* because of us? And you allowed this to happen because of what? Your precious knighthood? Your reputation? Your career as a member of parliament?"

"Harold, be quiet!" Mei Li found her voice and she was also angry. She stood and faced Beech. "My son finds it hard to accept the situation, Chief Inspector. He was not raised in Hong Kong, where the rules of colonial society dictate social and financial ruin if a man 'goes native' and marries a Chinese woman. If Anthony had chosen to take me as his mistress, no one would have thought anything about it. Such a practice is commonplace among British government officials in Hong Kong. But Anthony chose to marry me, in secret, so that I would never suffer the shame of bearing him a child out of wedlock."

"That does not excuse what has happened now!" protested the son.

"No, you are right," the mother said calmly, "but your father has important work to do and the British Empire is at war. Now is not the time for good men to be lost to government because of the actions of some spiteful and greedy woman."

Beech was impressed by the beauty and quiet dignity of the woman in front of him and he felt a sense of shame that she was forced to be kept hidden because of the narrow-mindedness of society.

"I understand that you had everything to lose – your position, your title, perhaps your money." Beech tried to be sympathetic, but he disliked the idea that Sir Anthony had sacrificed his family for his own self-preservation. "But I'm afraid that this gives you a very solid motive to murder Adeline Treborne."

"No!" Sir Anthony was outraged. "Whatever else you think of me, Chief Inspector, I am no murderer! I assume, from what you said earlier today, that this woman was murdered in her home. Well, I have – had – no idea where the woman lived. She came to see me at the Houses of Parliament, pretending to be a constituent. She told me what she knew about me, then she told me her financial terms and I was told to pay a certain sum into her bank account every month. Failure to do so would result in my family being exposed…"

"You took money out of our business to pay this woman?" The son's anger was refuelled by this thought.

"No! Harold, I would never do that! The business is in your mother's name. It is your business. The money came from my personal account." Sir Anthony turned back to Beech. "I never knew where the Treborne woman lived and I would never have killed her. As you must realise by now, I am not a man of courage." The son and the wife bowed their heads in shame at this statement, which they knew to be true.

"Where were you, Sir Anthony, on the night of the first of July and the morning of the second? The truth this time, please." Beech needed to go through the formalities.

"I can answer that," said the son. "He was here. It was my birthday and he came to celebrate with us."

Beech nodded and motioned to Tollman and Rigsby that they were done. The son followed them to the door to show them out. Beech looked back at the wife, who was seated once more, and he could see that Sir Anthony was now on his knees, presumably begging forgiveness. The son followed Beech's gaze and his lip curled.

"My father may lack courage, but I do not. If I had known about all of this, I would have killed the woman myself," he said menacingly. Then he closed the door behind them.

"Mr Beech! Look." Tollman had wandered down the side of the house and was pointing at the river frontage, where some repair work was being done on a terrace overlooking the river.

"I'm willing to bet those men are using waterproof cement," he observed with a grim nod.

***

The team meeting after dinner included Lady Maud briefly, as she was anxious to contribute to the gathering of information. Victoria explained that they had discovered this sewing circle, operating from a church hall at Hyde Park Corner, which they suspected might be a method by which some woman was obtaining pieces of scurrilous gossip about wealthy families. It would be meeting in two days' time.

"It may not be linked to the Treborne case, but it would be wise for us to investigate," she added.

"And how do you propose we do that?" Beech asked, trying to suppress a smile because he could see that Maud was desperate to explain the plan.

"Mother?" Victoria wisely offered the floor to Maud before she exploded with pent-up enthusiasm.

"Yes, well, Victoria and I have enlisted the help of Constable Rigsby's mother." Caroline and Tollman grinned at Billy, who shrugged and grinned back. "Elsie Rigsby has agreed to play the part of my lady's maid… someone who is widowed and has come back into service and I have taken her on because one simply can't get young maids any more – they all want to go and work in munitions or some such better paid occupation." Maud was relishing the story she and Billy's mother had woven between them.

"I have agreed that Elsie can gossip about me as much as she likes…"

"Whatever is she going to say about you, Maud?" asked Caroline in amusement.

"Well, the first thing we decided upon was that I have a drinking problem. I am a complete lush!"

Everyone laughed, and Victoria murmured, "It's true, it's true."

"Then Elsie pointed out that being a drunk was not really blackmailable, otherwise most of the women in Mayfair would be paying extortion money to someone, so we came up with kleptomania…"

"What?!" Beech was alarmed. "I do hope that if this person *is* anything to do with the Treborne woman, that it doesn't end up in the newspapers before we have a chance to arrest her! Otherwise your reputation will be ruined for ever, Maud!"

"Oh, I'm not too worried, Peter," Lady Maud said breezily. "I'm sure you'll leap in before things get out of hand. Besides, Elsie's only going to suggest that I am a little light-fingered when it comes to insignificant items in department stores. It is rumoured that Queen Mary suffers from the same condition, you know, so I shall be in good company."

Caroline was laughing so much that tears were coming into her eyes, while Billy suffered an unexplained bout of coughing and Tollman had to slap him on the back.

"Well, I must be off now," said Maud, quite oblivious to her effect on the assembled company. "I decided to visit

Ida Toller-Bridge this evening for a game of cards. Ever since reading her daughter's letter, which highlighted her mother's distress at being shunned by society, I realised that I have been remiss in offering some companionship. I shan't breathe a word about the letter or her divorce or anything. She seemed so grateful when I telephoned today, and it made me quite ashamed at my neglect."

Victoria kissed her mother's cheek. "Have a nice evening, Ma," she said fondly.

When Lady Maud had left, there was a universal sentiment expressed that she was, in Billy's words, 'a diamond', and Victoria felt quite proud.

The conversation turned to the Treborne case. Beech felt that they had made no further progress other than to add two more murder suspects to the list.

"We have no way of proving, at the moment, that Sir Anthony and his son have a cast iron alibi, as they are both vouching for each other on the night in question."

"The son looks very strong," commented Billy, "and he has a fierce temper. He could easily have lifted a dead body into a noose. I'm not sure I believe him when he says he didn't know about the blackmail situation."

"And there's the business of the cement," added Tollman.

"I've been looking at the blackmail list again," said Victoria thoughtfully. "I thought at first that 'SR M jew' meant that someone might be Jewish but then a thought occurred to me that it might be an abbreviation of 'jeweller'."

There was a surprised murmur of agreement from everyone as the possibility opened up before them.

Tollman suddenly said "Marchesi!"

"Yes!" Victoria agreed. "It has the Royal Warrant!"

"So, SR must be a person who works at Marchesi?" asked Caroline. "How do we find out?"

"I'll have to make a trip to the Inland Revenue offices in Parliament Square," said Tollman, pulling a face. Obviously, it was a job he had performed before and not enjoyed.

Victoria continued her analysis of the list. "I looked through all the letters of complaint again. I thought that 'Ruth B baby' might refer to a girl from a wealthy family who had become pregnant or had given birth out of wedlock, but I could find no reference to anyone called Ruth or even a reference to a baby. So that one is proving a dead end, at the moment. 'Kit B, Peachtree' eludes me as well."

"Well, we have two names to investigate tomorrow." Beech was feeling tired from his long walks around London during the day. "I suggest that Victoria and I tackle the QC – it might be useful to have some legal expertise by my side if the QC starts quoting the law at me – and Tollman, you make your investigations at the Inland Revenue. Let's all meet up here for lunch. Caroline? Are you working tomorrow?"

Caroline nodded. "'Fraid so. But then I have a few days off, so I can be of more help then."

Everyone began to go their separate ways, but Billy lingered to speak to Caroline.

"Doctor?" he said quietly. "How did you get on with David, the boot boy?"

"Not very well, I'm afraid," and she told him about her conversation with Mrs Bailey.

"Ah, well, I don't blame her," he said simply and turned to go.

"Billy," Caroline asked, her curiosity getting the better of her. "What was Sir Anthony Jarvis's wife like?"

"Beautiful... really beautiful and elegant. I can't understand why having such a wife is beyond the pale. I mean, marrying an American woman is fine. Plenty of the aristocracy do that. What's wrong with a Chinese wife?"

"Skin colour and colonial prejudices," said Caroline sadly. "'Those who profit most from the Empire look down the most upon its inhabitants', my grandfather always used to say. And I suppose we do. The British regard those with a different skin colour as their inferiors, even though they may come from civilisations much older and wiser than ours."

"The upper classes always look down on *everyone*," Billy said sarcastically, then hastily added, "present company excepted, of course."

Caroline smiled. "I wish it were just the upper class but, you know, the working class are every bit as bad, if not worse. We have two West Indian ladies in the hospital – volunteer orderlies – and many of the white working-class women complain if they are touched by them or they handle their food. It's disgraceful. I've lost count of the number of patients I've had to reprimand for being rude to those ladies. Let's hope this war removes all these prejudices."

Billy nodded but, privately, he doubted it.

***

Tollman was woken from a deep sleep by his eldest daughter shaking him.

"Air raid coming, Dad!" she said urgently, the rags in her hair bouncing around wildly as she shook her father again. Outside in the street, the air raid whistle was being blown with a shrill and insistent blast.

"All right, all right," he said grumpily as he reluctantly heaved himself out of bed and found his slippers. "What's the time?"

"One o'clock."

"Blimey, these bloody Zeppelin raids are getting beyond a joke." He looked out of the window and he could see the searchlights criss-crossing the sky from their emplacements along the river. Bloody fools, he thought. What's the point of all the houses and shops having to put out all their lights when the searchlights give the bombers a much better idea of important targets? He sometimes wished he lived somewhere else in London. He was very fond of his little house in Clapham, with its tiny rose garden and vegetable patch. But it was perilously close to two power stations, the massive railway station at the Junction, two candle factories and numerous important industries situated behind the wharves along the river at Battersea. All highly attractive to the Germans, he reminded himself, and all highly combustible.

With a sigh, he picked up his dressing gown and the storm lamp he kept beside his bed and padded down to the cellar.

His three daughters were already snuggled up together in the corner – two were already asleep. The eldest, and most sensible, Daphne, was the one who had woken everyone else up and she was waiting for her father to get settled down before she went back to sleep herself.

"All right, Dad?" she whispered. Tollman grunted. Taking that as a 'yes', she whispered again, "There's some hot tea in the thermos, if you want it."

He nodded and gave Daphne one of his rare smiles. She seemed content with that and settled down next to her sisters to try to get back to sleep. Tollman sank down into the old armchair that they had managed to get down the cellar steps and poured himself some hot sweet tea. He made a face. "Evaporated milk!" he muttered, and Daphne, eyes shut, smiled and murmured, "Be grateful for what you get."

Like all the other houses in the street, the Tollmans had converted what was their coal cellar into an air raid shelter. His daughters had scrubbed and whitewashed the cellar while Tollman had built a coal bunker in the front outside area (which could not be deemed a garden, as it was barely six feet long by three feet deep). Then they had 'furnished' the cellar, in a manner of speaking, with two fold-up camp beds, for the daughters to share, and the battered but comfy old armchair for Tollman.

He sat, sipping his tea, in the weak moonlight that was filtering through the two panes of glass in the window where the coal hole used to be. Strange, he thought. They had been told that Zeppelin raids only took place when there was no moon. He *was* grateful, he reflected, as he surveyed the rows of shelves he had put in, laden with canned goods for emergencies. He was grateful he didn't have to get out of a warm bed and make for the nearest Underground station or railway arch, like some families did.

He looked around at the well-stocked, if rather cramped cellar. There was a first aid kit, emergency lighting, a sealed drum of water and cans and cans of food – corned beef, Irish stew, pilchards, sardines, pears, plums, peaches…

Something clicked in his brain… peaches… Peachtree.

"Daphne!" he hissed, and she opened her eyes.

"What is it, Dad? I was nearly asleep!" For all her amiability and good intentions, she had inherited some of her father's tendency towards grumpiness.

"That place that you girls went for your works day out… where was it again?"

"What? That was last year! What do you want to know about that for?"

"Never mind, just tell me."

"It was Peachtree, Dad. A lovely place down in Kent, on the way to Gravesend. Can I go back to sleep now?"

"Just one more thing, Daphne. How big was this Peachtree place?"

"Oh, it was tiny. No more than about ten, fifteen cottages, one pub and a church. *Now* can I go back to sleep?"

"Yes, love. Thank you very much. You've been very helpful." Tollman finished his tea and settled back in the chair to go to sleep, with a small smile of triumph on his lips.

CHAPTER TWELVE

A Jezebel and Jewellery

Tollman decided that the Peachtree information could wait until this evening, but he stopped by the Mayfair house anyway, to pick up Billy.

"I thought you were going to go to the Inland Revenue on your own?" asked Billy, buttoning up his uniform jacket.

"Nah." Tollman shook his head. "I thought to myself last night, why go through all the nightmare of trying to get the Revenue to be co-operative, when I can just take along a uniform – that's you, son – and quote the Defence of the Realm Act at the shop manager."

"How do you mean?"

"Policeman's gift is DORA. You can basically use it as an excuse to get information or gain entry to anywhere you like. All I need to do is to say to the manager that we are doing a spot check on potential enemy aliens and he has to give me chapter and verse on all his employees. I don't know why I didn't think of it yesterday. Thing is, it's all so new, I haven't got used to it yet."

"Right. Well, lead on then, Sergeant! Where is this fancy jewellers, Marchesi, anyway?"

"Piccadilly – the posh end, up opposite Burlington House, so we can walk there."

As they strolled along in the morning sunshine, Tollman said, "Did you get much sleep last night, son?"

"Slept like a log. Why?"

Tollman looked at him in disbelief. "Zeppelin raid! Those anti-airship guns were going off all night. Mind you, they said this morning it was a false alarm. Apparently, the Admiralty decided to send some aeroplanes up to do a patrol but forgot to inform the Royal Marines who man the gun emplacements at Tower Bridge and Green Park, so they start firing at anything and everything. It's a good job they couldn't hit the side of a barn with those guns of theirs, otherwise we would be short of a good few precious aeroplanes by now! Didn't you hear anything?"

Billy shook his head. "Guns going off don't bother me, Mr Tollman. Never did in the trenches and a few bangs in London wouldn't even make me stop snoring!"

"It's supposed to be your job to look after the women of the household, Billy. You should have got them up and down into the basement."

Billy snorted in derision. "Huh, yes. The last time I tried that, a very ratty Lady Maud bit my ear off. She said, 'Peter told us that the Kaiser will never bomb the area around the Palace. That means us. So, if you don't mind, Constable Rigsby, I shall stay in my own bed!' So, ever since then, I haven't bothered."

"Gawd! How the other half live!" said Tollman, to no one in particular.

"Yes. Tell me about it," said Billy, with feeling, as they looked at the glittering array of jewellery in Marchesi's window in front of them. "Who can really afford this stuff?"

"Armaments manufacturers," said Tollman grimly. "I expect that every time a shell explodes, one of them buys his missus a new bracelet. They're the only people making a fortune out of this war. I hear that half the aristocracy are losing money hand over fist because they can't sell the goods from their companies in the far-flung places of the Empire. German U-boats blockading us in, like they are. Do you know," he added with feeling, "my local shopkeeper reckons that we shall run out of tea soon. Tea! Beggars belief!"

The manager and his mostly female staff were unlocking cabinets, dusting and generally preparing for the day ahead when Tollman and Rigsby walked in. The manager, a small man, looked up at the uniformed height of Constable Rigsby and visibly blanched. The female staff, on the other hand, cheeks suddenly a pretty shade of pink, simply smiled. Tollman pursed his lips and rolled his eyes. *The lad's catnip*, he thought in irritation.

"How can I help you, sirs?" the manager said warily, as Tollman produced his warrant.

"Defence of the Realm Act, sir," said Tollman breezily. "We're running a spot check on whether any female illegal aliens are being employed in West End shops." The women employees looked shocked and the manager bristled.

"Look, gentlemen, as I have told the Board of Trade many times, I can't afford to employ any staff with foreign-sounding names. None of our clientele would put up with it."

"So, you won't mind showing me your staff details, sir, will you?" answered Tollman tersely.

The manager looked resigned. "Come through," he said, going through to the back office. He rifled through a filing cabinet and laid down four buff files containing the details of the employees out in the shop.

Tollman quickly scanned them and frowned. "Is this all of it?"

"In this shop, yes. We have a workshop in Soho, where the jewellery is made or repaired, and we have a man from Soho come into the shop twice a week to collect and deliver."

Tollman nodded.

"Do you know all the workers in Soho?" he asked. "Only we're looking for someone with the initials SR."

The manager looked surprised and then a little flustered. "Well, the only person who works for Marchesi – here or in Soho – with those initials would be me," he said. "Samuel Robinson."

***

Victoria and Beech were having a pleasant end to a leisurely breakfast, chatting about their childhood memories and laughing, when Mary stuck her head around the door to inform Beech that there was a telephone call from Mr Tollman.

"Ah! I wonder what he has uncovered?" Beech looked optimistic as he left the breakfast table.

"Sir?" said Tollman on the end of the line. "I'm ringing from Marchesi, the jewellers. We've uncovered quite a little racket going on here."

"Oh?"

"Yes, sir. Apparently, the shop manager has been organising the making of fake jewellery for some of his clients, so that the real stuff can be broken up and sold. Strictly speaking, he's not doing anything illegal, unless one of his clients attempts to defraud an insurance company and Mr Robinson here would technically be an accessory."

"Interesting! So, this Robinson has been blackmailed by Adeline Treborne because of this 'service' he's been offering?"

"It would appear so, sir. However, and here's the interesting part, one of his regular clients is an American woman – Lady Patrick – the wife of the QC mentioned by Mrs E the other night."

"Good God! Do you want me to come down there, Tollman?"

"I think that would be a good idea, sir... perhaps with Mrs E... because matey here is supposed to have a meeting with Lady Patrick today."

"We are on our way!"

Beech put his head around the dining room door and said "Victoria! We need to be on our way! Grab your hat and coat and meet me outside. I'll tell you the details on the journey."

Victoria sprang to life, grabbed everything necessary and was at Beech's side in a flash.

"It's a lovely day, and we don't have far to go, so let's walk, shall we?" Beech suggested. Victoria took his proffered arm and they walked at a brisk pace while Beech explained the purpose of Tollman's phone call.

"What an incredible piece of luck!" Victoria exclaimed. "So, we shall interview this Lady Patrick?"

Beech nodded, then he added, "But do you know what I'm wondering? Whether any more of these wealthy people who have had their jewellery copied before selling the stones were also on Adeline Treborne's blackmail list? We only had an impression of that one page from the book. There could have been so many more names in there that we may never know about."

Samuel Robinson was seated in his office, looking distressed, when Beech and Victoria arrived.

"I really have done nothing wrong!" he protested, as soon as Beech walked in the door. "I've explained to these policemen that it is perfectly normal practice for clients to ask for their jewellery to be copied – especially if they are going to travel abroad and don't want their original pieces to be taken out of the country."

"Of course it is. My guess is, though, Mr Robinson," said Beech smoothly, after seating Victoria, "that your *other* trade in providing these copies and selling off the stones in the real pieces was rather unique, and this is why you were being blackmailed. I expect Detective Sergeant Tollman can give me chapter and verse." He looked at

Tollman expectantly and was rewarded by him laying a large ledger down on the table.

"A cursory glance, sir, would suggest in excess of one hundred such copies being made in the first half of this year," was Tollman's summary.

"I think that we need to discuss this further, down at Scotland Yard," said Beech, nodding to Billy, who put his hand on the trembling manager's shoulder.

"Wait! Wait!" Samuel Robinson was beside himself with anxiety. "I can't afford to be hauled out of this shop in broad daylight by the police! I will lose my position! Our customers will never come here again! Please! I'll tell you anything you want to know but, please, no scandal!"

Billy took his hand off the man's shoulder, which seemed to calm him down a little, then Samuel Robinson proceeded to tell Beech everything about the special 'service' that Marchesi offered its clients.

Some clients, he explained, did genuinely want replicas of their jewellery made, so that they could wear the fakes and put the real ones in a safety deposit box, while they grew in value.

"Diamonds, for example, are an investment that will never diminish," said Robinson knowledgeably. Then he went on to explain that, lately, they had had clients ask for replica necklaces and bracelets because they had 'cash flow' problems and wished to save face while their jewellery was broken up and reset, or left as individual stones, and sold to raise money.

"Several gentlemen in the City of London, who own overseas companies, are having difficulty selling commodities because of the war," Robinson confided quietly.

Tollman and Rigsby looked at each other and nodded. It was exactly the topic Tollman had spoken about earlier.

"There are others," – Robinson's tone grew more conspiratorial – "two ladies and one gentleman, who do this on a regular basis and require extreme confidentiality, which leads me to suspect that they are keeping the information about their activities from their spouses."

"Do you believe that these three people are in some distress?" enquired Beech.

Robinson thought for a moment. "Only one of the ladies." He leafed through the ledger and pointed to the name of Lady Patrick. "I believe that this lady needs sums of money and she cannot ask her husband for them."

"What about the other two 'regular' clients?" Tollman asked, pencil poised over his notebook.

Robinson smiled and shook his head. "The other lady," – Billy smiled at the fact that Robinson seemed unwilling to mention names – "here," – Robinson pointed to the name in the ledger of a reasonably well-known stage actress – "has many admirers and each time one of them gives her a piece of jewellery, she brings it in here to have it appraised. If it is valuable, she has it copied, and we sell the stones for her. She is quite frank, to me, that it is a way of supplementing her income." Beech raised an eyebrow, Billy grinned and Tollman pursed his lips in disapproval. Victoria privately thought it was rather enterprising.

"And the gentleman?" Beech probed further.

Samuel Robinson's lips curled in disdain. "One could hardly call him a gentleman." He pointed to a name in the ledger of a young MP, known to be a 'man about town', popular with the ladies. Robinson continued, "He always has the same method of operation. He brings a young lady in here and she chooses a piece of jewellery, he pays for it and he has an arrangement with us that we say it will be delivered to the young lady's address in a week. Meanwhile, we copy it and deliver the fake one to the lady, while he gets us to sell the real item in one of our other shops and refund him the money. That way, I assume, he gets to seduce the young lady at very little expense to himself."

Tollman looked even more disapproving, Billy's eyes widened, Beech shook his head in disbelief, and this time, Victoria was privately outraged.

"I presume you get a nice fat commission from all of these shenanigans?" demanded Tollman.

Robinson nodded and hung his head.

Beech continued to question. "Presumably that is why Adeline Treborne was blackmailing you?" Robinson nodded again. "Was she privy to the contents of this ledger?"

Robinson looked horrified. "No! Upon my word, sir, she was not!"

"Then how did she know that these 'arrangements' were going on?"

"The actress's maid had told someone who was a friend of Miss Treborne's – but I don't know how she found out about Lady Patrick. I was paying Adeline Treborne to *protect* my clients. She said that if I did not pay, she would make a note of everyone who came into the shop throughout the week and she would accuse them in the newspaper of having fake jewellery made, whether it was true or not. She said she would expose the trade of creating fakes. We would have lost our Royal Warrant!" Robinson looked thoroughly miserable.

"Where were you on the evening of the first of July and the morning of the second, Mr Robinson?"

"Why?" Robinson looked puzzled. Then he said, "I was at home with my wife and family. You can ask our neighbours. They came around for supper on the evening of the first. It was our wedding anniversary."

Beech looked at the others. Billy shook his head, so did Tollman, meaning that neither of them believed that Robinson was the murderer. After all, the man barely came up to Billy's chest, he was so small.

"You will be relieved to know, Mr Robinson, that Adeline Treborne is dead."

Robinson's face was a picture of relief, but then Beech added, "We believe that she may have been murdered." Robinson's face turned a nasty grey colour with shock. Beech continued, "However, we do not consider you to be a suspect in the murder enquiry." Before Billy could catch him, Robinson slid off his chair on to the floor, in a dead faint.

"Oh, dear! Poor Mr Robinson!" said Victoria in alarm. "Constable Rigsby, please do something!"

"Yes, Mrs E," said Billy with resignation, and he picked up the shop manager as though he were a sack of coal and laid him flat out on the table. Victoria produced a bottle of smelling salts from her bag and waved it under Mr Robinson's nose, which soon had him spluttering and coughing and fully conscious.

"There we are now, sir," said Billy helpfully, as he lifted Mr Robinson off the table, held him in his arms as though he were a damsel in distress, and then deposited him back on his chair.

Any further discussion was about Lady Patrick's appointment with Mr Robinson. It was decided that Mr Robinson should go home for the rest of the day, as he was obviously still in a state of shock. Victoria and Beech would stay, to talk to Lady Patrick. Rigsby and Tollman would go back to Scotland Yard, with Mr Robinson's ledger, to see if any of his clients had reported a burglary in the last six months, possibly with intent to defraud their insurance company.

***

As Tollman and Rigsby walked into the Yard, they found themselves almost knocked down by a stampede of detectives from CID, eager to get out of the front door as fast as they could. Bringing up the rear was Tollman's least favourite person in Scotland Yard, Detective Sergeant Carter.

"You still blowing the dust off old cases, Tollman?" asked Carter, trying to score points. "Only you'll have to excuse me... can't stop to chat... some of us have real police work to do."

"What? Like shining the shoes of West End gangsters who top up your pay packet, Carter?" Tollman thought he'd get one in, right below the belt.

Carter give him a contemptuous look. "Jealous?" he said softly.

"No, lad. You're welcome to your boot-licking. Just be careful it don't lead to your own personal hole in the ground one day. Gangsters have a way of disposing of people they don't find useful any more." Tollman gave Carter an equally contemptuous look.

"Mr Tollman, would you like me to take DS Carter around the back of this building and teach him a lesson?" asked Billy.

Carter laughed. "All right, Frankenstein's Monster, you can get back in your cage. Mr Tollman and me have an understanding and it doesn't have anything to do with you. All right?"

Billy was itching to thump him but unless Tollman gave him permission, he had to keep his hands by his side.

Tollman looked at Carter and smiled in a pitying way. "Now, Carter, I know that your little fragile ego is begging for me to ask what case you are on now. So, I am asking you, so you can get it off your chest and get out of my sight."

Carter grinned. "Crime of the century," he gloated. "Someone's just killed Ruth Baker." Seeing the smile disappear from Tollman's face, Carter assumed he had scored a point and the older detective was jealous, so he decided to put the boot in before he left. "Shame you won't be involved in the investigation – especially as you buggered up the last one into Ruth Baker. Never mind, eh?" Then he was out of the door, laughing to himself.

"What was that all about, Mr Tollman?" asked Billy, seeing Tollman's frozen face.

"Ruth B baby!" muttered Tollman. "How could I have been so blind? Ruth B baby! Of course! Billy! Follow me!" and he sped up the stairs with frantic haste, Billy racing after him. Tollman kept up the pace until he reached the Criminal Records Department, then he paused, panting, before pushing open the doors. The uniformed sergeant in charge, an amiable man called Horace Stenton, looked up from his paperwork and grinned.

"Been expecting you all day, Arthur! I expect you want the Ruth Baker file?" Tollman nodded, still too out of breath to form the words. Stenton handed it over and said sympathetically, "Never mind, Arthur. She appears to have got her come-uppance."

Tollman could breathe more easily now. "Did Carter say who the CID boys think did it?"

"Their money seems to be on the husband."

Tollman shook his head vigorously. "No. Not the husband. I know it won't be him." Then he turned to Rigsby. "Billy, be a good lad and get us both a cup of tea and then come and find me in Interview Room B. And I'll tell you the story of the greatest failure of my career."

Billy looked astonished and Stenton gave him a wink. "I hope you've got all day, lad," he said jovially. "Arthur's been known to harp on about the Ruth Baker case until the small hours!"

CHAPTER THIRTEEN

The Perfect Victim

Lady Patrick was an exquisite young creature, Victoria decided, rather like the most delicately featured porcelain doll, with her round blue eyes, plump pink lips and golden curls, framing a creamy complexion. She could see that Beech was overawed by the woman and was already being over-attentive – fussing over a chair for her and fetching her a glass of water. Victoria imagined that all men felt an instant attraction and sense of protectiveness when confronted by this doll-like creature. Victoria also sensed that it was probably not possible for women to feel jealous of her – envious, yes, of her physical attributes, but not jealous, because there was something almost childlike about her.

As Beech gently informed Lady Patrick that Adeline Treborne was dead and that they knew all about the fact that she was blackmailing various people, of which she was one, a single tear rolled down Lady Patrick's cheek. *She even cries beautifully!* Victoria was full of admiration for this living work of art.

Lady Patrick spoke in a soft, in volume and tone, American accent, as she explained the predicament she found herself in.

"Before I met my husband," she explained, "I was the mistress of another man." Beech looked at the floor in embarrassment and Victoria felt mean-spirited in her enjoyment of the fact that this exquisite young woman had a flaw. Lady Patrick continued, "It was not of my choosing. My mother… who was a much-admired courtesan from San Francisco… sold me to my… protector… when I was sixteen."

"Good God!" exclaimed Beech.

Damn, thought Victoria, *now I shall have to feel sorry for her again!*

"Fortunately, and fortuitously, my protector and my mother both died within a few months of each other – about five years ago – and I was free. I had a house that he had purchased in my name and jewellery that he had given me, so I was able to sell all of those and move to England. I changed my name and pretended that I was a widow. People were very kind and took me into their social circles and then I met my husband."

"I take it that your husband knows nothing about your past life?" asked Victoria, trying to be sympathetic but, judging by Beech shooting her a disapproving glare, she obviously hadn't succeeded.

Lady Patrick just shook her head sorrowfully, her golden curls trembling around her perfect face.

"My husband is a very honourable man and a very eminent lawyer. He has advised the Royal Family and many prominent figures in British society. If I told him, I am sure he would understand but I am equally sure that he would feel compelled to retire from his valuable work.

I would not wish to be the cause of such a brilliant man being lost to the legal profession."

"So, you have been selling the jewellery that your husband gave you, in order to pay Adeline Treborne, and having replicas made so that your husband would not suspect?" Beech asked gently.

Lady Patrick nodded and gave a small smile to Beech that was guaranteed to melt the hardest of hearts.

Victoria was then astonished to hear Beech say, "Well, I don't think we need bother you any further, Lady Patrick. Adeline Treborne will no longer be a problem for you and the secret of your past life is safe with us. We shall not mention your name in our report."

Lady Patrick's face lit up, like an amazed child at Christmas. The pink lips parted, and she smiled, displaying perfect white, even teeth. "Thank you, Chief Inspector," she breathed, and Beech escorted her protectively to the door. When he kissed her hand, Victoria thought she was going to explode with fury.

"Please, Lady Patrick, do not hesitate to call me, if you should need any assistance," Beech added. As the doll-creature left the room, Victoria realised that she had barely been the focus of the woman's gaze – even when she had spoken to her. Lady Patrick had concentrated only on Beech, answered Beech and reacted to Beech. It was as if Victoria did not really exist.

When Beech returned, his afterglow of briefly being Lady Patrick's saviour and protector was rudely stripped away when Victoria said, "Peter, you made a complete ass of yourself!"

"What?!"

"No wonder the Metropolitan Police Force needs the assistance of women! That creature just ran rings around you and you just lapped it up!"

Beech flushed with the realisation that he may have lacked a certain amount of professionalism in Lady Patrick's presence.

Victoria continued, "Not only were you not prepared to countenance the fact that she may be lying, but you have dismissed the notion that her husband could very well have known and could actually be the murderer! If she can get *you* to abandon your professional instincts, can you imagine what she could get a besotted husband, several years her senior, to do for her? The woman could be a criminal mastermind, for all you know! Just because she has the face of an angel does not make her above suspicion!" There was no doubt that Victoria was very angry, and Beech felt helpless in the face of such fury.

"I shall take myself home," Victoria announced, between gritted teeth, "I suggest you go back to Scotland Yard and brush up on your Chief Inspector skills!" With that, she swept out, leaving Beech confused, a little guilty and considerably embarrassed.

CHAPTER FOURTEEN

Who Killed Ruth Baker?

"So," said Billy to Tollman, after watching him sip his cup of tea for a while, "are you going to tell me, Mr Tollman, about this Ruth Baker, what she has to do with the case we are working on, and why your past dealings with this woman were such a failure?"

Tollman sighed. "Fifteen years ago, it was. We had a tip-off that a Mrs Ruth Baker was a baby farmer…"

"A what?" Billy had never heard the term before.

"A baby farmer," explained Tollman, "is a woman who offers to take illegitimate or unwanted babies and either look after them herself or find them new parents. All for a fee, of course. The problem arises when the baby farmer decides that she can make more profit from killing the infants than having to go to the bother of looking after them or finding them a new home."

Billy pulled a face of distaste.

Tollman nodded in agreement. "Someone anonymously tipped us off that Ruth Baker was one of these baby murderers. We investigated her, and her husband, but we couldn't find any proof. We dug up her back garden. No bodies. We dragged the canal near her house in Islington.

Nothing. We couldn't prove anything. She swore that all the children she had taken in were then passed on to 'loving parents' in Britain and abroad but she had no paperwork to prove it. She had no names to give us. She said everything was done confidentially and people gave false names. And, of course, there was no law, then or now, that said that what she claimed she was doing was wrong. Kids could, and still can, be bought and sold like dogs and horses and there is nothing the police can do about it unless we can prove bodily harm."

"Shameful," said Billy.

"The thing is," said Tollman, "her husband, the one that Carter reckons killed her, was like a faithful dog. Big dozy brute he was, a bit of a man mountain. Covered in tattoos. When he did work, he worked as a labourer. Ruth Baker was a slip of a thing. Small and dark, I remember her eyes were almost black. I think she had gypsy blood in her. But she had that husband of hers wrapped round her little finger. When we took her to the station for questioning, he cried like a baby. Great big ugly sod cried like a little kid. And when she was in the interview room, all she kept saying was, 'I need to get back to my Sydney. He's lost without me.' Really anxious about it, she was. Sydney Baker struck me as a bit simple, and he never wavered in his devotion to her. He would never kill her, I'd bet my own life on that."

There was a knock at the door and Stenton entered, with a file in his hand. "Mr Beech wanted these fingerprint reports as soon as possible," he said. "Told me to give them to you, if he wasn't around."

Tollman nodded and took the file. "Oh, Stenton, where did they say that Ruth Baker was living now?"

"Apparently, she was living, with her husband, at some house in the rough World's End area, off the New King's Road, not far from the Imperial Gas Works."

"Who reported the murder?"

"Neighbour. Went over about seven o'clock in the morning, before going to work, to pay into the Christmas Club that Baker was running and found her stabbed."

"Husband standing over the body?"

"No. The neighbour thought he had been there though, because he works as a night shift labourer on the Underground system and usually gets home around six in the morning. The husband's gone missing." Stenton held his hands up. "That's all that has been put down in the Morning Report. The printing department are working on photographs of the husband as we speak. Don't ask me anything else, Arthur, or Carter will make my life a misery."

Tollman nodded. "OK. Thanks for that, anyway."

After Stenton left, Tollman looked through the finger-print reports and said, with a note of disbelief in his voice, "This just keeps getting better!", and he turned the file round to show Billy.

"Identified fingerprints at 12 Trinity Mansions... Reginald Ingham... confidence trickster... etcetera... Sydney Baker... grievous bodily harm... arrested May 1911, Fulham. Charge sheets say that he was arrested for beating a man to within an inch of his life 'for speaking disrespectfully to his wife, Ruth'. Spent two years in

Pentonville. Fingerprints were found on the bedstead in Adeline Treborne's apartment and on the front door. Sounds to me like Sydney Baker is the most likely candidate, at the moment, for our hangman. He could have lifted up the Treborne woman with one hand tied behind his back."

"It says that there were other sets of fingerprints in the apartment indicating the presence of two other people," noted Billy. "Do you think that Ruth Baker was one of them?"

"It's possible," Tollman conceded, "but we would have no way of telling from the fingerprints. We didn't take suspects' fingerprints fifteen years ago and that's the only time, to my knowledge, she's been the subject of an investigation."

"So, we need to find Sydney," said Billy.

"If possible, before Carter and his mates," said Tollman grimly, "but that's going to be difficult as they will probably already be crawling all over the Underground system looking for him." Tollman stared ahead, at nothing in particular, and looked dissatisfied. "The thing is, Billy, if Adeline Treborne was blackmailing Ruth Baker, what was it all about? Unless Miss Treborne had proof that Baker had murdered those babies fifteen years ago…"

"Or Baker had started up her old business again…" Billy offered.

"Mm." Tollman wasn't convinced. "It's going to needle me until we find the truth," he said. "We need to talk to Mr Beech."

***

Elsie Rigsby savoured her cup of tea and Battenburg cake as she surveyed the gaggle of women sitting around at the servants' sewing circle. It was a lively group. The woman who ran it, a Mrs Leighton, was outgoing and friendly. Elsie had been welcomed with open arms, introduced to the others and immediately given refreshments.

She watched while Mrs Leighton circulated among the women and stopped now and then, appearing to have a little confidential chat with certain individuals. Elsie estimated that Mrs Leighton was in her mid-thirties. She was well-dressed, trying to be middle-class, Elsie thought, and there were flecks of grey in her blonde hair. She thought she detected a touch of powder and paint on the woman's face, but she wasn't sure. *If Sissy were here,* Elsie thought, *we would probably have decided that the woman was attractive but with pretensions.* That was the label that the two sisters apportioned to anyone who was trying to be better than they should be, whether it referred to age, class or education.

"So, how did you hear of us, Mrs Rigsby?" asked Mrs Leighton, sitting down next to her with a smile.

"Oh, my employer, Lady Maud Winterbourne, was told about it by Lady Donaldson. I believe you have some of her girls here?" Elsie replied, returning the smile.

"Yes, we do! Marjory over there and there's Daisy, who comes on our other meeting day. Do you know anyone here?" Mrs Leighton seemed very curious.

"No," answered Elsie, with a small, regretful smile. "I've only just returned to service. I was widowed, you see, and needed the extra money. Fortunately, a job came right up. Lady Maud's been having trouble getting youngsters, because they all want to go off and work in factories, where they earn more."

"Have another cake, Elsie. May I call you Elsie? I'm Louise, by the way." She gave Elsie a smile and nose-wrinkle that intimated they were going to be firm friends. Elsie decided, at that moment, that there was something suspicious about this overly friendly woman, but she was determined to play the game.

"This is such a lovely idea, to have a sewing circle, Louise," she said flatteringly. "How long have you been running it then?"

"Oh, about two years. I felt very strongly that ladies in service needed somewhere to go, on their days off. I mean, we can't go to pubs, like the men, can we?"

"No." Elsie felt like heading for the nearest public house right now. A gin wouldn't go amiss. All this cloying sweetness of 'all ladies together' was making her head ache. "Were you in service, Louise? Only you sound as though you understand what it's like for those who are."

Louise smiled. "I was, once upon a time," she said, thus confirming Elsie's suspicion that Mrs Leighton 'had pretensions'. "Lady's maid to a French Countess," she continued. *Ooh, la la,* thought Elsie, *'course, she wouldn't be just a normal maid, would she?*

Louise smiled again. "I travelled the world with the Countess! Monte Carlo, Cannes, Nice, Florence... oh, so many beautiful places." *Garn!* thought Elsie. *I bet she hasn't been anywhere further than Bournemouth.*

Louise was in her stride now. "But then I met my dear husband, Mr Leighton. He owned his own shop, selling luxury goods, and of course I had to leave my position with the Countess. She was absolutely bereft and didn't know how she would ever manage without me! But she did, of course. Our employers always replace us with ease."

Elsie tried to look suitably impressed and said, confidentially, "I don't think that our employers ever really think anything of us at all. We're just a convenience to them, aren't we?"

Louise Leighton looked interested. "Are you not happy in your place of employment then, Elsie?"

"Oh no! Don't get me wrong. Lady Maud is a good employer. She treats her staff well – what staff she's got." She lowered her voice for effect. "I don't think she's that well off, really, not since General Sir Richard Winterbourne died."

"Oh, poor woman!" whispered Louise, "I'm finding more and more that the upper classes are not doing very well, financially, since this war started."

"I know what you mean," Elsie agreed, "I think the worry of it is what drives Lady Maud to her... little eccentricities."

Louise's eyes widened, and her cheeks took on a slight flush. *Aha! That's got you interested,* thought Elsie.

"Eccentricities?" Louise was almost quivering with anticipation.

"Oh dear. I think I've said too much..." Elsie decided not to be too cavalier with criticisms of her 'employer'.

"Nonsense," whispered Louise. "You have to unburden yourself to someone. That's what this little group is all about. Somewhere for ladies to relax and talk to like-minded women, who understand the difficulties of being in service." She decided to go further in her efforts to convince Elsie to open up. "For example, Maisie, over there, works for Lady Patrick, who is American and quite odd, so she tells me. Whereas Doris, over there, works for Lord and Lady Sedgewood. Apparently, *he* is nice enough – what one would expect from an English lord – but *she* is foreign and is *very* demanding, to the point of unpleasantness, and has some very dubious relatives who are constantly visiting. Poor Doris is beside herself sometimes. If she didn't have us to come and talk to, she would be quite distressed."

"Oh, I can understand that," whispered Elsie sagely. "Her mistress sounds terrible. It's nothing like that with Lady Maud. She is always pleasant… when she's sober."

"Oh dear!" said Louise, her eyes widening. "That must be a trial for you?"

"It can be." Elsie was in her stride now. "I've got used to putting her to bed when she's insensible, poor woman. I think she drinks because she's lonely. Her daughter lives with her, but she's always out, and a daughter is not the same company as a husband, is she? The drinking and… the other little problem… are just the acts of a lonely woman."

"Other problem?"

"Sorry?"

"Elsie, you said… the other little problem."

"Oh," – she leaned towards Louise, who met her halfway – "I shouldn't say anything, really… but she steals things…"

"What?!"

"Shoplifts," and she nodded to Louise as though that were explanation enough.

"Oh. My goodness!" Louise was shocked, but a small half-smile played around her lips. "What sort of things does she steal?"

Elsie pretended to be puzzled. "Well that's just it… silly things really. Paltry things, that she doesn't really need. A cheap necklace here, a handkerchief there. She likes to spend her time in department stores. I'm surprised she hasn't been caught by now!"

"I believe it's called 'kleptomania', Elsie," said Louise knowledgeably. "A proper mania. I'm not sure that even a doctor can cure it."

Louise Leighton stood up and clapped her hands for attention. "Well, ladies," she said in a loud, firm voice. "I hope you have all enjoyed your little natterings today." A laugh rippled around the room. "But, sadly, we have to vacate the premises in half an hour and, yet again…" she said in mock reproach, "we seem to have done precious little sewing!" There was more laughter. "So, if you would just like to help me clear away and wash the crockery, I would be very grateful."

There was a bustle of activity. Chairs were put at the side of the hall, cups, saucers and plates were gathered up, cakes were wrapped in greaseproof and packed away in Mrs Leighton's basket. Elsie was just drying some crockery with a cloth when Louise said, "Wait for me, Elsie, and we shall walk together. I'm going your way." So, there was nothing Elsie could do, except smile and nod. Now she would have to walk back to Lady Maud's house, which was in completely the opposite direction to her own home.

Everyone scattered outside the hall and went off in groups of twos and threes. Elsie and Louise walked at a leisurely pace through the streets. During their stroll, Louise told Elsie how her husband, "who was sadly deceased and was the kindest man who ever lived," had come up with the idea of the sewing circle. "Louise, he said to me," she recounted, with a distressed look on her face, "Louise, it is our duty to help those who are less fortunate than us. Think of all the lonely days and nights you spent as a lady's maid. It is your job to give those poor souls a little cheer and companionship in life." She turned to Elsie. "And that is how the sewing circle was born."

"Fancy," said Elsie, trying to keep a straight face. *She's laying it on a bit thick*, she thought.

They were now outside Lady Maud's house and Elsie had to make the awkward decision to go inside, through the servants' entrance, of course.

"Well, here I am," she said breezily. "So I'll have to take my leave now. It's been a pleasure, Louise, and I shall look forward to coming along next week."

Louise smiled, and Elsie could see that she was taking in every detail of the house. "I shall look forward to seeing you."

She seemed reluctant to move on, so Elsie took a breath and darted down the steps to the kitchen door, praying that it would be open, and she wouldn't have to knock. Thankfully, it yielded when she turned the handle and she swiftly went inside and shut the door behind her. Her heart was pounding, and she leaned back against the door, hand on her chest, to quiet herself.

Mrs Beddowes looked up from her pastry-making with a startled and quizzical expression and Elsie quickly put her finger to her lips to indicate silence. She moved to the kitchen window and looked up the stairwell, noting gratefully that Louise Leighton was now walking away. She was joined by a curious Mrs Beddowes, who followed her gaze.

Elsie looked at her, held out her hand and said, "Billy Rigsby's mum – Elsie – pleased to meet you. You wouldn't happen to have a drop of gin about you, would you?"

***

Beech was back in Scotland Yard, having walked all the way from Piccadilly in frustration and confusion. Victoria's tirade had stung him. He thought he had been perfectly reasonable and gentlemanly while conducting the interview with Lady Patrick. It was true that such a beautiful woman had thrown him off balance. His judgement had been impaired. Damn it! Victoria had been right, of course. As a policeman, he should never have been swayed by a pretty face.

By the time he reached Scotland Yard, his leg was throbbing like fury and he was in a temper to match. To cap it all, he was faced with a pile of paperwork, which merely served to highlight his feeling that he was less of a policeman and more of a bureaucrat.

Tollman knocked on his door, with Rigsby in tow. He was clutching the fingerprint report, but first he had to tell Beech about the death of Ruth Baker, her connection to the Treborne case and the fact that her missing husband's fingerprints were found in Adeline Treborne's apartment.

To his surprise, Beech barked, "Right! That's it! No more prevarication. Tollman, I want the fingerprints taken of Sir Anthony Jarvis and his son, the two porters and the boot boy at Trinity Mansions, the live-out maid, the manager of Marchesi jewellers, the editor of the *London Herald* and the man who lives opposite the Treborne apartment. We need to find out if any of them match the unknown fingerprints in that report."

Tollman looked flabbergasted. "I thought we'd ruled out most of those people as not physically up to being the hangman."

Beech answered rattily, "I gave you an order, Tollman. Let's observe proper police procedure, please." Then he bent his head over his paperwork as a signal that they should leave.

Billy raised his eyebrows at Tollman, who, by the set of his mouth, had decided to be stubborn.

"Very well, sir, we will do that, even though I believe we should be out looking for Sydney Baker." Beech flashed him an angry look but Tollman continued anyway. "I am simply concerned that Sydney Baker will blurt out all he knows, or is involved in, on the Adeline Treborne case and the Commissioner will blame us for the news getting out."

Tollman's observation hit home. Beech sighed and threw down his pen. There was a moment's silence while Beech composed himself, then he said simply, "You are right, of course. How should we best proceed?"

Tollman breathed easily again. "Let me and Billy go out and find Sydney Baker. I have a few ideas of where he could be. But we need a letter from the Commissioner – something to show to the boys from CID – to say that… I don't know… that Sydney Baker may be involved in some case to do with the War Office. Anything, just so we get first dabs on him."

Beech nodded. "I can do that, if you wait for ten minutes while I appraise Sir Edward of the situation and get his signature on a letter."

"Yes, sir." Tollman was satisfied.

"Tollman?" Beech added. "What happens if the CID chaps find Baker before you do?"

"Then Sir Edward will have to step in and make sure that he is removed from their custody and placed into ours *before* any interviews take place."

Beech nodded. "Yes, of course. Wait downstairs and I will bring the letter to you."

After Beech had left, Billy heaved a sigh of relief. "What rattled his cage, then?" he murmured to Tollman.

Tollman shook his head. "Dunno, son. But he was limping badly again. Maybe he was in a lot of pain and not thinking straight."

They waited downstairs in the main foyer, Tollman flipping his hat between his hands with impatience. Suddenly Stenton appeared, slightly out of breath and clutching another buff file.

"You don't half get about, Tollman!" he complained. "I've been all over the building looking for you."

"What is it?"

Stenton sat down next to them and lowered his voice. "Fingerprinting has just come in from the Baker killing. They got them off the knife that was sticking out of her chest…"

"Weren't the husband's, were they?" Tollman said with certainty.

Stenton smiled. "You smarmy bugger! You're always right, aren't you?"

"So, whose were they?" asked Billy, butting in impatiently.

"They don't know, son," Stenton said, opening the file in his hand and pointing at the report. "All they know is that the fingerprints on the knife match one of the unknown sets of fingerprints in that file I gave you earlier."

CHAPTER FIFTEEN

The Hunt for Sydney

Billy had never seen such an old woman. She had wrinkles on wrinkles – her face was wreathed in them and her faded blue eyes looked him up and down and then she broke into a toothless grin.

"You're a big boy, aren't you? Like my Sydney."

Billy nodded and grinned back. Tollman returned from the bar with two half pints of stout, which he placed in front of the old woman.

"There you are, Mrs Baker. That'll keep you going for another eighty years!" The old lady cackled and shakily lifted one of the half pints to her eager lips and slurped noisily.

This was the third pub they had been in around Holborn, looking for Sydney Baker's mother, and finally they had found her.

"Carter and his boys don't know about Sydney's mother," Tollman had said confidently, as they strode around the streets that fed off Gray's Inn Road. Billy had noted that they were searching in some of the worst slum areas in London. The foetid back-to-back houses, with no running water, still with the Victorian standpipe in the centre of the cobbled street, were alive with grubby children and scowling women.

"The Germans would be doing us a favour if they bombed this lot," he had muttered, earning him a sharp rebuke from Tollman.

"What about the people crammed in these slums?" Tollman had said sharply. "Don't you care if they're bombed?"

Billy had blushed. "Sorry Mr Tollman. I didn't mean that…"

Tollman had softened. "No, I know, lad. Don't take any notice of me. I'm wound up about finding Sydney. You know," he had then decided to explain, "some people just get a raw deal in life. Take Sydney's mum. Violet. Born and then immediately put into the Foundling Hospital up the road here. Spent most of her life as an adult in and out of the Holborn Workhouse round the corner, while her feckless husband was in prison. Then she and Sydney ran a stall in Leather Lane, just next door, for about twenty years eking out a meagre existence. Then Sydney meets Ruth and marries her. But," he had said firmly, "Sydney has never, never abandoned his mum. Next to his wife, his mum is the most important person in the world to him and if anyone knows where he is, it's Violet Baker."

So, they had continued to search the places Violet was known to frequent. She regularly used to toddle up to the Booth's Gin Distillery in Clerkenwell where she knew the bottling plant foreman and he would give her a tipple of gin to set her up for the day – but she hadn't been there for a couple of days. Then there was Nicholson's Distillery, also in Clerkenwell, where she had a similar arrangement, and they were told that Violet had been and gone at about ten that morning. Finally, they went to Reid's Brewery, off Leather Lane, where people like Violet could partake of a pint of 'slops' (the run-off beer from the casking process) for a farthing. But she hadn't been there. A drayman was loading casks on to a cart and he knew Violet Baker.

"She must have a bit of money," he had said, helpfully, "cos I've not seen her in a bit. Look in The Jerusalem Tavern."

Tollman and Billy had then set off on a tour of pubs in the area.

"I get the impression Sydney's mum has a bit of a drink problem," Billy had commented sarcastically, after the second pub failed to turn up their quarry.

"You could say that, Billy," Tollman had replied. "Every time she went into the workhouse, apparently, she would have a bout of the DTs. But she's eighty-one and still going strong!"

"It's probably pickled her innards, that's why."

They had finally found her in the third pub, The Hand and Shears in Smithfield, and now Tollman had placed her favourite drink in front of her, it was time to talk about Sydney.

"Where's your boy Sydney, Violet?" Tollman decided to be direct.

A cagey look came into her eyes. "What do the coppers want my Sydney for? And tell him to sit down!" – she gestured at Billy – "He's making my neck ache, looking up at him all the time."

Billy took his helmet off and sat down. Violet smiled at him again. "You've got big shoulders, like my Sydney. You'll never be out of work if you're strong. That's what I always say to my boy." She took another long slurp of stout.

Tollman was patient but insistent. "Violet… Sydney's in bad trouble."

Violet looked frightened. "What sort of trouble?"

"Ruth's been killed…"

"Huh! Not afore time," was the surprising response. Obviously Violet Baker did not think much of her daughter-in-law. "Someone was going to do her in, one day," she continued, "I said as much to my Sydney – but he wouldn't have it. What do you want to take up with that gypsy witch for? I told him she would be trouble. She bewitched him, she did. Put the evil eye on him."

Tollman let her rant a little, then he said, "The coppers think Sydney did her in."

"NO!" Violet's outraged shriek temporarily quietened the pub and Billy noted that the landlord was looking over in concern, so he stood up.

"It's all right. Nothing to do with anybody here." The customers nodded and turned back to their conversations. Tollman put his hand over Violet's, reassuringly.

"*We* know that Sydney didn't do it, but we need to find him so that he can tell us what he knows."

Violet nodded. She took another drink and looked at Billy again. "You won't hurt my Sydney, will you?" she asked the only person she felt could take her son on in a fight.

"I'll do my best not to hurt him, missus," Billy said, honestly.

Violet leaned forward to whisper. Tollman narrowed his eyes and strained to hear what she said.

"He was working on the river thing between Farringdon Street station and King's Cross…"

"The what?" Tollman wasn't sure he understood.

"The thing they've built around the old Fleet river," she said. "He told me he'd been inside it and he'd seen the old river. He was fascinated with it. Gets these obsessions, does Sydney. Always has. Anyway, that was his latest one. Then they moved him to work on another bit of river at Sloane Square station. But he said to me that he wanted to go back and see the Fleet. There were two doors into it, he said. I'm willing to bet he'll be there."

Tollman nodded with grim satisfaction.

"You won't hurt him? You promise?" Violet pleaded with them.

"We'll do our best," Tollman assured her and he put some more money over the bar with instructions to give Violet another couple of stouts when she asked for them.

"Glad the bitch is dead," muttered Violet, as she raised her glass to her lips. "Now my Sydney can come back to his Ma."

It was a short walk to Farringdon Street station and Tollman negotiated with the stationmaster for access to the doors into the Fleet culvert.

"It means we will have to turn the power off and that will cause complete disruption of the timetable!" the shocked stationmaster said. "I'm not authorised to do that, unless there is an emergency!"

"This *is* an emergency," said Tollman urgently. "We believe there is a man down there who is extremely dangerous."

"How dangerous?" asked the stubborn stationmaster.

"He's killed several people with his bare hands," Tollman lied. "Why do you think I've brought him along?" He pointed at Billy, who tried to look suitably menacing.

The stationmaster acquiesced. "All right. I'll switch the power off for this section after the next westbound train. But, in any event, it's dangerous down there. We can't have you wandering about on your own." He left and returned with a man who was covered in dirt and grease and carrying an armful of equipment.

"Rubber boots," said the man cheerfully, dropping a sack full of assorted sizes. "Battery torches," he continued, giving one each to Tollman and Billy. "If you're going in the culvert, you can't carry a storm lamp, the gases could make it explode. These things," he tapped the torches, "are useful but the batteries don't last long. You'll be lucky to get ten minutes out of them. There will be some natural light down there because there are street gratings every so often. So only use the torches if you get a long stretch without them." He showed them how to switch on the torches and they both nodded. "I'll carry a storm lamp," he added, "because I'm not coming in the culvert with you. I'll wait outside the door. You're on your own in there." Again, they nodded.

"Face cloths," he said, and demonstrated by tying one round his nose and mouth. "It stinks down there. There's sewage and rats and all sorts. Put gloves on and you'll have to have a strip wash when you come out."

He grinned at the expressions on Billy and Tollman's faces. "You get used to it really quickly and after a while you don't smell it no more," he reassured them. He waited while the policemen took their own boots off and found rubber boots to fit. Then he said, "Follow me," and he led the way down to the Underground platform, making them pause at the end, just as a train thundered into the station.

The few people on the platform got on the train and one person got off. Once the train had departed, there was a loud clang and the traffic lights in the tunnels went to red.

"Right. The power to the tracks is off. Here we go," and he led them down some concrete steps and into the tunnel, his storm lamp held high and casting eerie shadows over the curved walls. Ahead, in the distance, Billy could see daylight coming through, where the railway line was open to the sky. He could remember when the trains on this line ran on steam and the openings were there to let out the accumulated smoke. They weren't really adequate, though, and a trip on the Underground, as a child, had meant that, at every station stop, the smoke would come into the carriages when the doors opened and make his clothes smell as though he had been standing in front of a coal fire all day.

"Here's the first door," said the man, pointing at a metal door in the wall. "Do you want to go in here, or the one further up?"

Tollman said it made no difference and they might as well go in here. The man nodded. "Inside, there is a short metal ladder down to the concrete walkway that runs alongside the river. If you turn to your left, when you are facing the ladder, you will eventually end up at the River Thames by Blackfriars. If you turn to your right, it will take you as far as Camden Town, before the river breaks into two tunnels. The Fleet itself should be way below the walkway because we've not had much rain for the last month. Try and avoid ending up in it, if you can. It's not nice. It's a sewer, basically. We never go down there unless we need to repair it and then we usually get some casual labour in to do the job, cos no one wants to do it."

Yes, like Sydney Baker, the poor sod, thought Billy. *What a way to make a living.*

The door opened with a clang of metal and a creak of rusty hinges. Tollman went first, stepping down on to the ladder backwards, and Billy followed. Once they were down and had switched on their torches, the man stuck his head in and pointed upwards.

"This is door fifteen," he said, as they shone their torch beams above the door to see the number. Look for this number when you come back. And, lads, try and be as quick as you can because all the time the power is switched off, the company is losing money." Then he shut the door.

"Cor, it doesn't half stink in here," said Billy, covering the lower half of his face with the cloth.

"Well, we were warned," said Tollman, doing likewise, as his eyes started watering.

"Which way?" Billy asked.

Tollman shrugged. "Let's go towards the Thames first. So, left."

The tunnel and the water exaggerated the sounds around them. Billy gave a shudder because he could hear, below them, the squeaks and rustles of rats, running along the water's edge. Occasionally, the tunnel would rumble alarmingly as they came close to a grating and heavy traffic trundled overhead. As they approached one grating, they were alarmed by several objects falling through and hitting the water below. Then they realised that it was horse manure, from a horse with its rear end conveniently above the grating.

"Lovely," murmured Billy. He didn't dare shine his torch down on to the water, at any point during the journey, for fear of what he might see. Then he sniffed and turned to Tollman. "Can you smell burning?" he whispered.

Tollman nodded. "And sausages!" he whispered back. He motioned to Billy to turn off his torch and, as they stood there in the gloom, they could just make out the glow from a fire in the distance.

Tollman tapped Billy on the shoulder, pulled down his face mask, and almost mouthed, rather than whispered, "Take off your helmet and jacket and leave them here. We don't want to frighten him." Billy nodded and did so, removing any items from the pockets and putting them in his trousers. "Undo your top button, make yourself a bit more casual." Billy followed instructions again. "Now," explained Tollman, "you go ahead and just talk to him normally, as though you've just come across him in a park. Just chat. See if you can throw him off guard a bit. I'll be following on behind."

Billy nodded and started to quicken his pace. The culvert was curved at this point and, in about fifty paces, Billy could see the large figure of a man, hunched over a small fire, trying to cook a sausage on a stick.

Pulling off his face mask, Billy said, "Hello mate, how are you?" as though it were the most natural place in the world for them to bump into each other. The man looked startled and scuttled backwards on his heels, as if in fear. "No, don't take on, mate. I'm just passing through. I'm not going to bother you."

The man seemed to relax. He stood up and faced Billy. They were the same height, but Sydney Baker was about twice as wide across the shoulders. Billy assessed him with a professional boxer's eye and immediately found his weak spot – the stomach. Sydney was strong in the arms and legs from lots of manual work, but he had a flabby belly. Billy reckoned that a swift jab to the stomach would floor Sydney. Shame I can't follow it up with a combination though, he thought, cursing his gammy left hand.

He decided to carry on with the charm, so he did an exaggerated double take and said, "Hold up! Aren't you Sydney? Violet Baker's son?"

A relieved look came over Sydney's face and he nodded. "You know my mum?"

"Know her?" Billy laughed. "I was having a drink with her in The Hand and Shears this morning!"

Sydney gave a big grin. "Is she all right?"

"She's as right as rain," said Tollman softly, coming up behind Billy. "Hello, Sydney. Remember me? DS Tollman?"

Sydney looked confused for a moment and then, suddenly, he bolted, running as fast as he could towards the River Thames.

"BILLY!" shouted Tollman, but Billy was already in hot pursuit after the fast disappearing Sydney.

For a big man, Sydney could run very fast indeed and Billy struggled to keep pace. Besides, the walkway was slippery in places; years of damp had caused mould and fungi to form in the cracks.

"We're not here to hurt you, Sydney," shouted Tollman, barely able to break into a canter at his age. His shout echoed around the cavernous tunnel. It was as much as he could do to keep fugitive and pursuer in sight.

Suddenly, Sydney slipped and fell into the Fleet river below. There were alarmed squeals from packs of rats that had been grazing through the detritus at the edge of the culvert. Sydney thrashed around for a moment in panic, until he realised that the water was barely two feet deep, then he regained his feet and began wading – not back to the walkway, but through the water and towards the Thames. "Bugger," said Billy, catching his breath and pulling his face mask up before he jumped into the water to follow Sydney.

"Sydney! We're gonna get sick from this water, you pillock!" Billy shouted, trying not to retch from the appalling smell.

Tollman puffed around the bend of the culvert and shouted, "We know you didn't kill Ruth!" Sydney suddenly stopped and turned around.

"I wouldn't touch a hair on her head!" he said, beginning to cry and dropping to his knees in the foul water. "My Ruthie…" he moaned, "someone killed my Ruthie…" Sydney looked up at Billy who had, by now, caught up with him and his face was a picture of anguish. "My beautiful Ruthie…" he moaned, the tears coursing down his dirty face and making white tracks in his skin.

"Don't you want to help us catch the person who killed Ruthie?" panted Billy softly. Sydney nodded, wiping his snotty nose with the back of his big hand.

Tollman had caught up on the walkway by now and was breathing heavily.

"I expect you'd like to see your mum, wouldn't you, Sydney?" The big, simple man nodded and stood up. "Let's get out of here then, shall we? Then you can have a nice wash and brush up and a cup of tea down at the Yard, while you tell us all about it."

Unfortunately, getting Sydney and Billy out of the river was impossible without Tollman himself getting covered in the stinking water. It was almost more than the fastidious detective could bear and he privately vowed that he would destroy his clothes, once he got clean again.

The sodden fugitive allowed himself to be led by an equally sodden Billy back in the direction of Farringdon Street station. Tollman kicked Sydney's makeshift fire into the Fleet river and it provoked a sound of hissing and screaming from rats scrambling out of the way of the falling embers. Billy shuddered again to think that he had just waded through that muck.

When they stopped to pick up Billy's helmet and jacket, Sydney looked surprised and said to Billy, "You're a policeman, then?" as if the thought had never occurred to him. *Poor simple sod,* thought Billy and he flashed Sydney a smile. "Well, someone's got to do the job, haven't they, Sydney?" and the big man nodded and grinned.

When the police van arrived to pick the trio up, the driver and his assistant at first refused to let them in, they all smelled so terrible. But after the wrath of Tollman was brought down upon them, they relented, although they complained all the way back to the Yard.

Beech was summoned to the mews around the corner, rather than Tollman, Billy and Sydney being allowed in the building, and when he arrived, he almost reeled backwards at a distance of about five yards.

"Good lord, men, what's that smell?!"

"The River Fleet, sir," said Tollman, with as much dignity as he could muster.

"Well, you'll have to strip your clothes off and have a wash before we can allow you all in an interview room," said Beech. "Sorry, Tollman," he said apologetically, then added, "but well done for finding Mr Baker here."

So Tollman, Rigsby and Baker were sent into one of the former stables, which now housed cars, made to strip naked and doused in disinfectant. Then they were given carbolic soap to wash with before being hosed down with cold water. Billy and Sydney laughed through chattering teeth. Tollman merely bore it stoically, in silence.

Fresh clothes were brought from the prisoner store (although Sydney's barely fitted) and the three of them, red-cheeked, wet-haired and smelling of carbolic, made their way down to the basement to Interview Room C. Billy noted that they had brought the amiable Sydney into the Yard without the use of any force or handcuffs. He would make sure to put that in the arrest report.

Hot tea was brought for everyone by Stenton, who winked broadly at them all. Tollman bristled. He had no doubt that this episode would be the talk of the Yard for years to come and he wasn't happy. Still, he managed a smile when he thought of how Carter's nose would be put out of joint by the fact that they had found Sidney Baker before he could.

Beech came in and Tollman immediately asked for a confidential word. Beech reopened the door and they stepped out into the corridor.

"I just wanted you to know, sir, that Sydney Baker is a simple soul. Bit like a giant child really. He came with us willingly and he is heartbroken about his wife's murder. We need to take it gently and not frighten him, otherwise he'll clam up."

"Point taken, Tollman. Let's see what we can do."

Beech began the slow, patient business of teasing information out of Sydney. A lot of the time he looked to Billy to take the lead in questioning, as he seemed to have struck up a friendship with the man.

Gradually, Sydney explained things as best he could. They started with Adeline Treborne. Sydney became upset and said that she was a bad woman who made his Ruthie cry. Tollman thought to himself that he would have liked to see that. The Ruth Baker he had interviewed fifteen years ago was probably the hardest woman he had ever met. The first time that Adeline Treborne visited, Sydney had been at work. The second time she came, to collect money, Sydney had been told to hide and then follow her when she left, to find out where she lived. This Sydney had done and discovered that she lived in Trinity Mansions.

In order to find out what number, Ruth devised a clever plan. She took an envelope and wrote on it 'Miss Adeline Treborne, Trinity Mansions, Sloane Square, Chelsea, London', then sealed the envelope and took it to Trinity Mansions herself.

When Ruth Baker went into the foyer, she said to the porter, "My employer asked me to deliver this letter to Miss Adeline Treborne, but he hasn't put the number of the apartment on it. Will it still get to her?"

The porter said, "Oh, she's in number twelve. Don't worry, I'll put it in her pigeonhole. It will get to her all right."

Beech remembered the envelope addressed to Adeline Treborne, and the blank piece of paper, in the wastepaper basket, when he had first visited the apartment.

Sydney said that Ruth decided they would go to see Adeline Treborne very early in the morning and frighten her. Warn her off, Ruth had said. "She'll take one look at you, Sydney, and she'll know to leave us alone."

Sydney had been working at Sloane Square Underground station, mending the large iron pipe that encased the River Westbourne, which was suspended above the station tracks. He worked a night shift, so that the trains wouldn't be disrupted.

"I suppose you used waterproof cement?" asked Tollman. Sydney nodded.

Ruth met him when he finished at 5.45. She took him round to the servants' entrance and she picked the lock. "Nimble fingers," said Sydney, smiling. "Not like me," and he held up his large, misshapen hands. Ruth had also picked Adeline Treborne's door lock and they had gone in.

"But she was dead!" Sydney said in a surprised voice. "We didn't know what to do! Then Ruthie pulled a rope off the curtains and said, 'String her up, Sydney! Just to make sure. Then she won't bother us no more.' She was already dead," he said feebly, shaking his head at the memory.

"So, you climbed up on the bed and hung her up? Is that right, Sydney?" asked Billy gently.

Sydney nodded. "Ruth said it was for the best. She was already dead, though."

"Then what happened, Sydney?" Beech chipped in.

"We went home! Ruthie said it had been a good day and we wouldn't have no more trouble. So, I went to bed."

There was a pause while Tollman and Beech stepped outside, leaving Billy to chat innocently to Sydney and keep him company.

"Sounds like the truth, Mr Beech," said Tollman. "I don't think Sydney is capable of lying."

"No. And yet… he didn't tell the truth when his wife was accused of murdering babies, did he?"

"True. But he was very controlled by his wife. Perhaps she told him exactly what to say."

"Well, we need to find out. Get him some more tea and we'll have a little chat with him about the babies and his wife's death. We might as well give CID a few crumbs."

Tollman sorted out some tea and they settled down to have another little chat with Sydney Baker.

"Who killed Ruthie, Sydney?" Tollman decided to get straight to the point.

Sydney's face crumpled. "I don't know," he said miserably. "I got home from work and she was lying there, knife in her chest. She was wheezing and trying to speak and I was upset. I didn't know what to do. She just said to me, 'Run, Sydney. Run and hide', and then she died. She stopped breathing and I knew she was dead. I did what she told me." He was crying now, remembering his beloved Ruthie. Billy put his arm around the big man's shoulders to comfort him.

"Sydney," Tollman said quietly, "do you remember when the police took Ruthie away to ask her about the babies?" Sydney nodded. Tollman continued, "What happened to the babies?"

Sydney shook his head. "Ruthie said never to tell anyone."

Billy looked at Tollman and Beech and they nodded encouragement to him to coax the big man into telling the truth.

"Yeah, the thing is, Sydney..." Billy said in a chummy tone of voice, "I was talking to your mum and she said that you don't have to keep a promise after someone dies. Your mum said you should tell people what happened to the babies, so that *their* mothers won't search for them no more."

Sydney appeared to see the logic of this and answered, "Well, it was their mothers' fault, Ruthie said. So, if I tell you, will that put it all right?"

Billy nodded. "Yes, mate. It will."

So, Sydney recounted the terrible tale of Ruth Baker and her murder spree – except Sydney, poor simple Sydney, had just believed his devil of a wife when she said that each baby had died 'for want of a mother's love'.

"Ruthie said that the women who gave up their babies were wicked and no matter how much Ruthie took care of them, they died because their mother didn't love them. I said 'Don't take the babies in no more, Ruthie. I don't like it when they die.' But she said that they were entitled to a few weeks of being looked after and loved and it was her duty."

"What happened to the dead babies, Sydney?" Tollman asked the question he had been waiting to hear the answer to for fifteen years.

"Gave them a Christian burial. Ruthie insisted. There's a big flower bed in the churchyard at St Patrick's Church in Clerkenwell. We'd bury them there at night. I would dig a deep hole and Ruthie would say a prayer. All Christian-like."

"Jesus, no wonder that churchyard has the most wonderful array of roses I've ever seen in my life!" Tollman couldn't believe it. He'd spent the last fifteen years visiting that churchyard whenever he could to marvel at the floral display.

"How many babies? Can you tell us?" Beech asked.

Sydney held up both hands and Billy realised that he meant ten. "Ten?" But Sydney closed his hands, then opened them again, twice more and Billy took a deep breath, "Oh my God. Thirty?" Sydney nodded.

All the men sat in silence at the thought of thirty small souls buried in a flower bed in Clerkenwell.

***

It took Tollman and Beech until ten o'clock that night to compile a report for Sir Edward and tailor a report for the boys in CID, which told them only about Sydney's innocence in the death of his wife and the grisly information about the bodies of the babies. Sydney was still charged with the murder of his wife, but when he protested, Billy told him it was a formality and they were going to look for Ruth's murderer.

Billy, after settling Sydney Baker down in the cells for the night, was sent home to Lady Maud's house to tell the others that Beech and Tollman would be working late and that they would all have a breakfast meeting in the morning.

"It may be that the Adeline Treborne case is closed for us now," commented Beech to Tollman, as they were writing their reports. "We can't prove that the drug overdose that killed her was anything other than an accident. Also, we are now handing over the Ruth Baker case to CID."

"Mm. Maybe, Mr Beech. But I still think Ruth Baker was killed by someone involved in the Treborne black-mailing business. Somebody took the book... why? Was that person going to carry on the blackmailing? We need to tie up the loose ends." Tollman was not happy. There were too many unanswered questions and he knew that it would keep him awake tonight fretting over them. Then he cheered up at the thought of putting his report, and the Commissioner's letter of authority, on Carter's desk before he left, and Carter having to tell the boys in CID that they had thirty bodies to dig up tomorrow.

CHAPTER SIXTEEN

Another Ghost from Tollman's Past

"I would imagine that the Ruth Baker infanticide will be all over the newspapers tomorrow," Beech said over breakfast, which had been a sombre affair once the men had revealed what had taken place yesterday.

Victoria spoke first. "It has long been a scandal, in my opinion, that there is no proper legislation to deal with adoption. If an unwanted illegitimate child in London is lucky enough to be placed in the Foundling Hospital or a Dr Barnardo's Home, then these institutions have procedures in place for adoption and do a certain amount of vetting of prospective parents. But there are too many desperate women who turn to unscrupulous back-street baby farmers. All of this traffic in babies should be regulated."

Tollman sucked his breath in and shook his head. "In some ways I agree, Mrs E. But once you start regulating things, it becomes a minefield. I wouldn't like to be the one who sets out the rules for who can and can't adopt a baby. But I agree, these little mites should be protected from the likes of Ruth Baker."

Beech decided to turn the conversation back to the Adeline Treborne case. "My personal opinion is that we have maybe gone as far as we can with the Adeline Treborne case…"

He was rudely interrupted by the women's protestations that there was so much more to do.

"We have to carry through with the sewing circle…" said Victoria.

"I'm sure that I will be approached as a blackmail victim," protested Lady Maud.

"What about the last name on the list?" asked Caroline.

Beech looked heavenwards. "I was about to say that, *however*, Mr Tollman has convinced me that we should continue and… as he said… tie up the loose ends."

"Quite right, Mr Tollman," said Victoria briskly. "We can't have any more slapdash policing." This barb was aimed at Beech, who gritted his teeth and ignored it, but not before Caroline had noted, with surprise, the coolness between them. Tollman just looked puzzled at the comment.

"Let us just recap what we have so far," said Beech. "Mr Tollman, you make a start."

Tollman looked at his notebook. "Right. We know that Ruth Baker and her husband, Sydney, went to see Adeline Treborne early on the morning in question, hoping to put the frighteners on her. According to Sydney, Treborne was already dead. Ruth told him to string the body up, presumably to make it look like suicide, which he did. We can definitely place Sydney there because his fingerprints were found at the scene and traces of waterproof cement, which he constantly used at work. Another set of fingerprints belonged to Reginald Ingham, aka the Major, and we know he was there, from witness statements and by his own admission. There were two unknown sets of fingerprints found in the apartment. One set could be Ruth Baker's, but we can't know because we can't get fingerprints off a dead body and we didn't have fingerprinting fifteen years ago, when she was arrested on suspicion of murder. We haven't matched the other set up yet – and we have plenty of others in the frame who would have loved to kill Adeline Treborne and get their hands on that book."

"One set of fingerprints must, surely, be the maid, Lily," said Victoria, scrabbling in her bag for the maid's address. "You could send someone round to fingerprint her. I have her address... but she doesn't seem to have put her surname on the paper."

Beech took the paper and said he would organise something, then he turned to Billy and asked, "Rigsby, remind us, from your notes, who could be suspects now... bearing in mind that we are not talking about the hanging element of it but, possibly, drugging someone and stealing the book..."

"Or, she drugged herself and the person was just there to get the book and took advantage of Adeline being insensible?" posited Caroline.

"Ah," interjected Victoria, "it would have had to be someone who knew what the book looked like and where it was usually kept, because don't forget that all of you went into the apartment after Adeline Treborne died and none of you reported it to be a mess, as though someone had torn the place apart looking for the book."

Beech nodded. "I feel we should rule her brother out. The Duke was so devastated when I told him his sister had been blackmailing people that I cannot believe he knew about the book."

Billy looked at his notes and said, "Sir Anthony Jarvis's son gave his dad an alibi, saying that they were together in Limehouse for the son's birthday. That could be a lie, or the father could have arrived late, or the son could have slipped round to Chelsea…"

The team all looked doubtful. Billy continued, "We only have the Major's word for it that he went to see Adeline just to have a chat and nothing else. He insists he didn't kill her and he doesn't have the book. We didn't find the book in his apartment and we searched everywhere…"

"Besides, it's not his style," said Tollman. "I've known about Ingham's activities for a long time and he's just a con man. He's never even swatted a fly."

Billy continued, "Don't forget that the crabby woman next door said she thought she heard two women talking at after midnight."

Tollman nodded. "Yes, I remember that. Could be something or nothing."

Billy closed his notebook and said, "The manager of the jeweller's shop has a solid alibi, in that he was celebrating his wedding anniversary all evening with friends and neighbours."

"Oh, by the way, the Yard have uncovered four of Robinson's customers who have reported burglaries in the last six months," Tollman added. "So I think we may have him as an accessory, unwitting or not, to insurance fraud."

"Well, I think we can leave that until we have closed the Treborne case," decided Beech.

Billy suddenly asked, "What happened at the interview with Lady Patrick, sir, because Mr Tollman and I had left then?"

Beech stirred uncomfortably. "Lady Patrick may have to be interviewed again," he murmured, trying to avoid catching Victoria's eye.

At this point, Lady Maud said, "Ah, Lady Patrick! This makes the sewing circle lady even more suspicious!"

"How so, Maud?" said Beech curiously.

"One of the first servants pointed out to Elsie Rigsby at this sewing circle was Lady Patrick's maid. And some gossip was repeated about her."

"Such as?"

Maud shrugged. "She was American, and she was odd." Victoria smiled sardonically, and Maud continued, "Elsie Rigsby said that the woman who ran the circle, a Mrs Leighton, was herself very odd and *very* nosy. She made a point of quizzing Elsie about her employer... me, of course... and then accompanying Elsie on her walk home, which, of course, was to here. Elsie said that she seemed to be sizing up the house and she lingered until she was sure that Elsie had gone inside. I shouldn't be surprised if I get a visit or a letter from the woman very soon, trying to extort money."

Mary stuck her head around the door and informed Beech that there was a telephone call for him from the Yard. After Beech left the room, Caroline whispered to Victoria, "Have you two had a falling-out?"

Victoria whispered back, "I will tell you about it later," which just made Caroline more intrigued.

Beech swiftly returned and said, "It appears that Lady Patrick wishes to speak to me again and is waiting at the Yard. Victoria, I would like you to come with me and interview her." He looked straight at Victoria, as though it were a challenge.

Victoria rose and answered "Gladly," in a defiant tone and marched out to get her coat and hat.

"Er, Mr Beech," said Tollman, anxious to get his request in before Beech disappeared. "I know the last name on the black-mail list, or rather, the place – Peachtree. It's a little village near Gravesend. Can Billy and I go and look for this Kit B?"

"Yes, of course. If nothing else, it will put another black-mail victim out of their misery when you tell them about the Treborne woman's death."

Caroline chimed in, "I'm not working today. Can I go with Mr Tollman and Billy? I'm sure I can contribute in some way!"

Beech looked at Tollman for approval. Tollman smiled. "I'm sure Dr Allardyce will be an asset to our investigation," he said formally, and Billy grinned.

As they all began to gather themselves together and go their separate ways, Beech turned to Lady Maud and said, "Maud, if you should receive any communication from this Leighton woman, do not agree to see her on your own. Let me know immediately of any contact. We do not want you to be in danger. Do you understand?"

"Of course, dear boy. I shall contact you at once."

***

When Beech and Victoria arrived at the Yard, Sergeant Stenton was waiting outside Beech's office.

"Begging your pardon, Chief Inspector," he said confidentially. "Might I have a word?"

Beech nodded, asked Victoria to wait for a moment and allowed Stenton to take him over to a large window facing Victoria Embankment. "See that gentleman there, sir?" he asked, pointing to a man who was sitting on a bench, ostensibly reading a newspaper. "He used to be in CID a few years ago. Name of Albert Wood. Bent copper who was shown the door and is now a private detective. Lady Patrick arrives here, this morning, in a state of some distress. Says she is being followed and she is in danger and wants to speak to you. One minute later, Wood turns up in another taxicab, looks dismayed because he can't come in here, and takes up residence on the bench over there. He's been there ever since."

"I see. Thank you, Sergeant. Let me know if Mr Wood moves away."

Stenton nodded and Beech moved over to Victoria to appraise her of the unusual situation that had cropped up. "Let us see what Lady Patrick has to say," he murmured.

The exquisite doll creature was glad to see Beech but, again, ignored Victoria. She wept a little and Beech waited for her to allow him to question her.

"Lady Patrick, one of my sergeants told me that you said you were being followed and are in danger. Is this true?"

"Yes," she said simply. "I became aware that a man was following me, yesterday, when I came to the jewellers. He's not very good at following people. He is very clumsy at keeping himself hidden, so I am always aware that he is there. And then, this morning, there was this…" She rifled in her clutch bag and produced a note, which she handed to Beech.

He immediately handed it to Victoria, who read the note out loud. "Adeline Treborne may be gone but I am taking over her enterprise. You will be given new instructions as to where and when to pay your next instalment. Payment must be made, or I shall tell everything that I know about you to the newspapers and your husband's career will be ruined."

Victoria noticed that the handwriting looked the same as the pink paper notes received by the editor of the *London Herald*, although this note was on white paper. "Lady Patrick, when did you receive this note?" she asked, and the American woman was forced to acknowledge her.

"This morning at breakfast," she said diffidently. "My butler brought it to me."

"Was it hand delivered or stamped?"

"Um, hand delivered. There was no stamp." Lady Patrick turned back to Beech with a pleading look on her face. "What do you think I should do, Chief Inspector?"

Victoria decided that she had had enough of Lady Patrick's little games and, before Beech could answer, she asked, "Is your husband still unaware of your past and the fact that you were being blackmailed?"

An expression of irritation crossed the doll-like face and she said curtly, "Of course! My husband has no idea what has been happening for the last few months."

Beech did step in now and he asked Lady Patrick why she felt she was in danger.

"Well, because of this man who is following me!" She was astonished that Beech would question her distress. Victoria realised that Lady Patrick was unnerved because she was not eliciting the usual response she expected from a man. This was a woman who was used to immediately triggering a protective instinct in the opposite sex and she sensed that Beech was being reserved.

"Lady Patrick." Beech had decided to tell her the information imparted by Stenton. "The man who is following you is a private detective. Unfortunately, he used to be one of our policemen but, apparently, a dishonourable one and he was asked to leave the police force. In my experience, private detectives, many of whom are *honourable* retired policemen, are usually employed by the legal profession when they wish to investigate, say, the other party in a divorce case or they are trying to find out information about the parties involved in a civil court case..." Beech trailed off as Lady Patrick had gone as white as a sheet and was trembling.

"Are you all right?" Victoria asked her anxiously.

"Could I have some water, please?" Lady Patrick asked in a mere whisper. Victoria immediately went out of the room to ask the duty sergeant for a glass of water. Lady Patrick leaned across to Beech and said in a stricken voice, "I think my husband may have employed this man to spy on me. This is why I feel I am in danger!"

Beech looked helpless. "Lady Patrick, I cannot interfere in domestic matters. If your husband suspects you of some wrongdoing, he is perfectly within his rights to hire a detective to follow you. I suggest that you tell him the whole truth about the blackmail situation. Secrets within a marriage can be corrosive."

Victoria returned with the water, just as Lady Patrick had risen and said haughtily, "You are not the man I thought you were, Chief Inspector. I came to you for some protection, but I see that I have wasted my time."

"Lady Patrick, we are concerned with the blackmailer. You must tell us when the blackmailer makes contact again. We have every intention of catching this criminal and putting him or her in prison for a long time."

The doll-like face had become quite hard and Victoria realised that this was how the young woman looked when she did not get her own way.

"I will keep you informed. Good day." Then she swept past Victoria and out of the office.

"Well done, Peter. You were thoroughly professional this time!" Victoria said encouragingly. "Although I fear that Lady Patrick will never forgive you for not being more gallant."

Beech looked a little sheepish and said, "Quickly! Let's see if this Wood chap really is following her!" They went out to the corridor to look through the window.

Sure enough, as soon as Lady Patrick got into her chauffeured car, Wood hailed a passing taxicab and set off in the same direction.

"I thought she was going to faint when you told her about private detectives being hired by the legal profession," observed Victoria. "I think she knows her husband is getting suspicious about something."

Beech agreed. "And now we have another blackmailer to worry about."

"And a definite motive for murder," said Victoria. "Obviously, this new blackmailer wanted the book, so that he or she could take over the very lucrative business of blackmailing all these people. That person possibly wanted the book enough to kill for it."

***

It was a sunny day and the train journey to Dartford was a treat for Tollman, Billy and Caroline.

"It's amazing how quickly the landscape changes from grimy city to pleasant countryside, when you travel into Kent," observed Caroline.

"I love it down here," said Billy. He was feeling relaxed because Tollman had told him not to wear his uniform today, as they were going to be searching for someone in a small village.

"We don't want the uniform to frighten them off now, do we?" Tollman had observed sagely.

So, Billy was in a mood to reminisce about his childhood holidays picking hops in Faversham. "We used to come mob-handed," he said, laughing. "My mum and her two sisters and my Aunt Ada's two children and me. We slept in a tin hut, on blankets over straw. My mum used to cook for us all in billycans over an open fire. It was always hot weather and hard work, but you could have a swim and wash off in the stream. We used to have a rare old time!"

Caroline laughed. "What about the men? Didn't they pick hops as well?"

Billy made a face. "Nah! Not really! There were some casual farm workers – mostly gypsies – who moved around all the time, but it was mainly women and kids. The men stayed in the smoke, doing their usual jobs. It was a paid holiday. Mind you, pay wasn't much, but to us kids, it was a fortune. A farthing a day will buy you a lot of sweets! Did you ever go hop picking, Mr Tollman?"

"No, son," was the answer. "I don't mind drinking the end product though."

The conversation continued in a jocular vein for most of the journey and Caroline basked in the rare companionship of the day. As they got closer to Dartford, their conversation turned to the business before them.

"We don't even know if we are looking for a man or a woman," Tollman pointed out. "Kit can be a name for either. Short for Christopher or short for Kitty, maybe."

"Where shall we start to look?" asked Caroline.

"Well, my daughters came down here for a works outing. Some picnic or other. All three of them work in Arding and Hobbs department store in Clapham. And my Daphne says that Peachtree is a very small village with one church and one pub. So, we'll start with the church, I think."

At Dartford station, the trio hired a horse-drawn hackney carriage to take them to Peachtree. It was about seven miles away, just past the village of Swanscombe. Caroline was dismayed to find that pretty countryside soon gave way to the ravages of the cement industry as they began to pass huge quarries and a great amount of industrial activity.

However, Peachtree seemed to have reclaimed a little piece of rural bliss, as they approached it down a winding lane, expertly navigated by horse and driver. Caroline noted, with satisfaction, that there were cottages with flower gardens, the church looked well-kept and a small river trickled by. There was not much activity. The sun was high and warm, and bees were humming in the hedgerow. A few women were buying fruit and vegetables from a cart near the pub. Tollman, Billy and Caroline alighted, and the driver of the hackney carriage was paid some money and promised more if he would wait for an hour or so to take them back.

They strolled over to the church and Caroline was on the verge of pronouncing the place 'idyllic' when they were confronted by a jarring sight on the church noticeboard. A large recruiting poster, which said 'Women of Britain Say GO!' and showed a woman and her children waving goodbye to marching soldiers, had been slashed across, diagonally, in what was obviously a protest against the sentiment.

"Someone doesn't like the war," muttered Tollman.

"I can't say that I blame them," commented Caroline. "Exhorting people to go off to their deaths has no place on a church noticeboard. These stupid posters make me angry. They only encourage women to tyrannise men into volunteering. It's the worst kind of propaganda."

"There's worse," said Billy. "I've seen 'em with pictures of children trying to shame their dads into going off to war."

Caroline gave a sigh of exasperation as they went through the gate into the churchyard. It was neat and tidy, and Billy noted that the same surnames kept cropping up on the headstones. Obviously, this village was a pretty tight community and had been for a few hundred years. He wondered who, in a village like this, could possibly be the victim of blackmail.

They entered the church. It was cool and dark, a little Victorian gem, with flowers in wall sconces and family-named pews. There was a movement of a curtain and the vicar appeared, wearing military uniform with his dog collar.

"Can I help you?" he called cheerily, as he advanced up the aisle.

"Detective Sergeant Tollman, Constable Rigsby and Dr Allardyce," announced Tollman briskly, his voice echoing up into the vaulted ceiling of the little church. "We have come from London to find someone and we wondered if you might be able to help us?"

The vicar shook everyone's hand, announcing himself as "Reverend, soon to be Captain, Peabody."

"I'm sure I can help you. Would you like to come through to the vestry, while I rustle up a cup of tea?"

Peabody led the way and soon they were all sitting in the vestry, making polite conversation about the village, while the Reverend boiled a kettle and made the tea. They learned that the village was named in the Domesday Book and that there were a few family names that had been a constant presence in this and surrounding villages since medieval times.

"Tight-knit community then?" Tollman ventured.

"Oh very! I've been here nearly ten years and they still stop talking when I walk into the pub." The Reverend found it amusing but Billy found it distasteful.

"So," the Reverend said, pouring tea and handing it round, "exactly who is it that you are looking for?"

"We just have an abbreviated name – Kit B – does that mean anything to you?"

The smile disappeared from the Reverend's face instantly and they could all see that the name Kit B meant a great deal to the man. "Yes, well, I'm not surprised that she is sought by the police," he said distastefully.

"Please do tell us more, Reverend." Caroline's interest was piqued as to why a man of the cloth should be so disapproving.

"Kitty Bellamy moved here, with her invalid husband, about six months ago. Her husband was wounded in the war and is… severely… disfigured. Fortunately, they live in a cottage at the very end of the village. No one sees the husband – which is just as well, because the sight of him would frighten most people, especially children. She… is a difficult woman. Various villagers have had run-ins with her, for one reason or another. She gets angry if the village children play up near her house, for example. And she is the one who, yesterday, slashed through the recruiting poster I had put up on the church noticeboard. A difficult woman. May I ask why you are seeking her out?"

Tollman shook his head and said firmly, "Sorry, Reverend, but the matter is confidential. You understand."

"Of course. I am leaving at the end of the week anyway, so whatever may affect the community will not really be my concern."

"What regiment are you going to?" asked Billy curiously.

The Reverend smiled. "I don't know yet. The Army Chaplains' Department will assign me when I get to basic training at Sandhurst. I go where I'm sent," he added with a smile. Billy didn't know whether he regarded padres as heroes or fools – all he knew was that *he* wouldn't like to be at the Front without a gun in his hand.

After receiving directions from the Reverend as to the exact location of Kitty Bellamy's house, they walked past groups of cottages huddled together and then up a lane to this one dwelling on its own. It was more than a cottage, being brick-built and having a tiled, rather than thatched, roof.

"I get the impression that this Kitty Bellamy and her husband like to be isolated," observed Caroline. She looked back down the lane and the village was now completely hidden from sight by the curve of the lane and the overgrown hedgerows.

Tollman knocked on the door and it was opened by a thin woman in her thirties, who looked as though she had been crying. What happened next took Caroline and Billy by complete surprise. There was a pause… Tollman seemed transfixed… The woman said "Yes?" in a weary tone of voice… Tollman produced his warrant card and then pushed into the house aggressively, pinning the woman against the wall. Then he said triumphantly,

"Kitty Mason, I am arresting you for the planning and execution of three separate terrorist attacks in London in 1913."

CHAPTER SEVENTEEN

A World of Hate

"Mr Tollman!" said Caroline sharply. "What is this?"

"This," replied Tollman, nodding towards the woman he had cornered, "is one of the most violent suffragettes ever to stalk the streets of London. One Kitty Mason. Responsible for a dozen arson attacks and at least three bombings where witnesses placed her at the scene." Tollman was almost laughing with glee.

"That may very well be, but this woman is also very ill. Let her go! At once!" Caroline's tone of voice snapped Tollman out of his exultation, as if she had slapped him across the face. He looked shocked and immediately backed off from Kitty Mason, who promptly slid down the wall in a dead faint.

"Billy!" Caroline urged. "Can you carry her into the next room?" Billy duly obliged, pushing past the dazed Tollman, who seemed overcome with embarrassment. Lifting up the woman, Billy reckoned that she weighed no more than a child, and he placed her gently on the sofa in the small living room. Caroline began undoing blouse buttons and fanning the woman with a newspaper she had picked up off the table.

"I'll get some water," said Billy, going through to the small scullery he could see through the door. He grabbed a cup and began pumping water from the standpipe outside the back door. As he was returning, he heard a howl... a terrible howl... like an animal in its death throes. Everyone froze, transfixed with horror. Then it happened again, a terrible animal noise, which died down to a strange keening, a subdued wailing of grief.

Billy could stand it no longer and he ran up the stairs, following the sound. He opened the door and his heart stopped. Before him, on the bed, lay a creature... no longer a man... no longer even human. The face was so badly disfigured that the left side was barely there at all. Also, the left shoulder and arm were gone. Billy couldn't see whether, under the covers, the left leg was gone as well. The man was making a terrible constant noise, somewhere between a moan and a scream, such was the level of his constant pain. Billy felt the tears trickling down his face. He couldn't stop them. He had seen dead bodies in this sort of state in the hell between the trenches at Ypres, but he had never seen anyone who had survived such terrible injuries.

Suddenly, the small woman, revived from her faint, pushed past him and ran over to the man in the bed. "Shush, I'm here, my love, I'm here," she said soothingly and stroked his hair. Billy realised that the man was blind as well. Then she prepared a glass syringe and expertly injected the man's only arm and gradually, he subsided into sleep. Billy turned away, rubbing the tears from his eyes, only to realise that Caroline had been standing behind him all the time. She fleetingly touched his shoulder and then went into the bedroom.

"Why is your husband not in hospital?" she asked Kitty softly.

Kitty raised a face full of anguish to the doctor and said, "He felt that he did not have long to live, and he wanted us to spend the time alone together. But he underestimated the strength of his body. Despite appalling pain and the fact that he cannot eat properly or see or hardly hear, he has lingered for six long months now. The doctor at the military hospital gave me enough drugs for two months. He said he wouldn't last longer than that. I have had to get more supplies from a local doctor in Dartford. Joseph…" – she laid her hand on her sleeping husband's chest – "…wants me to end his life. He has asked me again and again over the last couple of weeks. I love him more than my own life, but I cannot do it! God help me, I want to end his suffering, but I cannot do it."

"You have exhausted yourself," Caroline said. "I can see that you have pneumonia. How long is it since you have eaten?"

Kitty shook her head. "I can't remember. Food doesn't mean much to me, anyway, not since my spells in Holloway prison."

"How many times were you force-fed?" Caroline had encountered this health problem before with other suffragettes.

Kitty gave a low and bitter laugh. "Over two hundred times. Your stomach never gets over it." Billy made a sound as though he were choking.

Caroline looked at Billy. "Constable Rigsby, do you know how to make soup?" Billy nodded and headed down to the scullery again.

"Come downstairs now, Mrs Bellamy, your husband will sleep for a couple of hours." Caroline was firm. "Let us look after you, in the meantime."

"What? Get me better so that you can put me in prison?" said Kitty bitterly.

"We'll see." Caroline was thinking about all the options and she needed to talk to Tollman first.

Billy was in the scullery, peeling potatoes and onions. Tollman was making up the fire in the wood-burning stove. Caroline gently sat Kitty down and made her lie back against some cushions.

"Is it true? What Detective Sergeant Tollman said about you? That you committed arson and bomb attacks?"

Kitty nodded and stared into the distance, as if trying to recall her past life. "It all seems such a long time ago now," she said quietly. "Before the war, it seemed more important than anything else in the world that women should be the equal of men in all things. Then, when war broke out, we all realised that men may have the vote and the power of the law and control of the money but... there is a price to pay for that. They have to go and fight and die for their country. Suddenly, it seemed too high a price to pay for the privilege of having the vote. Most women in the suffragette movement drifted away. They got involved in the war effort, they made up food parcels for the men at the front, or, like me, they found themselves nursing a damaged and dying man sent back from the war to finish his days." She looked at Caroline, who could see that Kitty's chest was so congested that it was affecting her breathing and there was a blue tinge around her mouth. "None of it seems important any more. Men aren't the enemy. The Germans are the enemy. Most women don't care about having the vote now. They care about having their menfolk back in one piece."

"Rest. Sleep. I'll wake you when the soup is ready." Caroline had heard all she needed to hear. Kitty closed her eyes and Caroline went out into the scullery to talk to the men.

Tollman raised his hands in surrender. "I'm sorry, Doctor. I got carried away, I know, and I apologise. It's just that Kitty Mason – or Bellamy, as she is now – is – was – one of the most hunted criminals in London two years ago. The first bomb she set off was at a cottage that belonged to the Chancellor of the Exchequer. Twelve men were nearly killed. It was a miracle they weren't. Kitty and her friends bombed churches, post offices, railway stations and trains – the list is endless. They used to put incendiary chemicals in postboxes. One of my friends was a postman in Clapham. He was so badly burned by those chemicals when he was collecting the post that he hasn't worked since. And he's in constant pain because the chemicals scarred his skin so badly and it tightened up, causing pain and frequent bleeding. He's a mess. Because of her." He jabbed his finger towards the living room.

He continued, "The eighteen months before war started were the worst in my police career. You know we had letter bombs at the Yard from the suffragettes? Evil devices. MPs got them, other public figures too. Again, the postmen were in the front line, with the police, intercepting these letter bombs and defusing them. Lots of us got injured – policemen and postmen. Some of us got away lightly."

He pulled up his trouser leg to show an old, long scar, which went from ankle to knee. "Suffragette wielding a butcher's knife," he explained. "She'd just finished vandalising expensive clothing in a West End department store and when we tried to arrest her, she went for us. I got this and two of my mates got an arm and a face slashed. Blood all over the place. But," Tollman added passionately, "here's the thing. It's not the police getting injured in the line of duty that I mind about – I mean I *do* mind, of course I do – but it's part of our job. But the bombs… in public places. *Children* could have been killed. They didn't care! They put bombs in places where they knew there were going to be lots of people. It was just sheer dumb luck that no one was killed. But plenty of people were injured and their lives were changed for ever. Don't forget that. I never shall." Tollman tailed off. His voice had begun to crack under the strain of reliving the events and he had exhausted himself with his tirade.

Caroline rubbed Tollman's arm as a gesture of understanding, then she said simply, "She's dying, Mr Tollman. Her heart is about to give out and, even if I were to get her into hospital today, I doubt that I could save her, her pneumonia is so advanced. She hasn't been eating and she's exhausted. Has Billy told you about her husband upstairs?"

Tollman nodded. "We must do what we can for them, then," he said with resignation, and Billy agreed.

Soon, the soup was bubbling on the stove and Caroline, who had been checking Kitty's pulse and temperature, came back to the scullery, lured by the smell. "You're an awfully useful man, Billy," she said admiringly.

Billy gave a half-hearted grin. "It's the Army, Doctor. They teach you to look after yourself. Cook, clean, sew. 'The biggest, toughest Grenadier Guardsman should be able to sew like a lady's maid,' my old sergeant used to say. 'Keep your kit in order, lad, feed yourself and keep yourself clean. It's a matter of pride.'"

The soup was finally ready, and Billy had mashed it up a bit, so that Kitty could swallow it more easily. Caroline woke her up, Billy raised her up on the cushions a little, and Caroline began to feed her. They could see that swallowing every mouthful was painful. Finally, after no more than half a dozen spoonfuls, she declined to eat any more. The very effort was too much for her and her breath was coming in short gasps now.

Kitty clutched at Caroline's jacket desperately, and the tears rolled down her face. "I know I don't have much longer," she whispered, "but what will happen to Joseph?"

Caroline looked at Billy for support and she fancied that she saw it in his eyes. "I think I need to make you both comfortable," she said, swallowing hard. "Billy will carry you upstairs, so that you can be with Joseph, would you like that?"

Kitty nodded, and Billy gently lifted her up in his arms and started to carry her up the stairs. Caroline began to follow and Tollman grabbed her arm. "Don't take this on yourself," he warned softly. "You might not be able to live with it afterwards."

"I shouldn't be able to live with doing nothing," Caroline replied. "I have no choice."

Upstairs, Billy had laid Kitty next to her husband, on his undamaged side, so that she could hold his hand. At the touch of her fingers, Joseph's half face twisted into an approximation of a smile, before it twisted again into an expression of pain. He groaned softly but Kitty stroked his face and began murmuring to him, words of love and comfort.

"Let's leave them alone for five minutes," whispered Caroline and she and Billy stood out on the landing and closed the door.

They stood in silence for a minute, then Billy spoke quietly. "When I was in the trenches," he said matter-of-factly, "I heard this screaming coming from no-man's-land. It was like a child in terrible pain. Awful. I couldn't stand it. When I looked over the top, I could see it was a horse. Its back was broken but it was still alive and screaming in distress. So, I took my rifle and aimed at it from the trenches. Hit it right between the eyes and it was at peace. Never regretted doing it. I don't even like horses, but I couldn't see it in such terrible pain. 'Course, I got put on a charge for that – firing my rifle without permission and all that."

Caroline nodded. "You can stay out here, if you like, Billy."

Billy shook his head. "Nope. You're not doing this on your own."

Caroline opened the door and walked over to the table. She prepared a large syringe of the morphine solution and gave a final look at them both. Kitty kissed her husband, all farewells having been said, and mouthed "Thank you" to Caroline. As the injection went into Joseph's arm, he gave a sigh… the deepest sound of peace and relief… and he squeezed his wife's hand. Out of the corner of her eye, Caroline saw Billy press a knuckle hard into his mouth to contain his emotions.

Caroline filled the syringe again and said quietly to Kitty, "Are you sure?" Kitty smiled, her breath coming in short and painful bursts. "Never more sure of anything…" she laboured to whisper. Caroline administered the injection and then sat, holding Kitty's other hand for a while, until she was satisfied that both husband and wife had stopped breathing. "It's over," she said simply. Billy covered the couple with a sheet and Caroline began to cry quietly. Billy wrapped his arms around her and held her firmly, letting her cry into his shoulder for as long as she needed.

When they finally came downstairs, Tollman nodded and said that he would take the horse-drawn hackney carriage back to Dartford to fetch an undertaker's wagon and a local policeman.

After he had gone, Billy settled Caroline down in a chair in the garden in the warm sun and said he had something to do and would be back in five minutes. Then he marched purposefully down to the church to find the Reverend. He found him straightening prayer books in the pews.

"I just thought I'd let you know, Reverend, soon to be Captain, Peabody," Billy said in a menacing tone of voice that made the Reverend flush, "that Mr and Mrs Bellamy have both just died, in your parish. He of his terrible, terrible wounds and she died from malnutrition and pneumonia, wearing herself out looking after him. And *you*…" – Billy shoved the Reverend backwards into the wall – "never lifted a finger to help them. *You*," he said, jabbing his finger into the Reverend's chest for emphasis, "wanted her to keep him hidden away because the way he looked upset you. *You*," – another finger jab in the chest – "a man of the cloth, who wants to bring comfort to the troops, couldn't even bring yourself to take a bowl of soup up to a starving, broken woman." Billy's lip curled in disgust. "I hope you make a better padre than you do a vicar. You're going to see a lot of disgusting things on the front line. Let's hope you are man enough to deal with them. And I hope to God that you never treat a dying, disfigured man with the contempt that you showed to Joseph Bellamy. Just count yourself lucky that I don't punch your lights out!" was Billy's parting shot as he left the church like a whirlwind and, for good measure, tore the recruitment poster completely off the noticeboard and ripped it into little pieces.

Feeling as though he had got everything out of his system, Billy Rigsby marched back up the lane towards the solitary cottage containing the doomed couple who were finally at rest.

CHAPTER EIGHTEEN

Business as Usual

The newspapers, the next day, were full of the Ruth Baker story, with photographs of uniformed policemen digging up the flower beds in St Patrick's Church in Clerkenwell. People were appalled but, of course, attracted to the grisly nature of the crime and they flocked in their dozens to Clerkenwell in the hope of seeing a decomposed baby corpse. Tollman was cheered by the fact that one of the photographs clearly showed a harassed DS Carter trying to push back the tide of nosy, disrespectful humanity.

Tollman and Billy had spent the train journey home, yesterday, convincing Caroline that Beech did not need to know what she did for the Bellamy couple.

Tollman had been adamant. "He won't be able to cope with it. I know Mr Beech. If he thinks we are breaking the rules, he'll disband the team. Best we say that when we got there, the husband had already died from his wounds and the wife was on her way out. You just made her comfortable and she died from exhaustion."

"Keep things simple," urged Billy. "Need to know basis. Mr Beech doesn't need to know. You don't need to tell him."

Eventually and reluctantly, Caroline had agreed. It went against her nature to be anything other than honest, but she did not want to be the cause of the team being disbanded.

They had all realised, as the train drew into Charing Cross station, that they had never once asked Kitty Bellamy about the blackmail problem. It hadn't even occurred to all three of them – the day had been taken up with the immediate tragedy.

Something that had popped into Tollman's head as he had gratefully sunk into his bed was that Kitty Bellamy had successfully eluded the police for almost two years. How did Adeline Treborne find out about her? Now they would never know.

It was a sombre team gathering at breakfast. The Ruth Baker baby murders had cast a gloom over everyone, and when Tollman, Caroline and Billy recounted their experiences down in Kent, everyone just fell silent contemplating the awfulness of it all.

"I just don't think that Britain is prepared enough to deal with injuries on this appalling scale," murmured Lady Maud.

Caroline agreed. "Just the sheer number of artificial limbs that are now needed is going to be a problem. It takes, on average, about three months to get an artificial limb made to order by a company like Gillingham's in Somerset. At the rate that amputees are coming in to the military hospitals, the manufacturers can't cope."

Victoria could see that Beech was beginning to get restless. She had learned that he disliked conversations about the wounded, especially about amputation, because he had once confessed to her that when his leg ached, he feared that it would never heal properly, and he would eventually become an amputee.

"Anyway, everyone," said Victoria brightly, in an attempt to lighten the mood, "do we have any progress that we could discuss?"

Everyone around the table shook their heads so Victoria decided to relate the curious information about the manipulative Lady Patrick and the private detective that appeared to be following her.

"Albert Wood," said Tollman with a great deal of scorn. "Now there's a name to conjure with!" He elaborated. "Wood was never much of a detective and he was lazy. Liked the high life, did Wood. A bit like our mate, DS Carter. Wood liked to go out on the town and he got into a bit of debt, which laid him open to offers from the criminal fraternity. Anyway, nothing was ever proved, and he got chucked out of the force about fifteen years ago. Next, I hear that all the top legal chambers are using him as a leg man for their divorce cases and what have you. So, he must have had some friends in high places. He married, years ago, long before he got kicked out of the force, so she must be some long-suffering woman, and I heard that he was living over Marylebone way in quite a nice house, so business must be good. It sounds to me like Sir Michael Patrick is using him to get some dirt on his wife, so that he can offload her."

"Oh no!" said Victoria emphatically. "Patrick's chambers do work for the Royal Family! He would never divorce. It would put him beyond the pale."

Just then, Lady Maud said, "Peter! I can hear the telephone ringing and Mary is out this morning. Do nip out and answer it, please."

Beech loped out of the room and seemed to be gone a long time. When he returned, he said, with an amused look on his face, "I've just received a phone call about, coincidentally, Sir Michael Patrick. He's been shot!"

There were noises and words of surprise from everyone around the table.

"Did his wife do it?" Victoria asked mischievously.

"Well… yes!"

"Good God!" Victoria hadn't expected that answer.

"Sir Michael is in hospital and his wife is in custody. But he doesn't want us to press charges. He wants to see me, so I think, Tollman, if you would accompany me, I would be grateful."

Victoria was disappointed. "Oh, can't I come, Peter? I would so like to hear what his madam of a wife has been up to."

"Er, no, Victoria. I'm sorry." Beech was firm. "I think there are occasions when a man only wants to speak to another man about a subject that he finds embarrassing, like the fact that his wife has some deep, dark secrets and has just shot him."

Beech and Tollman left, but then Tollman swiftly came back with a clutch of letters for Lady Maud, which had been lying on the mat. He handed them over, tipped his hat and left again.

"The advancement of science has a lot to answer for," Maud announced, apropos of nothing at all.

"Sorry, Maud?" Caroline responded.

"Well, I mean, this is the first, what they are calling in the newspapers, 'industrialised' war. Aeroplanes, Zeppelins, gas, machine guns – who knows where the carnage will end? Plus, we apparently had suffragettes, just before the war, making sophisticated bombs that they put in letters, of all things! Who would have thought that advances in science would have led to such terrible things and not enlightened things?" Maud began to open her letters, then paused. "You don't suppose the Germans might resort to letter bombs as well, do you?"

Victoria smiled. "If they did, mother, I'm sure you would be a long way down the list of recipients. I think they would target most of the government first."

"Yes, of course. Silly of me. Good Lord!" The letter in her hand caused her to express shock. Then she handed the letter over to Victoria, with a triumphant, "Well, my dear, it appears that we were right. The woman at the sewing circle must be a blackmailer."

Caroline and Billy got up and came around behind Victoria, as she read out loud,

"Lady Maud Winterbourne, it has come to my attention that you are in the habit of stealing from department stores. If you do not want this information to appear in print in the London Herald, you will need to pay for the privilege of secrecy. Bring £20 cash to the bench opposite the Duke of Bedford statue in Russell Square tomorrow at 11 a.m. Someone will meet you. Come alone, if you value your secrets. Do not inform the police or your details will be published immediately in the newspaper."

Victoria's eyes widened at the reality of the situation. "Mother, we must tell Peter immediately!"

"Yes, of course." Maud appeared elated but shaken.

"Don't worry, Lady Maud," said Billy reassuringly, "you won't be alone. We'll fill the square with plain-clothes policemen. They'll be ready to pounce at the slightest suggestion of any trouble."

"Thank you, Constable Rigsby, that's a comfort," Maud said weakly with a wan smile. "Planning was so much more fun than the execution," she observed.

***

Beech and Tollman entered the discreet doorway of the private hospital in Fitzroy Square where Sir Michael Patrick had been admitted under the care of his personal physician. They found him sitting up in bed, his arm in a sling, recovering from the removal of a bullet from his shoulder. Fortunately, it was from a small-calibre gun, apparently carried by his wife in her bag, and had created little damage other than a minor painful wound and a bruised ego.

"Thank you for coming, Beech," said Sir Michael, in his usual commanding voice. Their paths had crossed before, when Beech had been asked to give evidence in some notorious bank fraud cases, perpetrated by gentlemen in the City of London. Sir Michael, of course, had represented the defendants and managed to get them acquitted. As usual, the relationship between the police and the legal profession was delicate. They did not always see eye to eye – particularly with defending barristers who managed to help criminals evade justice. Beech braced himself for a round of bargaining.

Tollman opened his notebook and Sir Michael said sharply, "I don't think that is necessary!"

Beech said smoothly, "Sir Michael... as I'm sure you know by now, we are investigating a case of blackmail involving several people, and what you do not know is that this case is attached to one of murder. Therefore, it is essential that we make notes of anything that may be of relevance to our current case."

Sir Michael looked frustrated. "I understand," he said cautiously, "but in light of the fact that I will not be pressing charges, I do not wish the details of my private life to be written down anywhere."

Beech considered this for a moment and then said, "DS Tollman will write down anything that I deem of value to the case that we are investigating, but nothing else." Sir Michael appeared satisfied with this arrangement.

"Now," Beech continued, "please be so kind, sir, as to tell us the full story of how your wife came to see me, in fear of her life, and how you ended up in this hospital today."

Sir Michael began his story. He had had his suspicions that all was not quite right with his wife for some time. She had been behaving oddly, spending several hours out and about in London seemingly to no purpose. He had feared the worst – that she was having an affair. So, he had engaged Albert Wood to investigate and, specifically, to follow her. Wood had discovered that Lady Patrick had made many trips to the jewellers but did not buy any new pieces. She had also paid several visits to an hotel in Kensington, where she had stayed several hours each time. Wood had ascertained that she was visiting a gentleman in room twenty-seven who was registered as a Mr Cyrus of San Francisco in the United States. This information had convinced Sir Michael that his wife was having an affair and he had confronted her about it.

"The whole sorry tale came out," he said, avoiding looking at either of the policemen in front of him. "My wife turned out to be not a respectable widow called Ann Miller, but the mistress of a California property speculator and her name was Ann Elliot. What is more, she had been in contact by letter with said Californian throughout our entire five-year marriage. Apparently, he was in financial trouble and had come to, basically, I suppose, blackmail her into supporting him. So, my wife was being blackmailed by two people – her former lover and the Treborne woman – hence the copying of jewellery that I had given her. In my wife's defence, the pressure that she was under must have been tremendous. When she told me of all this, I lost my temper, I'm ashamed to say, and she, thinking I was about to attack her, produced a small pistol and shot me. Our butler telephoned the police, as I am afraid that I blacked out, otherwise my wife would not be at Marylebone Police Station at this moment."

"Excuse me, sir," asked Tollman, trying to be as respectful as possible while inwardly enjoying the downturn in fortunes of a prominent QC, "but when did you hire Albert Wood? Was it before or after your wife started being blackmailed by Adeline Treborne?"

Sir Michael looked confused. "Um… I'm not sure. I hired Wood about six months ago. I think that, during our argument, my wife said she had been the subject of blackmail for four months. Payments to this property speculator started first."

"Thank you, sir."

"What will you do, now, Sir Michael?" Beech asked.

"Divorce is out of the question, of course. I've already paid large sums of money to this Californian man, I'll be damned if I'm going to pay with my career and reputation as well. I shall probably give my wife some money with the proviso that she returns to America, with her lover, and never, ever returns. I will have her British passport taken away and I shall forbid her from using my name ever again. If you could, please, just get her out of Marylebone Police Station before the press get wind of it, I would be most grateful."

"Of course," Beech replied. "We will go there straight away. Thank you for your assistance and we will be in touch if there is anything further."

"I shall be at home after lunch," Sir Michael added. "My wound can heal just as well there as here. And I need to supervise my wife's departure. I don't want her stealing all the valuables in the house in my absence." He gave a small mirthless smile.

As they stepped out again into the street, Tollman said, "Something has been worrying me, Mr Beech, and I think that Sir Michael may have provided the answer…"

"What's that, Tollman?" Beech hailed a taxicab and Tollman waited until they were inside the cab and the partition was closed before he continued.

"Well, some of the blackmail cases could be put down to straightforward servants' gossip but some of the others can't. Like the Major, for instance. How would a blackmailer find out about the Major's fraudulent activities?"

"I suppose it could be information from a servant of one of his victims?" offered Beech.

Tollman shook his head. "No, sir, because they don't *know* that they are victims. He tells them about the poor horses, they give him some money, end of story. And then there is the Ruth Baker case. No servants there, either. Then, yesterday, Kitty Bellamy and her husband. Not only no servants, but isolated way out in Kent. How would anyone find out about these people, in order to blackmail them? The MP, the QC, the shop manager, I can understand that could be servants or shop employees being persuaded to spill the beans... but not the others. Then it came to me, when Sir Michael said that he employed Wood two months before his wife said that the blackmail started. Some of the blackmail information has to be through a police connection and Albert Wood is right there in the frame, as far as I can see."

When Beech and Tollman finally reached Scotland Yard, there was a message from Victoria regarding Lady Maud's blackmail letter and Sir Anthony Jarvis's son was waiting outside Beech's office, displaying very little patience.

"My father can't be here, for obvious reasons," he said testily when Beech invited him to take a seat. He passed a letter over the desk and continued, "We assumed, after your visit, that because the Treborne woman had died, this business was at an end. It would appear not, judging by this extremely offensive letter. What do you intend to do?"

Beech scanned the letter.

"Sir Anthony Jarvis, it has come to my attention that you have a secret family. Your wife is Chinese, and your son is a mongrel. What would the Houses of Parliament say? If you do not want this information to appear in print in the London Herald, you will need to pay for the privilege of secrecy. Bring £30 cash to the bench opposite the Duke of Bedford statue in Russell Square tomorrow at 11.30 a.m. Someone will meet you. Come alone, if you value your secrets. Do not inform the police or your details will be published immediately in the newspaper."

Beech exhaled loudly. "Mr Jarvis…"

"My name is Chen. My father prefers that I do not use his name and since I have reached my majority I do not care to do so, anyway."

Beech bowed his head in acknowledgment. "Mr Chen. We have only just become aware, this morning, that someone has, shall we say, 'taken over' Adeline Treborne's blackmailing business. We think it may be the person who murdered her and took her book of contacts. This morning, we have heard of one other letter…"

There was a knock at Beech's door. A constable opened it and Beech could see, in the background, the sweaty and anxious face of Samuel Robinson, the manager of

Marchesi jewellers, who was clutching in his hand a white envelope, presumably containing the same sort of letter as the one on his desk. He said, "Wait a minute, please!" and the constable closed the door again. Beech turned back to the young Mr Chen and said, "I beg your pardon, we have now become aware of *three* blackmail letters, including your father's, and we must formulate a strategy to deal with them. Could I possibly ask you to be patient until later today, when I will call you on the telephone and we can discuss procedures?"

Mr Chen nodded. Beech continued, "I presume, Mr Chen, that if we were to suggest that your father met with this blackmailer, his safety assured by a strong police presence…"

Chen interrupted. "He would not agree to co-operate, I can tell you that now. My father has kept our existence a secret for many, many years. He is a prominent public figure and cannot be seen on a park bench handing money over to a stranger. However, I would be willing to do so, in his place. The writer of this letter obviously knows that I am part Chinese – a mongrel, as they so delicately phrase it. The blackmailer would surely accept money from me?"

"Probably." However, what concerned Beech was the young man's ability to keep calm in a stressful situation or whether he would relish causing the blackmailer some physical harm.

After Chen had left, it was Mr Robinson's turn to see Beech. He was in a state of great anxiety when he presented his letter. Beech read once more the instructions:

"*Mr Samuel Robinson, it has come to my attention that you are in the habit of assisting your wealthy customers to replicate their jewellery – possibly to assist them in defrauding their insurance companies. If you do not want this information to appear in print in the London Herald, you will need to pay for the privilege of secrecy. Bring £20 cash to the bench opposite the Duke of Bedford statue in Russell Square tomorrow at 10.30 a.m. Someone will meet you. Come alone, if you value your secrets. Do not inform the police or your details will be published immediately in the newspaper.*"

"Yes, Mr Robinson, someone appears to have taken over Adeline Treborne's business," he explained yet again. "We do not, at this stage, know who that person is, and we are hoping that you will assist us in capturing this blackmailer…"

"Me?" asked Robinson with a note of hysteria in his voice. Beech had not forgotten that Robinson had fainted during their last encounter. He did seem to be rather highly strung.

"You will be surrounded by plain-clothes policemen, I assure you, Mr Robinson," Beech stated. "We will do our very best to protect you."

It was clear that Mr Robinson did not find the thought comforting at all. There was a knock on the door again and Beech was bracing himself to reprimand the constable who had interrupted him before when he saw that this time it was Tollman, who said quietly, "Sorry to interrupt, but could I have a word outside, sir?"

When Beech stepped outside he could see that Tollman had, in his hand, a sheaf of notes on pink paper. "I've just had a visit from the editor of the *London Herald*, sir," he said ominously. "It appears that our blackmailer has not only taken over Adeline Treborne's list of victims but has also taken over writing the gossip column. The editor received these notes and a letter demanding that payment be made today to a Post Office box number at the General Post Office by Trafalgar Square."

"I would say, Tollman, judging by the notepaper and handwriting, that our blackmailer has *always* written the gossip column, wouldn't you?"

Unwilling to let Mr Robinson go until they had finally thrashed out plans for the money exchange, Beech told the constable to get the shop manager a cup of tea and to tell him that Mr Beech would be right back. Then he and Tollman adjourned to a nearby empty office.

Beech got no further than the first item of gossip. "God help us!" he said loudly in shock. It read:

The Duke of Penhere should take himself round to the churchyard in Clerkenwell and say a prayer for the body of his illegitimate son, that he sired with a housemaid sixteen years ago.

CHAPTER NINETEEN

The Empty Mousetrap

The Duke of Penhere was devastated.

He has the look of a man who cannot fathom out why life keeps delivering blow after blow, thought Beech. He reflected that he had, in his time, known many young men like the Duke, who had lived a youth of privilege and excess, barely giving a thought to the structure of the society that assisted them in their lofty position. *The war has changed that,* Beech decided. *Living in trenches, watching men from all levels of society dying, has changed the sense of privilege the upper classes enjoyed.*

Finally, the Duke spoke. "It is true," he said simply, "that I did, stupidly, take advantage of my mother's personal maid and she... became... pregnant. My mother never knew. Neither did my father. He was too busy at the time, desperately trying to shore up the family fortune, which had dwindled away because of his poor and reckless investments. It was my sister who said she would sort things out in my absence. I gave her a substantial amount of money for the maid and I went back to Oxford. I was twenty-one at the time. It was the stupidity of youth. When I came back, Adeline said that it had all been solved. The maid had left and had the child and it was immediately taken for adoption through the Catholic Church. I am ashamed to say that I thought no more of it."

Beech nodded. "If this piece, intended for the newspaper, is correct, then I'm afraid that the child ended up in the clutches of a baby farmer who murdered all her charges."

The Duke put his head in his hands in despair. "I admit that I was cavalier and thoughtless when I was young. That's how men of our status are allowed to be, aren't we?"

Beech noted that the Duke considered them equals – something that would not have happened before the war – but he didn't feel that the observation warranted a comment.

The Duke continued, "We are encouraged to be reckless, embrace our privileged position and dismiss the needs of the lower orders. Sow our wild oats before we settle down to family responsibility and guarding the Treborne name." He uttered a brief, bitter laugh. "What family name do I have to protect? Aside from my mother, we have all disgraced the dukedom and the family name – and this war will deliver the final blow to the aristocracy, I am sure of that. I must make amends. I'm not sure how, but I shall find a way."

"What was the name of the maid who bore the child?" asked Beech, as he rose to depart.

The Duke looked blank. "I am ashamed to say that I cannot remember. Not at all. I can't remember how she looked or spoke, or anything. What a despicable person that makes me."

***

Tollman and Billy, once more in plain clothes, were in the cool, vaulted interior of the General Post Office just off Trafalgar Square. The editor of the *Herald* had sent the payment over by hand, addressed to the appropriate box number. They had spoken to the manager and had arranged that the woman on the counter that dealt with Post Office box numbers would give them a signal, by blowing her nose loudly with a white handkerchief, when someone appeared asking for any correspondence for Box 1978.

As with the bank that they had staked out earlier in the week, most of the counter staff were women. Older men were seen in the background, fetching items from the storerooms, lifting parcels and carrying sacks of mail.

The post office was filled with foreigners and servicemen, whether visiting or resident it was impossible to tell, but the poste restante facility, whereby customers could have their mail directed to the post office on a temporary basis, seemed to be extremely busy. In fact, so busy that *two* women were working it, ensuring that no time was wasted in trying to whittle down the long queue that snaked from the counter to the door.

It seemed as though servicemen from all over the Empire were represented in the queue. There were young black men in sailor blue and brown-skinned soldiers in khaki wearing turbans. Billy pointed out to Tollman soldiers whose uniforms signalled that they were from New Zealand, Canada and Australia.

Poste restante was the best way for some foreign soldiers to get letters from and to their families before they shipped out to France and Belgium or even further afield. Also, once in the field, rather than risk letters going astray through the Royal Engineers (Postal Section), they would just pick up a batch from the post office while on leave, reply to them and post the replies before they went back to the Front. Sailors also found the poste restante convenient, as all their mail had to go through two different Navy post offices in Scotland, then be delivered to the relevant flagship to be dispensed among the fleet while in convoy. It could be weeks before letters arrived at either end. The volume of mail to and from the men in action was enormous. Tollman had read in the newspaper that two thousand bags of letters a day were coming into Mount Pleasant Depot. This was equalled, apparently, by the number of parcels going *out* of Britain. To deal with those, the Post Office had actually built a new wooden structure in Regent's Park, which covered five acres and employed hundreds of men and women.

What a palaver, thought Tollman, *all for a blessed letter!* He doubted that poste restante would be available for much longer. He had heard that the Armed Forces were clamping down on all avenues of mail, except that which went through the Army and Navy, due to the need for them to censor everything.

He looked at all the different posters and notices up on the wall alongside the poste restante counter. One said:

WARNING. Defence of the Realm Act. Discussion in Public of Naval and Military matters may convey information to the enemy. BE ON YOUR GUARD.

Billy made a tutting noise of disapproval at another poster.

The New Armies... More men are needed at once, it said. What provoked Billy's disapproval were the statements at the bottom of the poster that said *Enlist for the period of the War... Standards have been lowered.*

"Bloody hell!" he exclaimed. "Lowered to what?"

"As long as you can walk and breathe at the same time, probably," commented Tollman sourly.

"Perhaps they'd take me back then," Billy grinned.

Tollman looked alarmed. "You've done your bit, lad. The work here is just as important. Don't get any ideas about taking yourself off back to that hellhole again, or I shall take it very personally. You stay here, where I can keep an eye on you. You make a bloody good policeman and they're going to be hard to find when this war is over."

The afternoon dragged on. There was no signal from the woman behind the counter. Billy was hungry and Tollman needed a mug of tea, so they were thankful when the post office closed its doors finally and they could walk briskly down past Buckingham Palace and back to the house in Mayfair.

In the study, Beech and Victoria had actually drawn up a giant map of the layout of Russell Square on the back of an old roll of wallpaper they had dug out of the attic rooms. It showed every last bench, statue and flower bed and they had pinned it up on an old easel – another remnant of Victoria's childhood from the attic. Tollman was impressed. He liked detail.

"It's probably not to scale," apologised Victoria.

Tollman smiled. "It doesn't matter, Mrs E. You've done a smashing job."

Lady Maud came in, bearing a tray of jars of pickles, followed by Mary carrying plates of sandwiches.

"I'm afraid it's only ham and cheese," she said. "But as supper won't be until eight, I felt that there may be some need of sustenance."

Billy restrained himself from falling upon the food immediately, but he was so hungry he felt he could eat both plates by himself. Fortunately, Mrs Beddowes had anticipated Billy Rigsby's appetite and entered pushing a trolley with further plates of sandwiches and a large pot of tea. Tollman sighed with pleasure. If only he could take his shoes off and put his feet up, he thought, life would be perfect.

Caroline came in and immediately made Tollman envious by slipping off her shoes and curling her legs up on the sofa in an unladylike manner.

"Mabel should be here any moment," she announced. "She says she has something to show us. Did you bring the perambulator down, by the way?" she asked Beech.

"Blast! I forgot! Rigsby, would you be so kind as to run upstairs and fetch the perambulator? You know where it is. Good chap," Beech said as Billy sprang to his feet and disappeared out of the door.

As soon as Billy had bumped the perambulator down the last step and into the hallway, the front door bell rang, so he opened the door and was astonished to see the trio of Mabel Summersby, his mum and his aunt, who seemed to be getting along like a house on fire.

"I didn't know you were coming!" he said in amazement as the ladies stepped in to the house. Mabel hung back, smiling, as the other two women made a fuss of Billy.

"Mr Beech called us," said Sissy breathlessly. "Said he wanted all the team together."

"Fancy!" added Elsie. "Me and Sis! Part of a police team! We'll be making arrests next!"

Billy laughed and opened the door to the study.

"Acting policewomen Elsie Rigsby, Sissy Bates and Mabel Summersby," he announced loudly, with a flourish, and Caroline led a round of applause.

"Daft 'aporth!" murmured Elsie to her son. She and Sissy were flushed with pleasure to be part of the team.

Everyone found seats, Lady Maud introduced herself to an overawed Sissy and exhorted everyone to help themselves to sandwiches and tea, and then they all subsided into respectful silence as Beech outlined his plan for tomorrow.

"Firstly, ladies, may I say how much I value you being part of this operation," Beech began. "But I need to tell you now that you are there for two reasons only. One, to make the square look as normal as possible by having women in various guises doing various things, so it is not just full of men, which would look suspicious. Two, you are there to identify the blackmailer and could be called upon to speak about that identification in court. Let me stress that on no account are you to involve yourself in any interaction with the suspect – that is apart from Lady Maud, who has to play the part of a victim. Do you understand me, ladies? Involvement only at a distance. We do not want to have to worry about the safety of anyone except Lady Maud."

The women all nodded their heads.

"Right," Beech continued. "Now, Tollman and Rigsby will be in charge of two groups of police officers that we have borrowed from H Division. We don't know why the blackmailer chose Russell Square but it could be that it is close to home, in which case it seemed advisable not to use policemen from the local area, as they may be recognised. So we are bringing them in from Whitechapel and... this should be right up your street, Tollman... you are all going to be dressed as gardeners and will be tending the flower beds. The local council have been advised and they are providing tools etcetera, but they have asked us please not to make too much mess. So, gardening clothes for you men."

Tollman winked at Sissy, which was noticed by Elsie, who raised amused and questioning eyebrows at her sister.

"Now," Beech carried on. "Ladies. You will all have your roles to play. Firstly, Mabel, I believe you have something to show us?"

"Oh, yes." Mabel began fumbling in her holdall and produced a small black oblong about the size of her hand, with brass circles on the front and top.

"What is it?" asked Caroline.

"It's a camera," explained Mabel, opening up the plate over the lens. "It's a Leica handheld camera that uses thirty-five-millimetre film rolls. I bought it in 1913 when they first came out. It's awfully useful for taking pictures outdoors without any of the paraphernalia of a big camera and tripod. It's German. Sorry." She felt she needed to apologise.

"What, that little thing takes proper pictures?" Billy was amazed. "It's even smaller than a Box Brownie," he said, referring to the portable cardboard box camera that was so beloved by the troops at the Front.

"Yes, it takes quite good pictures actually. But you need to be about twelve feet in front of your subject for the best quality."

Beech interjected. "Mabel here is going to be a nursery nurse, wheeling her charge around the park in a perambulator – with the camera secreted inside, so that she can pause and take pictures of the blackmailer without taking the camera out of the perambulator. That is the idea, isn't it, Mabel?"

"In theory, it should work. As long as the lens is not obstructed."

"So, no one will realise that you are taking a picture?" Victoria was impressed.

"No," Mabel replied. "I should be able to lean over the perambulator, as though tending to the infant, and press the switch to take the picture. If I get the angle right, it should work well. But I need to have a practice."

"We'll do that in a moment, Mabel." Beech wanted to finish his organisation of the team. "Now, Mrs Rigsby, I am concerned that if the blackmailer does turn out to be this Mrs Leighton who runs the sewing circle, then she will recognise you. But I think we should continue the fiction that you are Lady Maud's maid and you should accompany her but be sent off shopping before she enters the square. Anyone watching from a distance would find this quite normal."

Elsie was disappointed at not being in the thick of things, but she tried not to show it.

Beech continued his plan. "Sissy, I was wondering if you could walk that splendid dog... Timmy?" Sissy nodded. "If you could walk him around the square, stopping occasionally to sit on a bench, or perhaps play with him?"

"Oh, Timmy'll love that," said Elsie, and Sissy smiled.

"And finally, Victoria, Caroline and I will sit on the grass and pretend to have a picnic. Rug, basket and all that."

Everyone understood the roles that they were to play and nodded agreement.

"Finally," – Beech wanted to wrap everything up – "we know of three blackmail victims who have been asked to turn up at Russell Square tomorrow. It is possible that there could be more, as we only had a copy of the details of the last page of Adeline Treborne's book. Therefore, we need to assemble in Russell Square, gradually, from about nine in the morning. I have written down a timetable of when each person should arrive." Beech handed out a list to everyone of timings, which showed the ladies arriving at fifteen-minute intervals, starting with Mabel, who would be first.

"Needless to say, but I shall say it, the blackmailer could very well be a murderer as well. We do not know whether Adeline Treborne self-administered the drugs that killed her or whether someone else gave them to her." He noted that Maud had begun to fan herself, as though she were unbearably hot, and he felt a pang of concern.

"Maud," he said gently, "if you feel that this is too much for you to cope with, then let someone stand in for you. The blackmailer doesn't know what you look like and we can swap around roles between the ladies."

"Good gracious, no!" Lady Maud was outraged at the suggestion that she could not play her part. "I am confident that you and your men will protect me. Good Lord! I only have to hand over some money, for goodness sake! The question is whether I can restrain myself from slapping the Leighton woman's face!"

Her response made everyone laugh and then general chatter broke out, while Billy took the large teapot downstairs to get it refilled and the remaining sandwiches were mopped up.

Elsie, Sissy and Tollman departed, with Sissy murmuring about giving Timmy a bath when they got home. Elsie gave her a funny look.

"You're going to walk him round the park tomorrow," she said acidly, "not offer him as a model for Pears Soap posters."

Sissy decided to ignore her. Mr Tollman waved cheerily as he walked off down the road and the two women waved back.

"Nice man," observed Elsie. "Seems to have taken a fancy to you."

Sissy blushed and muttered, "Don't be daft."

Elsie allowed a small sardonic smile to play about her lips. "I bet you a penny he winks at you tomorrow in the park." She knew she was right.

Back at the house, Mabel spent about an hour creating a little platform for her camera inside the perambulator, using an old soap dish and some wire she had produced from her holdall. Then she spent a further half hour making minute adjustments to the angle of the platform and cutting a lens-sized hole in the fabric of the perambulator hood. Victoria produced an ancient doll from up in the attic rooms, plus her old nurse's uniform and some blankets to put in the perambulator.

"What an incredibly ugly doll," murmured Caroline, staring into the depths of the baby carriage. "I do hope no one stops you, Mabel, and asks to look at the baby. They'd get a shock if they did."

"Don't worry," Mabel replied, "I shall model myself on my old nanny and be very fierce. No one will want to speak to me or view the infant, I promise."

CHAPTER TWENTY

Under the Duke of Bedford's Gaze

It was a fine July morning and there was a heavy dew, as Billy found out when he decided to sit on the grass and take in the surroundings. He sighed as he put a hand on the big wet patch on the seat of his trousers and stood up again. Tollman chuckled.

The policemen from Whitechapel were beginning to assemble at the north-western corner, as they had been instructed. Tollman decided he would wait until the full dozen were there before he went over and introduced himself.

Billy looked around. It was a big square, not one that he recalled ever having visited, and it was larger than he had anticipated. Everything was in its full summer glory and he realised that they would have to get quite close to the southern end of the square, where the statue was, in order to be within striking distance.

Finally, the twelfth man appeared to have arrived, as well as a horse and cart loaded with spades, hoes, scythes and buckets of plants.

"Right," said Tollman briskly. "The men and the council wagon are here. Let's go, lad."

Billy and Tollman marched up to the assembled men and introduced themselves, and they all set about unloading the garden tools and plants from the cart. Tollman was given a key and shown where the maintenance shed was in the square. "Leave the tools there, when you've finished," the man said. "We'll pick 'em up tomorrow."

Tollman led the crew down through the lime walk to the shrubbery on the south-west of the square and gathered them around.

"The suspect will be conducting business on that bench there, opposite the statue. The Chief Inspector says that we are not to apprehend the suspect until after the 11.30 appointment. He will give me the signal to move. Obviously, if something goes wrong before that time, I will give you a shout to move, so be alert. Meantime, we have to look busy. The council said we can dig over the bed in front of the shrubbery, here and the one opposite, and plant these flowers. Anyone from Whitechapel know anything about gardening?"

Two of the men raised their hands. "Right, you two are in charge over there. Take five other men and make a start on the flower bed. Best work slowly, lads, we could be here a long time today."

So, they began to dig. Other people began to come into the park – some just passing through, some sitting on benches to meet others or just rest.

"What do we do about the public getting in the way?" asked Billy.

"Nothing we can do, lad," was Tollman's reply. "We can't close the square, because we need the blackmailer to have free movement. We just have to hope that we can work round it. Just keep your eyes peeled."

The first lady to arrive was Mabel Summersby, looking every inch the efficient nursery nurse in her uniform, pushing along the perambulator slowly. She came in at the north-western entrance and slowly traversed the giant horseshoe-shaped path that led down to the Duke of Bedford statue. About three-quarters of the way down the path, she stopped, sat down on a bench, took a book out of the perambulator and started reading. Billy smiled, wondering how she had fared with loading the baby carriage into a taxicab and whether the cabbie had caught sight of the porcelain 'baby' and thought she was probably a madwoman.

Fifteen minutes later, Beech arrived with Caroline on one arm and carrying a picnic basket and rug in the other hand.

"Well, don't they look like they're off to Henley Regatta," said Tollman flippantly, remarking on Beech's natty straw boater and Caroline's flowery frock, hat and parasol.

"Where's Mrs E, then?" asked Billy, suddenly anxious.

Tollman pulled a disapproving face. "Billy, if you'd have read the timetable properly, you'd know she isn't due to arrive for another fifteen minutes."

"Sorry," Billy mumbled.

Beech looked around and noted the men in position, digging and weeding, then he spread out the rug near a tree a good fifty yards from the statue, and he and Caroline sat down.

"I'd better sit facing the statue," Beech said, "as I need to see what's happening."

When Victoria arrived, in an equally fetching summer outfit, she joined them on the picnic rug. "Anything happened yet?"

Beech shook his head and Victoria sat down on the rug. Caroline opened the basket, in which she had secreted her medical bag, in case of emergencies. She groped around underneath and produced a thermos flask. "Tea, anyone?" she said with a smile.

When Sissy arrived with Timmy, her heart was pounding, but as she came in the south-eastern entrance, she saw the reassuring presence of Billy and she began to relax. Unfortunately, Timmy also spotted Billy and yanked the lead from Sissy's hand as he made a bolt for one of his favourite people with a series of excited yelps. He flung himself at Billy, who was crouched down, and licked him furiously all over.

Tollman grabbed the squirming terrier and, with a confused Timmy in his arms, he marched over to Sissy and said loudly, "Kindly keep your dog under control, madam!" and gave her a broad wink.

"Yes, of course, I'm so sorry," said a flustered Sissy. *Damn,* she thought. *I've just lost a bet with Elsie about Mr Tollman giving me a wink in the park.* So, with Timmy's lead firmly in her grasp, she continued along the path, dragging behind her a reluctant dog, who didn't understand why he couldn't go and play with Billy.

Nothing happened for a while but then Tollman spotted a young woman coming up the lime walk.

"Billy!" he hissed, "get behind the tree, quick!" Billy obeyed and Tollman swiftly joined him. "We've got a problem," he continued. "That's Lily, Adeline Treborne's maid. She can recognise us – and Mr Beech and Mrs E, too."

"Bloody hell! What's she doing here?"

"It looks like she may be our blackmailer," said Tollman grimly, as they both watched Lily sit down on the bench opposite the Duke of Bedford's statue.

Beech had spotted her too. "Victoria, cover your face with your parasol," he said urgently, as he bent his head down, hoping his straw boater would obscure his face.

"What is it?" asked Caroline.

"The woman sitting on the bench by the statue is the live-out maid of Adeline Treborne," said Beech, head still bowed.

Victoria was aghast. Suspecting Lily had never entered into their deductions. "Are you sure it's her?"

"Absolutely."

"Perhaps it's a coincidence," Caroline ventured.

Beech shook his head. "No, I think that would be stretching the bounds of reality too far."

Just then, one of the undercover policemen 'gardeners' came up to a tree near the trio and began inspecting its roots and trunk.

"Mr Beech," the man said, without looking at the group. "Message from DS Tollman, sir. He said he is aware of the situation regarding the woman on the bench and he and Constable Rigsby are keeping out of sight in the shrubbery. He advises that you move behind this tree, in the shade, and keep yourself hidden as much as possible."

"Thank you," Beech responded. "Please tell Tollman I will take his advice."

The man nodded and moved away. Beech and Victoria stood, their backs to the suspect, while Caroline packed up the basket and gathered up the rug. She then spread the rug out behind the tree for the others to sit on.

"I'm afraid you are going to have to be our eyes, Caro. Make sure you have a good view of everything." Beech was frustrated. He turned to Victoria. "I can't, somehow, believe that this Lily is the criminal mastermind behind all of this."

"Nor me," agreed Victoria. "If she is, then she must be an astonishing actress, because her shock and tears after finding Adeline Treborne strung up seemed incredibly real to me."

"Her shock *must* have been real," observed Caroline. "Don't forget, we now know that the Bakers hung Adeline's corpse. When Lily came in that morning, she was expecting to find Adeline peacefully dead on her bed, probably, not swinging at the end of a rope!"

"That's true." Beech took a deep breath. "But I still feel that there is a missing part of this. Lily is, what, fifteen years old? Adeline Treborne has been writing this gossip column for two years – or rather, someone with very neat writing and using pink paper has been writing the column for two years. That can't be Lily. It means she would have started doing it at the age of thirteen! That's hardly likely."

"Ah, there's a development!" said Caroline excitedly. "A small, sweaty man has arrived at the bench and it looks as though he is going to sit down."

***

Samuel Robinson was terrified. He had spent all morning being terrified. His mouth was dry, and his heart was fluttering in his chest. He knew he was sweating – as he always did when he was nervous – but there was nothing he could do about it. He clutched an envelope containing four large £5 notes and his hand was trembling. He deeply regretted allowing himself to be persuaded by the police to engage in this exchange and he wasn't sure what frightened him the most – being confronted by a violent criminal or his own cowardice, which could induce him to faint at the slightest provocation.

So, it was a somewhat confused Samuel Robinson who arrived at the bench opposite the Duke of Bedford's statue to find a young girl sitting there. He decided she must be sitting there accidentally and that at any moment the blackmailer could turn up, so, unsure as to how to proceed, he concluded the best thing to do was to sit down.

His confusion was replaced by surprise when the young girl said, "I do hope you have brought the money, Mr Robinson."

He started and looked at her. She was about the same height as he was, which was really quite small. Her face betrayed nothing. It was neither hard nor frightened. She was calm and looked at him directly. It was a bold look, without any shame, and it made Samuel Robinson replace his fear with a small spark of annoyance. To be blackmailed by this chit of a girl! He almost felt insulted!

The girl noticed the change in his face and said quietly, "Please don't think about protesting or walking away, Mr Robinson. I did not come here alone. At this very moment there are people watching us who will not be pleased if you try to change our arrangements. And, don't forget, you really don't want all your little business dealings in the newspapers, do you?"

Samuel Robinson felt afraid again and he looked around nervously. There was no one in immediate sight, except a nurse wheeling a perambulator, who had paused to comfort her infant. Wherever these people were who were watching, he could not see them. Reluctantly, he handed over the envelope. And the girl put it in her dolly bag.

"Am I going to have to come to this park bench every month?" he asked, irritably. "That's going to be rather unpleasant in the winter."

The girl smiled. "Maybe one more time here, Mr Robinson. Then you will be contacted and given details of a bank account in which to pay your money. Don't worry, you won't have to freeze in winter." Then she added, "You may go now."

Robinson felt another surge of annoyance at being treated as though he were a pupil being dismissed by a teacher. He got up awkwardly and left the square feeling foolish and only marginally comforted by the fact that the girl would soon be in police custody.

***

Elsie Rigsby had come prepared to support Lady Maud and when they stepped into the taxicab in Mayfair and sat down, she discreetly passed her a hip flask of brandy. Maud gave her a grateful smile as she put the flask in her bag.

"Belonged to my late husband," said Elsie. "Billy's dad. He always took it with him everywhere and he used to say to me, 'Else, I just take one gulp before I go into battle, and I'm as right as rain.'" She turned her face away from Lady Maud, as she could feel a tear prickling her eye and she didn't want to appear foolish.

Maud understood and patted Elsie's hand. "It's not an easy life for army wives," she said softly. "You spend your whole married life worrying about the worst happening and then, when it does, it takes you completely by surprise."

Elsie smiled. "I forgot you were an army widow too, Your Ladyship. And you're right, when a soldier dies, it doesn't matter whether he's high born or low born, his widow still grieves the same as all the other widows."

They sat in companionable silence for the journey to Russell Square. Once they alighted, they assumed their roles. Lady Maud was the bossy employer and Elsie the meek employee.

"Rigsby!" Lady Maud said loudly, in her most autocratic voice. "You can make yourself scarce while I take a turn around this charming square. Here's some money. Take yourself off to a café somewhere and report back here in half an hour. Then I shall want you to accompany me to Gamages department store in Holborn."

"Yes, madam," said Elsie, giving a brief curtsey, and she watched Lady Maud enter the gardens. "Fingers crossed," she murmured to herself and she took herself off to a small café she could see on the corner of Southampton Row. From there, she would be able to see the south-eastern gateway to the square.

She had settled down with a cup of tea in the front corner of the café, by the window, when she realised that she could see the unmistakeable figure of Louise Leighton sitting in the shadows on a bench just inside the gates. So, it was her, Elsie thought. Devious minx. But she wasn't sitting in the right place. Mr Beech's plan showed the statue was right in the centre of the south side of the square. In fact, right where the Leighton woman seemed to be looking.

***

Lady Maud entered the square with a certain amount of trepidation, but she was reassured by all the familiar faces she saw around the area, performing their assumed roles. She couldn't see Beech or Victoria, but she had no doubt that they were there. Caroline was sitting on a rug, seeming to be reading a book. Sissy was strolling down through the tree-lined walk, with her little dog in tow. Mabel was sitting on a bench with the perambulator in front of her, gently rocking it. There were lots of men digging in the two flower beds on either side of the square, so Maud felt quite safe.

As she approached the designated bench, her brows knitted in concern. A child? Surely not? She sat down gingerly and decided to have a surreptitious sip from Elsie Rigsby's hip flask, just to give her some Dutch courage.

As she raised the flask to her lips there was a soft laugh from the girl sitting on the bench. "I heard you were a drinker, Lady Maud," she said, "but I didn't think it was so bad that you had to have a snifter at this hour of the morning."

Maud was astonished but decided to play her role fully and replied haughtily, "How dare you! This is for medicinal purposes only, young lady."

"I don't care what you do, Lady Maud," was the brazen response. "You can spend all day blind drunk and lying in the gutter. As long as you have the money we asked for. That's all I care about."

Maud noted the use of the word 'we'. She would relay that to Peter Beech later. She decided to try another approach, so she said, in a voice of concern, "Is someone coercing you into blackmailing people? If you are in fear of someone, I'm sure the police could help."

The girl threw her head back and laughed loudly. "The police?! I'm sure that most of them are too busy being on the take themselves to bother with the likes of me. Besides," she added, "I answer to no one. I am my own mistress. Now, stop wasting time, Your Ladyship, and hand over the money."

Maud rifled around in her bag and produced a roll of twenty £1 notes, held in place by a rubber band. She passed them over to the girl, who put them in her coat pocket.

"It's a pleasure doing business with you, Your Ladyship," she said with a sarcastic smile. "You can go now, we'll be in touch."

Maud rose, trying to walk away with dignity, but she couldn't resist turning back to the girl and saying, "You know that you will be caught and punished one day, don't you?"

The girl just stared at her sullenly and said, "How's the shoplifting going, Your Ladyship?" Then she cleverly echoed Maud's words and said, "You know that you'll be caught and punished one day, don't you?"

As Maud walked away, she realised that Mabel had been taking photographs all the time she had been having a conversation with the girl. *I do hope she doesn't have a picture of me about to have a snifter from a hip flask,* she thought worriedly.

As she came out of the gates, she saw Elsie gesturing to her from the corner of the street and she made her way towards her. Seeing that Elsie was outside a café, she said dramatically, "I need a very large cup of tea and, possibly, an iced bun."

***

Harold Chen was angry. Here he was, about to go and pay someone money because his father had never been honest about having a Chinese wife and son. In fact, it stuck in his throat. He had spent his entire life concealing his true identity – for what? Even his mother was beginning to find her own explanation of their life of concealment a little threadbare. She had always told him that his father was a great man, a member of the British parliament, his work was more important than anything else and, now there was a war on, he was needed to help run the country. But the revelation that Sir Anthony Jarvis had allowed himself to be blackmailed, rather than reveal the truth about his perfectly legal family, had been one concealment too far for mother and son.

Ever since the police had visited their home in Limehouse and revealed that his father had been black-mailed, Harold had watched his mother slowly crumple, as though years of disappointment had finally overwhelmed her, and she had realised that she was never going to be acknowledged as Lady Jarvis and her son given his rightful place at the side of his father.

Harold had a more pragmatic view of the situation. His simmering resentment of his father and the treatment his mother had received at the hands of her husband had coalesced into cold, hard vengeance. The import/export business was in the names of the three of them but Harold, this week, had had papers drawn up to remove all direc-torships from his father. Sir Anthony had signed them with reluctance but realised that he had no choice. The debt he owed his wife and son was too great to quibble about his control of the companies in London and Hong Kong.

Then yesterday, Mei Li had informed her husband that she would be returning to Hong Kong for ever. Harold had decided to join her, as soon as he had appointed a general manager for the Limehouse company. It was time for him to embrace his Chinese origins and stop hoping that he would be accepted as an Englishman. A public-school education had already taught him much about his position in life. To the other boys he was always the 'Chink with money', just like his friend, the son of the prime minister of Persia, was always the 'Wog with money'. It had been offensive and designed to tell him, bluntly, his exact position in society. It was a situation he could bear no longer.

Therefore, when Harold Chen sat down on the bench next to the pale girl, he was not in a mood to be trifled with.

The girl said, after a moment's hesitation, "Who are you?"

Without looking at her, Chen said, "Believe it or not, I am the son of Sir Anthony Jarvis and I am here to pay the blackmail money that you have extorted from him."

The girl sounded nervous, which rather pleased him. "This isn't what should happen," she said. "Sir Anthony Jarvis should be here."

"Well, it's not going to happen!" said Harold aggressively, between clenched teeth. "You either accept the money from me or I will walk away, and you can say what you like in the newspapers."

He wanted to frighten the girl by grabbing her and threatening her. He knew that he was strong and intimidating. He was toying with the idea of upsetting the police plans and physically harming the girl when some nurse pushing a perambulator stopped a few feet away and began fussing with her baby.

Suddenly, a beautiful, elegantly dressed woman came almost running into the square and straight up to the bench.

"You have ruined everything!" she screamed in anger at Harold and the girl and promptly drew a gun and shot them both at close range. There were several screams from women nearby and, in an instant, the men digging close at hand descended on the woman with the gun to disarm and restrain her. Lily slumped to the floor and Harold Chen clutched his chest.

"Lily! Oh, Lily! Speak to me!" Another woman had run from the nearest gate to crouch over the girl's body.

"Lily!" a man roared, and came running from nowhere. "What have you done?" he shouted at the dazed woman who had fired the shots, and tried to grab her around the throat, only to be restrained by one of the plain-clothes policemen.

Caroline reached the bench at the same time as Beech and she immediately knelt beside the girl, Lily. "She's still alive," she yelled to Victoria, who was still running towards the bench. "Get my medical bag!" Then she turned to Harold Chen, who was sitting completely still on the bench. Caroline prised his hand away from his chest and discovered a perfectly formed bloody hole in his shirt, no more than an inch away from his heart. It was obvious that he was having trouble breathing.

Beech looked at the human damage and then spoke to the woman who had fired the shots. "Good God, Lady Patrick. What have you done now?"

Tollman had arrived, and immediately shouted, "Billy! Grab that man! It's Albert Wood!" Billy was moving to arrest the man who had tried to strangle Lady Patrick when Wood lunged and headbutted the policeman restraining him. The man staggered back, his nose broken and bleeding, and Wood grabbed the nearest woman to him, which happened to be Mabel Summersby. Suddenly, everyone was aware that Wood had a handgun pointed at Mabel's head and everything went quiet.

"Wood," said Tollman in a warning voice. "Let the lady go. Don't be stupid, now."

Wood gave a hollow laugh. "Arthur Tollman. I might have known they'd bring you back on the force."

"Bert, don't make things worse," said the woman who was crying over Lily.

"Shut up, Louise!" Wood was in no mood to bargain. "It's over. It's all gone wrong. If Lily's dead, what's the point?"

Caroline spoke. "Lily's not dead. But she will be if you don't let me get her to hospital immediately."

Wood nodded. "Do it then. But I'm taking this lady and I'm going to walk out of here. I'm not going to prison."

Then he began to walk backwards, out of Russell Square, dragging the helpless Mabel with him. At the gate, he turned, placed the barrel of the gun in Mabel's side and, with his other arm firmly around her waist, started walking north.

CHAPTER TWENTY-ONE

The Family Enterprise

As Wood disappeared out of the gate, everyone was galvanised into action.

"Billy!" Tollman pointed after Wood. "Take four men and follow him at a distance. Don't give him any opportunity to pull that trigger. I'll take the rest of the men – except him and him." He pointed to the copper sitting on the path with blood streaming from his broken nose and the one restraining Lady Patrick. "We'll go parallel and see if we can get ahead of him and pick up some uniforms on the beat to join us. We'll try and head him off – see if we can trap him, between us."

Billy and the four men nearest to him sped off after Wood. Tollman looked at Beech, suddenly realising that he had overridden his seniority in issuing instructions.

"Yes, that's fine, Tollman," said Beech, who was busy holding Harold Chen while Caroline was applying a pressure bandage to his chest. "Get on with it. I'll supervise the hospitals and arrests. I'll join you as soon as I can."

Tollman nodded and raced off with the six Whitechapel men in tow.

Sissy appeared with the dog. "I'm going to follow Billy," she said anxiously.

"No..." Beech protested, but it was too late, Sissy was marching off. "Be careful, please, and keep out of the way of everything!" he shouted after her. Sissy raised a hand to signal that she understood. Beech saw, despairingly, that she had met up with her sister and Lady Maud at the gate. "Victoria! Stop them! We can't have them following Sissy's example!"

Victoria ran across to the gateway and Beech could see that Victoria was remonstrating with the three women, but Sissy and Elsie broke away and were gone. To his relief, Victoria started coming back with Lady Maud alongside her.

"I'm sorry, I couldn't stop Elsie from wanting to follow Billy. She is his mother, after all. They are both worried about him," said Victoria apologetically.

"Well, let's hope they don't put themselves and Billy in danger." Beech was distracted. Lady Patrick and the woman holding Lily's hand were crying. Caroline had now turned her attention to Lily and was trying to revive her. Victoria retrieved the picnic rug from the grass and folded it up to put under Lily's head. Then she took some gauze from Caroline's bag and started to clean up the policeman.

"Mother – is there a drinking fountain nearby?" she asked, trying to wipe off the caked blood, which was now drying in the sun.

"What about this?" Lady Maud proffered the hip flask.

Victoria looked amused but gratefully accepted it. She moistened the gauze and began to wipe the blood away.

Caroline stood up. "I think Lily has a bullet lodged in her pelvis, just by the groin," she said. The woman cradling

Lily audibly sobbed. "I need to summon ambulances. I can take Lily to my hospital, but this gentleman will have to go to University College Hospital. I need to telephone…" She looked around anxiously.

"There will be a telephone in the Underground station," Beech said.

"Right." Caroline quickly ran up the long tree-lined walk.

Victoria had finished cleaning up the policeman. Beech and Maud helped him up and sat him on the bench next to Harold Chen, who was labouring to breathe.

"Constable, what's your name?" asked Beech.

"Thomson, sir," was the muffled reply from the man, whose top lip was beginning to swell, and his eye sockets were starting to look bruised.

"Well, Thomson, you look in a bad way and you need proper medical attention, so I'm going to send you in the ambulance with Mr Chen here. If you could take care of him and make sure he is settled before you get your own injuries dealt with, I would be grateful." Thomson nodded. "Good man," Beech added and patted him on the shoulder.

Then he moved across to the woman sitting on the ground by the unconscious Lily.

"Can I have your name please, madam?"

Without taking her eyes from Lily's face, the woman said, "Louise Wood. Albert's my husband and Lily's my daughter."

***

Billy and the other men were walking at a steady pace, keeping Wood and Mabel in sight at all times. Wood had looked back a couple of times and seen them, but he had just grinned, pulled Mabel closer to him and continued his onward march.

Billy had looked back at one point to discover, to his horror, that his mother, aunt and dog were following at a distance. He motioned to them to go back but they just ignored him. He resigned himself to the fact that they were too stubborn to take any notice of him and he resolved not to look back any more. He was worried about Mabel. He didn't know how resilient she was. *She's a lady pharmacist of a certain age*, he reasoned, *I don't know if she can cope with all this.*

Wood was proceeding past Woburn Square garden now and as he reached the main thoroughfare, Billy saw him look to his right and shout something. Then Wood turned abruptly left.

"Let's see if we can head him off through Woburn Square," shouted Billy and his band of men turned left into the square and began to run, diagonally, across the lawns. As they burst out of the north-west corner, Billy saw that they had just missed Wood, who was now crossing the road and hurrying down the side of Gordon Square. As Billy looked to his right, he could see Tollman advancing up the main road with his band of men and two uniformed officers in addition.

"Right, lads, let's do another sprint up through Gordon Square and see if we can head him off at the next junction!" So, they sprinted across the road and entered the square.

As they ran, Billy could see through the trees and foliage that they had passed Wood, who was walking as briskly as he could on the pavement outside the railings. *Mabel is slowing him down*, Billy thought, and he felt another pang of pity for the poor pharmacist who had willingly volunteered for this adventure.

As they hurtled out of the top of the square and turned back, they had overtaken Wood by about a hundred yards.

"Fan out across the road," Billy commanded.

Wood stopped dead, faced with a line of men obstructing his way. He looked back and saw Tollman and his policemen advancing. Suddenly, he pushed Mabel sideways and she almost stumbled, but Wood grabbed her again and propelled her up a side street.

"Bugger!" said Billy. "He's going into the university!"

Tollman realised the same thing and both groups ran to join each other and follow Wood. As they headed up the driveway, and the imposing Georgian buildings of University College loomed ahead of them, they could see Wood dragging Mabel up some steps. She stumbled again, her skirt having caught in her boot, and Billy saw her put her hand out and then collapse. "Oh my God! She's had a heart attack!" he said out loud, but then he saw Wood drag her up and she managed to walk up the final steps, clutching her wrist with the other hand. Then they disappeared inside a door.

Tollman shouted, "Billy, take the main entrance! Three men go round the back! We'll follow him in this door!"

They split up into their groups and Billy's men started up the staircase that led up to the colonnaded entrance to the building. As they neared the top, they heard a shot, followed by many screams, and suddenly people came streaming out of the building and Billy found himself fighting to get through the tide of humanity. He grabbed one young woman and shouted, "The man with the gun, where did he go? Which way?" She fearfully pointed to the right of the main entrance and Billy pressed on.

Inside, the people were still trying to push past. One of Billy's men shouted "Rigsby!" and pointed up the corridor, where the figure of Wood was bundling Mabel through a door. They ran as hard as they could and then ranged themselves either side of the door. Billy carefully opened the door a crack to see that there was a flight of stairs, which seemed to go all the way up to the top level of the building.

"Take your boots off, lads," he said quietly. "We need to follow him up this staircase as quietly as possible."

Everyone started unlacing their boots, just as Tollman arrived with his men.

"What's the score?" Tollman asked breathlessly.

"Wood's dragged Mabel up a long flight of stairs. I think she's hurt. She fell over and I think she might have broken her wrist. We're going to follow him up as quietly as we can."

Tollman nodded, looking grim. "I'll be up in a minute," he said. "Don't do anything until I'm up there. Maybe I can talk him round. Meanwhile, I'm going to get these other men to evacuate the building. Lads, get your warrant cards out and start getting people out of the way. Get them right out of the area. We don't want Wood taking potshots at people through a window."

All the men scattered, and Billy's group slipped in through the door. As he looked up, Billy could see Wood's long mackintosh flapping through the struts of the handrail as he made his way up the seemingly endless flight of stairs.

***

Lily was in surgery and her mother was refusing to leave the Women's Hospital until she knew her daughter was alive and well. Beech took over Caroline's consulting room so he could interview her.

Lady Patrick had been taken off to Scotland Yard to cool her heels in one of the cells until Beech returned – but not before her bag had been taken away and she had been subjected to a body search by Victoria.

"Who knows how many guns this woman has, tucked away," Beech had said irritably.

Lady Patrick had looked defiant, even though Victoria had intruded upon her person by raising her skirts and feeling both of her thighs to make sure she wasn't wearing a garter belt with guns tucked into them.

Victoria had then volunteered to supervise Lady Patrick at Scotland Yard, although she desperately wanted to go and help release Mabel.

Lady Maud had been persuaded to go home, with the perambulator and Mabel's precious camera, on the understanding that she would be telephoned with news the moment that Mabel was rescued.

Beech was deeply concerned that he should be supervising the operation to capture Wood, but he knew that his damaged leg did not allow him to move quickly and he would probably hinder progress. Besides, he trusted Tollman and Rigsby to do the best that they could.

Louise Wood had been given a cup of tea and was now sitting anxiously awaiting news of her daughter.

"Mrs Wood," Beech began, "Am I correct in assuming that you also go under the name of Louise Leighton and run a club called the Servants' Sewing Circle?"

Louise nodded.

"Can I also confirm that your daughter, Lily, worked for the late Adeline Treborne?"

"We all did," she replied quietly. "It was a family business, you might say."

"I think you had better explain everything to me, in as much detail as possible," said Beech firmly, grabbing a notepad and pen from Caroline's desk.

CHAPTER TWENTY-TWO

Ladies of Crime

In Scotland Yard, Detective Sergeant Carter eyed the refined-looking woman and the scruffy-looking man with dirt on his boots with suspicion.

Word had got around the Yard that a copper in plain clothes from Whitechapel had brought in the wife of an eminent QC, who was cussing and shouting like a fishwife down in the cells. Carter had come to see for himself. He couldn't see the woman in custody, but he could certainly hear her. She sounded American and she was letting rip in the cell, occasionally banging on the door for emphasis.

"Do you think I would have married that pompous bastard," she was yelling, "if it wasn't for his money?! I've never been so bored in my life!" She kicked the door and screamed, "Aagh!"

The refined-looking woman seemed to be writing it all down, and occasionally the man in grubby clothes shouted, "Mind your language!"

"Need any help down here?" Carter asked from the doorway.

"No, thank you, sir," said the man. "Just waiting for Chief Inspector Beech."

Carter nodded and retreated.

Upstairs he sought out Sergeant Stenton, the fount of all human knowledge in Scotland Yard.

"What's all this palaver downstairs, with the American woman and the copper from Whitechapel?" he asked confidentially.

Stenton, like many of the uniformed section, did not have a lot of time for DS Carter but he was too wise to show it. He shrugged and said, "Something to do with Chief Inspector Beech and a shooting at Russell Square."

"A shooting?" Carter was getting more and more interested. He was still aggrieved at being outsmarted by Tollman over the finding of Sidney Baker and he was getting a little peeved about this little 'team' of Rigsby, Tollman and Beech. "You don't get many of them to the pound, now. Anything else?" he probed.

Stenton smiled. "I don't mess with Chief Inspector Beech's cases, son, and you shouldn't either."

Carter was irritated at being warned off. "Why? What's so special about Beech's cases then?" he asked shirtily.

"He's got the special favour of the Commissioner, that's why. So back off, if you know what's good for you."

Carter was stung but he couldn't think of a reply, so he walked away.

***

Louise Wood had told the story of her involvement with not just Adeline Treborne, but the whole Treborne family.

Beech learned that Louise Leighton, as she then was, had been a housemaid for the Treborne family. She had worked for them since the age of fourteen and it was when she was sixteen that she caught the eye of the son of the house and was seduced. The resulting pregnancy was hushed up. She left the Treborne household without references because she did not give a period of notice. No one, except the son and daughter of the household, knew that she was pregnant and the daughter, Adeline, had been deputed by her brother to deal with the situation. Adeline found a place for her at Ivy House in Hackney – an unmarried mothers' home run by The Salvation Army – because ordinary maternity hospitals would only help married women give birth. After the birth, Adeline took the child and told Louise that she had organised an adoption through the Catholic Church. Louise was sad but content that her child would have a good home. Then Adeline forged some references from her mother, so that Louise could get employment in a modest household in Richmond.

After a year, when Louise was almost eighteen, she had met and married Albert Wood who was, at that time, a serving policeman. Albert, it appeared, was making good money from all sorts of little side ventures, not altogether honest, but they were able to rent a decent house in Marylebone and have middle-class pretensions. That year, their daughter, Lily, was born.

Albert was eventually thrown out of the police force, but not before he had made enough connections to be able to work as a private detective, mostly for the legal profession.

The Treborne family, meanwhile, had lost everything and a chance meeting between Adeline and Louise, about two years ago, had revealed that Adeline Treborne was very bitter about being without money and filled with rage at the way society had treated her, now that she was penniless.

That was when Albert had come up with the idea of Adeline being a gossip columnist. He and Louise would feed the gossip to Adeline and she would get paid for it – giving them a commission for the information. They also persuaded Adeline to employ their daughter, Lily, as a maid. Lily was thirteen at the time. Louise wrote the gossip column for Adeline every week. She would visit her very late at night and write down everything that Adeline dictated. But Adeline got greedy and creative. It was then that Louise realised that Adeline was deliberately leaving some of the gossip out of the newspaper column because she was blackmailing people.

Albert was furious. Not only had she left them out of the blackmail operation but she was also becoming increasingly dependent upon drugs and alcohol and was likely to spill the beans inadvertently at some point and put them all in danger. Albert decided that she must be 'got rid of'. Louise was fearful of taking such a step.

Albert said it would be a simple thing to do because, as Louise explained to Beech, she was the one who, over the course of the last six months, had been obtaining the drugs and injecting Adeline with heroin on a regular basis.

There was something else, though, and this was when Louise became truly tearful and Beech had to summon a nurse to administer a mild sedative. It transpired that, the week before Adeline's death, in one of her drugged states, she had revealed to Louise that, sixteen years before, she had *not* taken her baby to the Catholic Church Adoption Society, but she had given it to Ruth Baker, the baby farmer. Adeline had given Louise's son – the child she had never forgotten and thought about every day – to a woman who had been suspected of killing all the babies put in her charge. When Adeline also revealed that she had found out where Ruth Baker lived and was now blackmailing her, it had proved too much for Louise. She went home and agreed, wholeheartedly, to Albert's plan to kill Adeline Treborne.

There were a few details that puzzled Beech.

"How did you know where these people lived? The people Adeline was blackmailing?" he asked Louise. "Were their addresses in the book?"

Louise nodded. "But most of them had been found by Albert anyway. He had some contacts in the police that he drew on and he had other methods. He's a good detective. He found Kitty Bellamy and Reginald Ingham and Ruth Baker. Anything to do with the aristocracy and others, I found out from the maids gossiping at my sewing circle. The thing is," she added, "Albert didn't know about the baby I had before I met him. He didn't know about the importance of Ruth Baker to me. He didn't have anything to do with her death. That was me. She opened the door, I said 'Ruth Baker?', she said 'Yes?' and I stabbed her. It was premeditated. I took a kitchen knife with me and I stabbed her. I said, 'That's for my baby, you evil witch! May you rot in hell!'" Louise began to cry again. "And, Chief Inspector, I tell you now, even though I know I will hang for it… I would do it again."

There was silence for a while, as Beech allowed her to cry and get everything out of her system. Then he asked another question.

"Did your daughter, Lily, know that you were going to give Adeline Treborne an overdose?" Louise nodded. "Then why was she so upset on the day that we interviewed her?"

Louise looked at him and said, "Because she wasn't expecting to see Adeline hanging from the ceiling! She was deeply shocked! We had told her that Adeline would be just lying on the bed – because that was how I had left her, the night before. She hadn't quite stopped breathing but I could see she was on her way out. I found the blackmail ledger and cut the pages out, so I could stuff them in my handbag, then left, down the back stairs. My Lily was terrified when she saw Adeline swinging there! She couldn't understand what had happened. I never thought for one moment that the stupid woman would revive from the drugs and decide to hang herself!"

The Wood family did not know, of course, that Ruth and Sidney Baker were the ones who had strung up Adeline Treborne.

"Just one more thing, Mrs Wood," Beech said. "Did you have a key to the back door of Trinity Mansions?"

"Of course! Lily had one and I had one. Albert never went there. It was just Lily and I who went in and out."

Beech said quietly but firmly, "Louise Wood, I'm afraid that I shall have to charge you with two counts of premeditated murder."

She bowed her head and said nothing.

There was a knock at the door and Caroline entered, looking tired and hot as she pulled off her theatre gown and hat.

"Lily will be all right," she said simply, and Louise dissolved into yet more tears. "The small-calibre bullet had actually lodged in her pelvic bone. She will probably suffer some pain and it may plague her with arthritis in later life, but luckily it missed a main artery and she has not suffered any great loss of blood."

"When can I see her?" Louise asked anxiously. Caroline raised questioning eyebrows at Beech and he nodded.

"I'll take you up there now," said Caroline. "She'll be awake soon." She led Louise down the corridor, with Beech trailing behind.

As they came through the reception area, Beech could see that one of the Whitechapel men was there, accompanied by a uniformed policeman.

"Chief Inspector!" he said, "Message from Mr Tollman!"

"I'll be with you in a moment," was Beech's response, then he turned to Caroline. "I'm going to have to break the rules of this wonderful establishment," he said, pointing to the sign that said NO MEN ALLOWED BEYOND THIS POINT, "as Mrs Wood has now been charged by me and will have to be taken to Scotland Yard. So, this policeman here will have to accompany you upstairs."

Caroline said she understood. Beech summoned the uniformed police officer and took him over to a quiet corner to explain that he had charged Louise Wood with double murder and, once she had seen her daughter, she was to be taken down to Scotland Yard to the cells and processed. Beech would summon transport to be waiting outside the hospital. The policeman nodded, and Beech turned back to the man from Whitechapel for his report.

"Mr Tollman said that Albert Wood is cornered in University College in some museum. He is trapped and there is no way out for him. Tollman is going to try and negotiate the lady's release and he says could you please come, and could you requisition a rifle and ammunition from King's Cross Police Station for Constable Rigsby."

CHAPTER TWENTY-THREE

A Modest Little Museum

Albert Wood had now gone beyond desperation as he realised that he was cornered, with no way out. He had chosen the wrong staircase, thinking that it would lead him to a floor where he could traverse the building and go out of an exit that was not being watched by police. He had misjudged and ended up at the top of the university building, under a bank of skylights, in the Petrie Museum of Egyptian Archaeology. Now he was sitting on the floor, with the woman he had kidnapped, looking down the hallway at the stairwell, where the police had gathered. And as if that wasn't enough of a humiliation, he was being talked to by Arthur Tollman – a detective he had always loathed.

Wood looked around at all the bizarre exhibits in their glass cases. There were rows and rows of glass cases, with endless, neatly labelled pots… pots as far as the eye could see.

"Who cares about bloody pots!" he said loudly, to no one in particular.

"I expect the man who dug them all up cares about them very much," Tollman's voice echoed from the stairwell.

"You've always got a bloody answer for everything, haven't you, Tollman?" Wood said wearily.

Tollman said nothing in return, realising that he was getting on Wood's nerves.

Mabel was lying on the wooden floor, gratefully. She was exhausted and had curiously gone beyond fear. She knew that her wrist was broken, and the pain was keeping her alert. She felt frustrated that her usually analytical and scientific brain had let her down, in a situation that had needed quick thinking, physical agility and strength. Those things had always been beyond her capabilities. Even as a child she had been slow and methodical and had loathed sport. She decided to speak.

"Could I have a glass of water, please?" she said quietly, and Wood looked at her with surprise.

"Well! Aren't you the posh one! What are you? You're too posh to be a nanny." Wood looked at her with suspicion.

"I'm very thirsty." She was not going to engage him in conversation.

"D'you hear that, Tollman?" called Wood. "Her Highness here says she's thirsty and she wants some water. I think that's down to you, mate," he laughed.

"We're on it!" Tollman called back and Wood could hear some muffled exchanges on the stairs and then some movement.

"So, you're working out of the Yard these days, Tollman," said Wood. "What's it like, working at headquarters?"

"It's all right." Tollman began to feel a small amount of hope that Wood was co-operating. "I've worked at HQ before – when I was in Special Branch."

"Oh, of course," Wood said sarcastically, "I forgot what a high flyer you were. Arthur Tollman, he who knows everything and everyone."

Tollman didn't rise to the bait. One of the Whitechapel men came back with a curious-looking leather water bottle, with two metal cups, all attached to a leather belt.

"We've got the water and cups," called Tollman. "Are you going to let one of my men bring it to you?"

"As long as it's not you!" was the answer. "I don't trust you, Tollman. You're a devious bastard. You send a youngster, stripped down to his vest. No jacket where he can hide a handgun. I want to see his hands above his head."

Tollman nodded at a young copper. "You heard him. Take everything off. Leave your trousers and vest on. And, lad," he said in his sternest voice, "no bloody heroics. That woman in there is in a bad way, Wood knows that there is no way out. He could start shooting if you make him nervous. Just take the water and put it down." The man nodded. "Coming up!" yelled Tollman.

The young policeman picked up the water bottle and cups and gingerly raised himself up, with his hands above his head. Then he walked up the steps and into the corridor.

Wood pointed his gun straight at the policeman as he slowly advanced.

"Bring it to the doorway, put it on the floor and then back away."

The policeman did as he was told and put the water bottle and cups on the ground in the open doorway.

Wood looked at them and laughed. "What the hell is this? Something that fell off the back of a camel?"

"This is the Petrie Museum of Egyptology. That water bottle likely belongs to Professor Petrie. Something he takes to Arabia with him when he's digging in the desert," Tollman replied.

"Get away!" called back Wood, as he scrabbled for the bottle, all the while keeping his eye and his gun fixed on the retreating policeman. "I might keep this as a souvenir!"

Wood unscrewed the top of the leather flask and poured some water into a cup, which he gave to Mabel. She drank greedily and mumbled, "Thank you."

Wood gave her a funny look. "Like I said before, you're no nanny," he declared, in a menacing tone of voice. "No, you're so posh, you even say thank you to the man who's got a gun trained on you. So, come on, love. Stop messing me about and tell me what you really are."

There was a silence while Mabel weighed up her options, then realised she had none, so she said quietly, "I'm a pharmacist."

"A what?"

"I'm someone who makes medicines…"

"I know what a pharmacist is! I'm not stupid! So why were you dressed up as a nanny and pushing a baby carriage?" There was a silence and Wood's face changed from curiosity to fury. "Tollman!" he bawled. "You've gone back on your principles!"

"What?!" Tollman was genuinely confused.

"I remember..." shouted Wood, "I remember you making some speech to us all when we were preparing to police a suffragette march... and in that speech you said that women would work in the police force over your dead body. So why is this bloody woman here, sitting next to me, working as part of your team?"

Tollman's heart sank. Wood had worked out that Mabel was working undercover and now he truly feared for her life.

***

When Beech arrived with the rifle, he stepped out of the car to find Rigsby pacing up and down, reading the riot act to his mother and aunt. Also, some small, middle-aged woman was constantly buzzing around Billy, tugging at his sleeve and trying to get his attention.

"What's happening, Constable Rigsby?" he asked. "Anything I can help with?"

"Yes!" the small woman said forcefully. "There most certainly is!" She introduced herself as Margaret Murray, assistant to Professor Petrie and the woman in charge of the museum currently being occupied by the fugitive. "The museum has, literally, only just opened. The artefacts in there represent several lifetimes of dedicated work. Frankly, I'm terrified at the damage that may be caused by this madman in there."

"Madam, this madman, as you call him, has a female hostage and is threatening to kill her. We will do our best to avoid any damage, but we cannot guarantee it. What is more important is saving a life."

Margaret Murray looked embarrassed and dwindled into a few ineffective protests but had to content herself with waiting and watching, like everyone else.

Beech turned to Rigsby. "You seemed to be having words with your family, when I arrived. Is there a problem?"

Billy made a sound of exasperation, "No, sir, no problem – except that I can't get them to go home. Women, eh?"

Beech smiled and handed over the rifle. "What's your plan, Rigsby?"

"Matey has boxed himself in. He's sitting on the floor in a room opposite the stairwell. Tollman and the boys are sitting on the stairs. He's getting desperate and he could do something stupid. We think that Miss Summersby has broken her wrist…"

"Oh God! Poor Mabel." Beech was devastated that things were going so badly.

"Anyway, sir," said Billy confidently, as he held up the rifle, "I am taking this up on to the roof. The whole room where Wood is holed up is in the roof up there…" – he pointed at the south end of the building, past the great dome over the entrance – "and it is covered with skylights. I should be able to pick off Albert Wood without him even knowing I'm there. It will have to be a kill shot though, sir. We can't risk him being wounded and still being able to shoot."

"And you can do that, Rigsby?" Beech was surprised.

Billy grinned. "Army Rifle Association medallist four years running, sir. I can do it."

"What about your hand?" Beech looked at Billy's rigid left hand, covered in its usual black glove.

"As I tried to tell the Army when they discharged me, it doesn't make any difference. It's not my trigger hand. But they wouldn't listen."

Beech agreed to the plan and Billy marched over to his mother and aunt, planted a kiss on both of their cheeks and told them to keep quiet, no matter what they saw. "Mabel's life depends on it," he said firmly. Then he tapped the professor's assistant on the shoulder and she led him into the building to show him where to access the roof.

About five minutes later, Beech saw a hatch open near the dome, and Rigsby appeared. He slung the rifle across his back, lay down on the roof and began pulling himself slowly forwards, using his forearms to drag himself forward. At that point, Beech decided to go inside and see if Tollman needed any support.

***

"Anyone's entitled to change their mind, Albert," said Tollman, in response to Wood calling him a hypocrite. "Forget the suffragettes. What they did is history now. It's what women are doing now that's important. Look at them, man. All over London – taking over the jobs left empty by men who've gone off to war. You can't deny that they're doing a good job."

"Ach!" Wood was scornful. "Tisn't right. Women should be at home, looking after a husband and kids! What happens when all these blokes come back from war to find women have taken over their jobs, eh? What happens then?" He was getting more belligerent by the minute and Tollman decided that he should try to end this discussion.

"You and I both know that a lot of those men are never coming back, Albert. The Prime Minister said in February that over one hundred thousand men were killed in the first six months of the war. That's just the British and those figures were for four months ago, before the Germans started gassing our troops in April, so I can't imagine how many more have been killed."

There was a silence while Wood digested this, and then he said, "Yeah, well, I don't suppose I'll be around either. You'll have me hanging at the end of a rope, won't you, Tollman?"

Beech had arrived and was crouching next to Tollman. He decided to speak.

"Mr Wood, this is Chief Inspector Beech…"

Wood laughed, "Oh, we've brought the heavy brigade in now, have we? Pleased to meet you, sir. I would salute but I'm not in the police force any more, as you very well know."

"What you were saying earlier, about hanging," Beech continued. "It may not be so. The courts have, er, been advised to, er, limit death sentences during time of war. Convicts are more useful making things in prison to contribute to the war effort." Beech was being creative.

He had a feeling that someone had mentioned such a policy at a headquarters meeting but it had been nothing more than a proposal.

Wood gave another sardonic laugh. "Nice try, Chief Inspector, but you and I both know that there's nothing the public loves more than a good hanging. I'm for the end of a rope and I know it. The thing is…" – he raised his voice – "I might as well be hanged for a sheep as for a lamb… so which one of you am I going to take with me? Eh? The lady here? Or one of you coppers? Or both?"

"Don't be hasty, Wood! Think about it, man. What about your daughter?" Beech added.

"Is she alive?"

"Very much so."

Beech heard Wood panting, presumably trying not to shed any tears.

"Maybe it would be better if she had died," Wood said. 'Cos she's going to spend a long time in prison and her mother and me won't be there for her."

***

Billy had crawled into a position where he could see the back of Wood, who was facing towards the open doorway. He could also see Mabel, who had given in to her pain and was now lying prone on the floor. He realised that he would have to compensate for the bullet going through the glass in the skylight and make the shot good, before Wood had a chance to react and shoot. But it was a short distance and the bullet, he reasoned, should not be too affected by passing through glass. There was no way of opening the skylights from outside. He would just have to risk it.

To get a decent shot meant that he would have to stand up. He had a ten-round box magazine on the rifle, which was standard Lee-Enfield, but he doubted whether he would be able to get off a second shot.

He slowly stood up and balanced himself. He raised the rifle to his shoulder and looked down the sight, balancing the barrel in between the first finger and thumb of his rigid gloved hand. As he adjusted his aim and applied his finger to the trigger, Wood appeared to have staggered to his feet. He could hear him shouting but he couldn't quite make out the words. Billy realised that Wood was aiming his handgun straight down the corridor.

***

"So, I've decided to take *you* with me, Tollman, you bastard!" Wood shouted angrily. "I've decided to rid the world of one know-it-all copper who gets right up my nose and always has! So, come out from your hiding place, Detective Sergeant Tollman! Don't be a coward, man. Give your life instead of the lady's here."

Tollman was about to stand up, despite Beech trying to drag him down, when suddenly there was a sound of a shot, almost simultaneous with shattering glass and a thud.

"Man down!" shouted Rigsby, from up on the roof, and Beech thought he could hear some cheering and whistling from outside the building. All the policemen stood up to see Albert Wood lying, dead, face down on the wooden floor of the museum with a perfect bullet hole in the back of his neck.

"Well done, lad!" shouted a grateful Tollman, who thought he had been about to face his Maker, and he ran to help Mabel.

Beech looked up at Rigsby, standing, rifle in hand, on the roof. The skylight had shattered from the close range of the bullet and shards of glass were scattered all over the display cases of precious Egyptian artefacts. But no harm seemed to have been done. "Yes, well done, Constable Rigsby," he called up and smiled. Billy gave a casual salute and disappeared.

Mabel was carried downstairs by one of the Whitechapel men, even though she protested that there was nothing wrong with her legs, and, once downstairs, was taken by police car to the Women's Hospital, accompanied by Sissy.

Elsie declared herself 'worn out' by the 'goings-on' of the day. Timmy was exhausted, as the little dog had been walked for the best part of eight hours, and he had slept through all of Billy's heroics on the roof.

Margaret Murray, the keeper of the Petrie Museum collection, was almost in tears with relief that the precious artefacts were unharmed, save for one pot shard that had detached itself from its display position, fallen to the bottom of the case and cracked.

"Bloody thing was already broken, wasn't it?" muttered Tollman under his breath to Billy. He was not a man who was impressed by the detritus of antiquity.

The men from Whitechapel departed, with a promise from Beech that they would all be commended in his report to their divisional chief inspector.

Students and staff began returning, hesitantly, to the building. Some of them, those who had watched events from a distance in the quadrangle, paused to pat Billy on the back as he retrieved his boots from the bottom of the staircase.

A body wagon arrived to remove the corpse of Albert Wood and another vehicle arrived to transport those remaining to Scotland Yard. Elsie and Timmy were loaded in, with the promise that the vehicle would carry on to Belgravia. As they all sat in weary silence, Beech suddenly remembered, with a jolt, that Victoria was still at Scotland Yard, supervising Lady Patrick and, hopefully, taking note of anything the woman said or did.

When Beech finally rescued Victoria from the depths of the Yard cells, he was profusely apologetic and reassured her that everyone else was safe and sound.

"Did she say anything?" he asked, indicating towards the cell where Lady Patrick appeared now to be taking a nap.

Victoria laughed and produced over fifty pages of notes. "I warn you, Peter Beech, some of her utterances were quite vulgar. How such language could have come out of that rosebud mouth is beyond me. The poor policeman who accompanied me kept blushing from ear to ear! Anyway, I have signed the notes and he has countersigned them, so there is no doubt that they are a true record."

"Well done you," said Beech fondly. "In fact, well done everybody. This has been a devil of a case."

EPILOGUE

The Commissioner pronounced it the most fascinating report he had ever read, and Beech was gratified. In fact, so impressed was Sir Edward by Mabel Summersby's report that he sent her a personal letter praising her methodical approach and inviting her to lunch, when she had recovered, so that they could discuss in detail the subject of a forensic approach to policing.

Such was the complexity of the cases they had encountered in investigating the murder of Adeline Treborne that it had taken a week of the combined efforts of Beech, Victoria, Caroline and Tollman to put all of the notes together into one report and then separately make the notes into reports for each crime. So, at the end of the week, they had provided the Commissioner with recommendations for prosecutions for six individuals:

1. Reginald Ingham, to be charged with multiple counts of larceny: false pretences.
2. Samuel Robinson, the best they could come up with as a charge was 'corruptly taking a reward' from customers who had shown intent to defraud the insurance companies.
3. Lady Patrick, three counts of attempted murder.

4. Sydney Baker, aiding and abetting infanticide, thirty counts.
5. Louise Wood, two counts of murder – Adeline Treborne and Ruth Baker.
6. Lily Wood, threatening to publish, with intent to extort, six counts.

Tollman had made a passionate plea, within the report on Sidney Baker, for the man's mental capacity to be taken into consideration. He argued that Sidney was not capable of understanding that his wife had committed the crimes and that Sidney had truly believed that the babies had died of natural causes.

Victoria had felt strongly that they should argue in Louise Wood's report that she should be spared the death penalty, arguing that grief over the discovery that her illegitimate child had been murdered had upset the balance of her mind. Beech and Tollman disagreed but, after strong and relentless argument from both Caroline and Victoria, Beech had agreed to a recommendation for a medical assessment to be included in the report.

So, everything was handed over to Sir Edward for him to read and discuss with the Director of Public Prosecutions.

Meanwhile, the team had funerals to attend.

Victoria insisted on accompanying Caroline, Rigsby and Tollman to the funeral of Joseph and Kitty Bellamy at the Brookwood Cemetery in Surrey. Joseph could have been buried in the military section but then Kitty would not have been able to lie in the same grave and Caroline, who had organised the funeral, knew that neither of them would have wanted that. She had put a notice in *The Times* to announce the deaths of *Kitty Bellamy née Mason, one-time prominent member of the Women's Social and Political Union, and her husband, Corporal Joseph Bellamy, late of the Queen's Own Royal West Kent Regiment.*

The advertisement gave the date and time of the funeral and Tollman was discomfited to find himself surrounded by a full honour guard of the WSPU, complete with sashes and armbands and a wreath in WSPU colours to lay on the grave. Victoria was quietly astonished when she saw out of the corner of her eye, at a particularly moving point in the funeral, Caroline holding on to Billy's hand for several minutes.

The following day, there was an official interment of the thirty babies that had perished at the hands of Ruth Baker. An anonymous donor had purchased a private plot in the churchyard of St Philomena's Catholic church in Chelsea. The public had lost interest in the babies by then, so it was just a small knot of people at the ceremony – representatives of the police, the parish and Beech's team, including Elsie, Sissy and Lady Maud, but not Mabel, who was still recuperating.

"It is apt," said the priest, as they all stood by the plot in the dappled shade of the trees, "that the donor chose this church because St Philomena is the patron saint of babies, infants and youth. In the fullness of time, a specially commissioned memorial stone will be laid here, which will say, *Psalm 127, verse 3, Behold, children are a heritage from the Lord, the fruit of the womb a reward.*"

Beech, looking out past the trees, reflected that Adeline Treborne's old apartment looked out over the churchyard and it was a mere ten-minute walk to where the murderer of the babies lived. Then he noticed a familiar car parked in the street and through the open rear window he could just about see the veiled face of the Duchess of Penhere. *Ah, so she knows,* he thought, and he realised that she was the anonymous donor.

So, after a gruelling two weeks of investigations, report-writing and emotional aftermath, it was a pleasant surprise when every one of them received a handwritten invitation card, which said,

Elsie and Sissy of Belgravia request the presence of .... at their residence on Saturday at 11 a.m. for a 'Doing Your Bit' party. Vegetables and fruits will be planted to aid the war effort. Wear gardening clothes and bring tools if you can. Lunch and tea will be provided.

Lady Maud was thrilled, and Billy laughed. "It's nothing to do with me, honest!" he said. "This is the first I've heard of it!"

Tollman was chuffed. "Right up my street, this is."

"We must break Mabel out of her enforced rest and take her along," said Caroline. "She will love supervising everyone digging and planting."

"Constable Rigsby," said Lady Maud, "do you suppose your mother and aunt would mind if we contributed some food to the festivities?"

Billy laughed again. "Lady Maud, do my womenfolk look as though they mind anyone giving them food?"

Victoria had a thought. "Peter?" she said, turning to Beech. "Do you actually *have* any old clothes?" Everyone looked at the usually immaculately suited Beech and waited for an answer. He looked uncomfortable. Victoria beamed. "You don't, do you? Mother, can we turf out some of father's old clothes for Peter to wear?"

"Of course! You'll have to have a rummage in the attic, though."

***

Saturday came, and an excited team descended on the Belgravia house that was looked after by Elsie and Sissy. Billy had borrowed a gramophone and some records from a friend and a tinny version of a Strauss waltz was playing as, one by one, they entered the walled garden.

"What a wonderful idea this is!" enthused Lady Maud, as Sissy relieved her of a basket of scones and showed her to a chair. "I do wish we had a garden in Mayfair," she added, "because I do so miss the gardens in Berkshire."

Mabel was fussed over and given a chair in the shade, with arms, so that she could rest her plaster cast on something. "It's so hot and uncomfortable," she complained. "All I want to do is scratch inside. Ladies? Do you have a knitting needle, by any chance?" Elsie went indoors and fetched one and Mabel poked it inside her cast with a look of bliss on her face.

Tollman had come fully equipped for gardening with three spades, two rakes and several trowels. Sissy marvelled at how he had got them all on the omnibus. "Oh, I take my gardening seriously," he said with a wink, and took them over to the corner of the garden. Billy murmured in Sissy's ear, "You've given the old bloke a nervous tic, he's winking at you so much," which earned him a thump.

Beech finally arrived, looking distinctly uncomfortable in cricket flannels and a checked shirt, courtesy of Lady Maud's late husband.

"You look rather fetching, Peter!" said Caroline, with an amused look on her face. Beech wasn't convinced. He couldn't remember the last time he had worn anything other than a uniform or a suit. At school, probably.

There was a clinking of a spoon against a teacup, signalling a speech, and Elsie Rigsby stepped forward to a modest round of applause.

Elsie explained that she and Sissy had had the idea of writing to their employer, Lady Murcheson, after seeing a picture in the paper of Queen Mary visiting a school that had turned part of its grounds into a vegetable garden. The newspaper had intimated that everyone, if they had a garden, should try to grow their own food to beat the U-boat blockade. Lady Murcheson had written back to say she was happy for the garden to be turned over to a good use for the duration of the war and she had even sent packets of seeds donated by her gardener on her country estate. "So, there we are," concluded Elsie, "seeds and tools at the ready! But let's have a pot of tea first!"

Tea and scones were served, with promises of pork pies and home-made pickles for lunch, with a drop of Elsie's home-made elderflower wine from 1914.

Epilogue

Mabel and Tollman started an earnest discussion about the scientific planting of the proposed vegetable plot, working out the trajectory of the sun and which vegetable to plant where.

Timmy was snuffling around hoping for titbits to fall from people's plates. Sissy nudged Billy. "Watch this," she said with grin and she lifted up Timmy's lead from the garden table. "Timmy!" she trilled. "Walkies!" Timmy gave a yelp and immediately shot under a bush where he lay down and looked fearful.

"What's that all about?" asked Billy.

"It's ever since I took him on an eight-hour hike around Bloomsbury," she explained. "He thinks we're going to do it again and he's not having any of it."

Tollman had begun digging and Billy joined him. Beech felt duty-bound to do so as well, even though he really had no idea what he was doing. Elsie and Lady Maud were having an earnest conversation about the merits of carrots, and which varieties were best, while Victoria and Caroline were poring over the record selection.

"This one," said Victoria simply, and put it on. As the music came, sweet and pure, from the gramophone, one by one, they joined in the song.

"Just a song at twilight, when the lights are low, And the flickering shadows softly come and go…"

Caroline tapped Beech on the back and offered her arms for a dance. Victoria did the same with Billy, and an unusually forward Tollman swept Sissy into his grasp. Slowly they danced around the small garden, all singing.

"Tho' the heart be weary, sad the day and long,
Still to us at twilight comes Love's old song,
Comes Love's old sweet song."

"This is such a perfect day to be in a garden," said Lady Maud softly, smiling at Elsie.

"Even today we hear Love's song of yore,
Deep in our hearts it dwells for evermore.
Footsteps may falter, weary grow the way,
Still we can hear it at the close of day.
So till the end, when life's dim shadows fall,
Love will be found the sweetest song of all."

Their voices and the music lifted above the walls of the garden and into the street. A passing bus conductress, the omnibus paused at traffic lights, smiled and began to hum, which quickly formed into the words of the song.

"Just a song a twilight, when the lights are low,
And the flickering shadows softly come and go,
Tho' the heart be weary, sad the day and long,
Still to us at twilight comes Love's old song,
Comes Love's old sweet song."

Two women on the bus laughed and joined in with her and soon the whole lower deck of the omnibus was singing the song. The bus then pulled away, trailing the sound of happy voices in unison behind it and taking a little gift of joy down the street and into Buckingham Palace Road.

Also by Mirror Books

Murder Under a Green Sea
Phillip Hunter

Max, a newspaper journalist, is married to Martha, the daughter of a wealthy family – who are less than keen on their son-in-law. When he discovers members of his old platoon from Passchendaele are being mysteriously murdered one by one, he also finds himself the prime suspect.

With humour, reckless capers and a little help from Winston Churchill, can Max and Martha uncover the truth behind the murders – and prove his innocence?

An exciting, stylish and nostalgic murder-mystery adventure.

Also by Mirror Books

Murder in Belgravia
Lynn Brittney

London, 1915. Ten months into the First World War and the City is flooded with women taking over the work vacated by men.

Chief Inspector Peter Beech, a young man invalided out of the war in one of the first battles, is investigating the murder of an aristocrat and the man's wife will only speak to a woman about the unpleasant details of the case. Beech persuades the Chief Commissioner to allow him to set up a clandestine team to deal with this case and pulls together a small crew of hand-picked women and professional policemen. Their telephone number: Mayfair 100.

Delving into the seedier parts of WWI London, the team investigate brothels, criminal gangs and underground drug rings that supply heroin to the upper classes. Will the Mayfair 100 gang solve the murder? If they do, will they be allowed to continue working as a team?

The first in an exciting series of fascinatingly-detailed stories involving the Mayfair 100 crimebusting team working London's streets during the First World War.